CTC

(Conspiracy Theory Corps)

Induction

"Knowledge does away with darkness, suspense and doubt; for these cannot exist where knowledge is. …In knowledge there is power."

- Joseph Smith

"We crave for new sensations but soon become indifferent to them. The wonders of yesterday are today common occurrences."

\- Nikola Tesla

Induction

Book one of the CTC (Conspiracy Theory Corp) Series

First Edition, 2025

Published by Wolfdog Publishing

ctcuniverse.net - conspiracytheorycorp.com - admin@conspiracytheorycorp.net

ISBN: 979-8-9936044-0-4 (e-book)
979-8-9936044-1-1 (paperback)

Cover design by Gavin Rice
Interior formatting by David Rice

Printed in the United States of America

Prologue

Thursday, October 28th, 1943

The world was on fire. Echoes of war, carnage, genocide, and destruction engulfed everyone's thoughts like a plague. The only cure for this outbreak was faith - not from perfect knowledge of the future's outcome, but from having hope for deliverance, justice, vengeance, and peace, knowing that these things were truly within reach. Faith fueled the desire for some to charge forward as the world's savior from the evils that infested it. For others, it sparked the will to survive, knowing that faith without action meant death. Pearl Harbor had ignited that spark for the U.S., and now the flame burned abord the U.S. Navy destroyer escort USS Eldridge, docked at the Philadelphia Naval Shipyard.

A slight breeze chilled the air that morning along with the eerie silence from a lack of activity in the Shipyard. It was usually bustling with activity. For some reason, it had been cleared out. Only the Eldridge showed signs of life on board. From preparing breakfast to checking the mechanics, sailors were peppered throughout the ship, performing their regular maintenance duties. The thermometer on the deck read 52 degrees. Two sailors had the privilege of swabbing the already clean upper deck. One was an anxious new recruit that had that fire burning inside him. Yet here he was, repeating the same tasks day after day with little explanation as to why a brand-new ship was still at port.

As he swabbed the deck, fantasies of personal wartime heroism played out in his mind. Those fantasies were interrupted by the sound of a honking goose calling to its mate as it flew by. As he was jerked back into reality, his grip on the handle of the mop tightened from frustration. The strokes on the deck became more aggressive. Annoyed, he carelessly dropped the mop head into the bucket, splashing his crewmate's legs with soapy water.

The slightly older, more experienced crewmate froze as drops of water spattered him. His brow furrowed at his crewmate's carelessness, yet he kept his composure. "Something on your mind, sailor?"

The sailor didn't notice he'd splashed his crewmate. Instead, he looked up at his companion while shaking his head in disgust. "I don't get it Matt."

Matt again continued to swab the deck. Without looking up from his task, he replied in a deep monotone voice, "What don't you get, Jim?"

Jim hit the ship's wall with the side of his fist. "We've been sitting at the dock on this brand-new ship for a couple months now doing the same pointless tasks over and over. When are they going to be done with their so-called "modifications"? When are we going to see some action?"

Matt looked at him with a grim smirk. "Why, are you anxious to die? Other ships are getting slaughtered out there by those Nazi U-boats." Putting his head down again, he continued to swab the deck.

Gripping the handle of the mop again with both hands, Jim looked at his crewmate with contempt. He pulled the mop out of the bucket, slammed the mop head on the deck, then threw the handle to the floor. "Exactly! Nazis are killing thousands of people and here we are swabbing the same brand-new deck over and over again. We need to be out there! We need to stop them!"

Matt stopped and looked down at the mop on the floor. With his eyebrows down and lips tight, he looked at Jim with an icy stare. Jim recognized that look. It was the "you better pick it up" look. He immediately complied. Matt released Jim from his stare and continued swabbing the deck. "This is your first real assignment, isn't it?"

An eyebrow lifted on Jim's face. He stood up taller to compensate for the belittling comment that was thrown at him. Brazenly raising his voice, he replied, "Yeah, why does that matter? Others I trained with are already out at sea and have seen all sorts of action. I'm sure they've already given a lot of them Nazis a one-way trip to hell. And here we are, swabbing an already clean deck."

Matt didn't react to the anxious sailor's heated response. Instead, he kept his composure as he continued to swab the deck. "And have your heard at all from your friends from training?"

Jim's chest deflated slightly as he thought for a second. "N…no. What's your point?"

Matt still didn't look up but calmly continued with his task. A slight grin appeared on his face. "Relax. Our time will come sooner than you think. When that time hits, we'll see if you're still anxious."

Jim, unwilling to listen to reason from his crewmate, dipped his mop back in the bucket and then slapped it hard back on the deck in frustration. He shook his head in disgust as he continued to swab while saying under his breath, "What a load of crap." All he could think about was how his friends were battling to protect the freedom of his country that he loved while he was stuck in port.

Hundreds of miles away, two sharply dressed men in dark, neatly pressed suits escorted President Franklin D. Roosevelt down a well-lit narrow hallway. One pushed his wheelchair while the other marched in front of them. The hallway had plain white walls with wood panels from the waist down and a red-blue-swirled carpet over the cement floor. At the end was a metal door, painted to simulate wood. The lead man opened it, holding it as the other pushed President Roosevelt through. He followed, shut the door, and stood at attention next to it.

The well-lit, highly decorated room was about fifty feet wide and two hundred feet long. It had one entrance with no windows. In the middle was a long rectangular conference table that stretched most of the length of the room. On the opposite side was a long desk mounted against the wall. On the desk were several decoding machines designed to send out secure messages. Three of the machines were manned by soldiers on standby. The Secret Service agent pushed President Roosevelt's wheelchair at the head of the conference table. There were five men already sitting. On one side sat Admiral William D. Leahy, the Chief of Staff to the President and Admiral Ernest J. King, Chief of Naval Operations. On the other side sat Albert Einstein. Next to Albert sat two quiet men dressed in all black suits. After positioning the president, the Secret Service agent joined the other agent at the door.

Roosevelt gave a quick glance at the men at the table. "Gentlemen. How are we looking?"

Admiral King sat at attention. "Sir. Both ports have cleared the area of all civilians. The USS Eldridge as well as the SS Andrew Furuseth are both ready and on stand-by. The commanding officers on the Eldridge have been fully briefed and waiting to give disclosure to their men sir. As far as how much disclosure, that is up to you, Sir."

Roosevelt gave a sharp nod. Maintaining a serious tone, he turned his head towards Albert. "And what about your team Mr. Einstein?"

Albert was much less stiff than his counterparts on the other side of the table. "The equipment has been checked and seems to be in working order. Franklin Reno is safely on the shore in viewing distance of the Eldridge as well as his team with cameras to record the event to study it later…" Albert pauses for a second, as if in thought. "Mr. President, I must say again although we have had success on smaller scale subjects, I am not completely comfortable rushing to such a large-scale experiment so fast."

Admiral King put both fists on the table and stared at Albert. "We've had this discussion already. As we speak thousands of men on our ships are in danger of those U-boats out there. Thousands have already died. We've run out of time!"

Admiral Leahy stepped in with a calm but commanding voice, "Admiral King is right. It was already decided that we move forward. Mr. President, everyone is in place and everything is ready to go. What are your orders, Sir?"

The President sat there for a moment with his head down in thought. He lifted his head in confidence. "We will proceed as planned. The men on the Eldridge will be given full disclosure and sworn to secrecy. Allow anyone that does not feel comfortable participating in the experiment to exit the ship with no repercussions."

Admiral Leahy nodded in approval. "Yes sir. Although, I know those men and I'm pretty certain that we will have a full crew on board when the experiment goes forward." Admiral Leahy looked across at one of the soldiers anxiously waiting to send an encrypted message and nodded. The soldier turned towards his machine and started typing aggressively.

Back in Philadelphia, a soldier sitting at a decoding machine aboard USS Eldridge frantically wrote down the incoming message. He folded the message and handed it to a sailor waiting next to him. The sailor took the folded message and ran it over to the captain. After reading the message to himself, the captain walked over to a small room where his commanding officers were patiently waiting for the news. He stood tall in front of the officers with his hands by his side. "The President has ordered us to proceed. All on board are to be given full disclosure while sworn to secrecy, punishable by court martial. He has also ordered that anyone that does not wish to participate can leave the ship with no repercussions. Go spread the word. Dismissed." The officers immediately jumped up and booked to their assigned locations.

Over the ships loud speakers, a whistle sounded and the orders "Report to your debriefing stations" stretched across the whole of the decks. All the sailors on the ship immediately marched to their assigned locations where they found their commanding officers waiting for them. They all stood in rows at attention. The officers proceeded to give the message to their groups. They all carried the same message but delivered it with their own tone.

One of the officers spoke to his men with authority but also with sincerity. "We have been stationed here at this port for a while and you have been given no explanation as to why. The President of the United States has just authorized you now to know and understand why. Needless to say, this information is top secret. What you are about to hear, you never heard. What we are about to do, as far as you are concerned, we never did. Failure to comply is punishable by court martial. We have had hundreds of ships sunk by the German U-boats. Thousands of sailors have lost their lives. Thanks to breakthroughs in science and research, the U.S. has come up with a new technology that allows us to jump from one location to another far away location instantly. This will eliminate much, if not all of the threats from the U-boats. This technology is incredible. That is why it must never fall in the wrong hands. No matter what happens today, you must protect its secret. Our enemies would do unspeakable damage to us if they had this type of ability. Do I make myself clear?"

All the sailors replied in sync, "Sir, yes sir!"

"Needless to say, this has never been attempted with a ship this size before, nor with so many people. If successful, we will be able to win this war without the loss of thousands, if not millions. But since there are risks involved, you have been granted an opportunity to leave this ship while we are conducting the experiment. There will be no repercussions to you if you choose to do this. All those who wish to leave the ship, step forward now." Not a single sailor stepped forward. "Very well. Let us proceed. When I am done speaking, you will report to your stations and stand perfectly still while the experiment is happening. Do not touch anything. We will be relocated instantly to another location and stay there for a few minutes. It is important for you to stay in your location and stand perfectly still. We will then be returned to our original location. At that point the experiment will be over. Is that understood?"

All the sailors barked out in unison, "Sir, yes sir!"

"In that case, report to your stations. Dismissed."

The sailors quickly ran to their respective positions and stood at attention. There was little chatter as they obediently went to their posts. A mixture of wonder, pride, determination, and fear appeared on their faces. Once the captain was notified that everyone was at their positions, he turned to the soldier at the decoding machine and told him to let the President know that they were in position and ready to go. The soldier immediately started to type.

Back in the room with the President, a soldier at one of the decoding machines received the message from the Eldridge and quickly wrote it down on a piece of paper. The man sitting next to Albert got up and grabbed the message from the soldier. After sitting back down, he read it to the group. "The USS Eldridge is in position and ready to go."

President Roosevelt and Albert looked at each other. The President gave a nod to Einstein to proceed. Einstein took a deep breath and turned to a soldier at a second decoding machine. "Please message Mr. Reno that everyone and everything is ready to go. Begin the experiment." The soldier turned to his machine and started sending the message.

Back in Philadelphia off the shore to where the Eldridge was docked, Scientist Franklin Reno stood behind a concrete wall that was about four-and-a-half feet tall along with a person that had a motion picture camera and three other men holding note pads, ready to take notes. A soldier was sitting at a table set up behind them with a machine to send and receive messages as well. The machine jumped to life. The soldier wrote down the message. He stood up and turned to Franklin. "Everyone is in place and ready to go sir."

Franklin turned around and clapped as he looked at the soldier. "Very good." He turned to his crew and with much gusto started giving orders. "Start the picture recording. Keep an eye on what happens and take notes of every detail. Take note of the times." He picked up a radio sitting on the table next to the decoding machine and pushed on the side button. "Start up the machine."

A voice on the radio replied, "Starting it up right now."

Franklin and his team cautiously ducked below the wall with only their heads exposed to watch the ship. The men watched anxiously with their note pads at hand. A few seconds later they heard a soft humming sound. A bluish-green fog snaked around the ship. The men quickly wrote down what they saw while the person holding the camera focused in on the event.

On the Eldridge the men nervously stood still as the humming got louder and the fog surrounded the ship. They didn't know what to expect and feared moving a muscle. The fog thickened over a minute. For a brief moment everything around them seemed to become distorted, as though someone took the very moment that they were seeing and twisted it like a wet rag being rung out by hand. This distortion lasted for a couple of seconds until the humming stopped. The fog started to clear. As it cleared the men noticed that their surroundings were very different. They were no longer in Philadelphia.

In Norfolk, Virginia, the SS Andrew Furuseth sat on the water in Chesapeake Bay. The ship's crew were commanded to stay below deck. They obediently and anxiously awaited below deck as ordered. Two of the men managed to position themselves where they could see outside. One of the sailors, named Carl Allen, turned to the other with a shocked look on his face. "Hey, do you see that?"

The other sailor looked at him in confusion. "Carl, what are you talking about?"

Carl pointed to the porthole. "Right there. That ship. It just appeared. It came out of nowhere."

Carl's shipmate looked out the porthole and noticed the Eldridge sitting on the water. "I'm sure it just pulled up. You just didn't notice."

"No, it didn't just pull up. It appeared out of nowhere. I'm going to let someone know above deck."

"We were ordered to stay down below. You better stay down here." Carl's shipmate grabbed his arm in an attempt to stop him.

Carl didn't care. He knew what he saw. He pushed away from the sailor. "This is too important not to let someone know. I'll be back." Before his shipmate could say anything else, Carl ran up the stairs to the deck.

Noticing someone coming up the stairs through his peripheral vision, the commander turned to see him coming up deck. "Allen! What are you doing up here? You were told to stay below deck!"

Carl wanted desperately to get his discovery known. "But sir I…"

The commander interrupted Carl. He didn't want to hear his excuses for breaking orders. His face started to turn red. "I don't want to hear it! Get below deck now!"

Carl turned around and quickly went back down below. The commander, William Dodge, watched to make sure Carl went back down. Steam was almost coming out of his ears. He didn't want any distractions from what was taking place. Quickly, he turned his attention back on the Eldridge that just appeared in the bay. His face started to turn back to its normal color. As he looked at the Eldridge his eyebrow changed from down to up. He couldn't believe what was happening. Picking up his binoculars, he scanned the ship for anything out of the ordinary. After scanning for several moments, he lowered his binoculars and turned to a soldier that was sitting at a portable table with their own decoding machine. The soldier quickly typed everything that the commander spoke. "Everything seems to be intact from here. No signs of damage or displacement. All parts of the ship are in place. The water below them seems to be calm as well. No signs of any wake."

Back in Philadelphia, all the men behind the wall were cheering from the fact that the ship was no longer in front of them. In its place was a thin green line on the water that outlined the shape of the ship. Inside of that outline was a slightly different shade of blue water, contrast to the rest of the bay. Franklin noticed. He turned to one of the men beside him and pointed at the water. "Look at the different color of the water. It must be a result of the displacement from the other side. That's got to be Chesapeake Bay water. Quick, run over and get a sample before the ship returns!"

The man dropped his note pad, turned sharply, and ran to a crate that was behind them full of supplies. He frantically looked through it but all he could find to help tackle the task was a long rope. He turned back around, grabbed his cup of coffee that was sitting on the floor, dumped out the coffee and took off sprinting toward the dock. When he got there, he took the rope that he found in the crate, pushed it through the handle of the cup, tied a knot to secure the cup to the rope, and lowered it down to the water. He dipped the cup in the water several times in attempt to clean it out. Bringing it back up, he used part of his shirt to wipe it down. He ran to another part of the dock and lowered it down in attempt to fill the cup with the different colored water. When he lifted the cup back up, he untied the rope, carefully turned toward the wall, and walked as fast as he could, trying not to spill a drop of the collected water. As he approached the wall, he noticed Franklin relaying everything that he witnessed to the soldier on the decoding machine. The soldier was typing as fast as he could. There were a few occasions when he had to tell Franklin to slow down and repeat what he just said.

In the room with the President all three soldiers on the decoding machines were frantically writing the messages that the three locations were giving. As they finished writing a message, they put it to the side of them and waited for the next message to appear. The man sitting next to Einstein got up and collected the messages. He read them to the group. First, he read the messages from Franklin and then from the SS Andrew Furuseth. Both Admirals, Einstein, and the President seemed very happy from what they were hearing so far. He read another message from the Eldridge. "Everything seems to be in place and in working order. The machinery is charging up and will trigger in seven minutes. The crew seem to be fine." He read the next message. "Reports of disorientation and nauseousness are coming from the crew. Seems to be getting worse by the second. They are being reminded to stay in place. Two minutes until jump."

Einstein shook his head in disapproval. A bead of sweat rolled down his brow. "It is imperative that the crew stand perfectly still and not touch anything when they jump back!"

Over on the Eldridge many of the sailors struggled to maintain their balance. Two sailors puked. Down below deck one sailor fell forward and caught himself with both hands on the wall of the hallway where he was standing. He rested his head against the wall as he continually dry heaved. A few other sailors were either on a knee or resting their hand or hands on the walls and equipment around them to maintain their balance. The situation on the deck was no different. The loud speaker continually reminded the sailors to stand at attention. The hum was back and the bluish-green fog started building again. The countdown began. "Ten seconds to jump. Nine. Eight. Seven. Six…." A sailor on the top deck was on his knee. He tried to get up as the count-down continued. For a second, he managed to stand up but then tumbled forward and stumbled over the side of the ship. A sailor standing next to him saw what was happening and instantly lunged after him to save him. Unfortunately, he was also very dizzy. As a result, both men fell over the side just as the countdown hit one.

"They're gone!" Commander Dodge yelled out as he stood on the SS Andrew Furuseth. He looked out at the space where the Eldridge used to be. All he could see was the bluish-green fog that slowly disappeared. A ring of discolored water outlining what used to be the ship's haul was all that was left. He described what he saw to the soldier sitting at the decoding machine, adding words like "unbelievable", and "incredible", as well as, "I don't believe it." The soldier typed his words.

On the shore in Philadelphia, Franklin and his team were cheering and celebrating as they stared at the returned Eldridge. Unfortunately, the celebration was short lived. Franklin looked carefully at the ship. His excitement went from cheering, to curiosity, and then fear. He turned to his team with that fear in his eyes. "Hold on, hold on. Look. Look! There is a lot of commotion going on with the sailors on the ship. There seems to be something wrong."

On the Eldridge the sailors and officers were either on their knees holding their heads or running around in panic. A sailor who saw their fellow crewmates fall quickly yelled out "man overboard!" and ran over to where they fell, expecting to see them in the water. There was nothing there. Down below deck was a horrific sight. Sailors' hands and arms fused together with ship parts they'd held or leaned against. One poor sailor had his head and arms inside the wall of the ship while the rest of his body hung lifeless. On the level below, one man was draped on a large pipe screaming with one of his legs fused to that pipe while his other leg rested on top of the pipe, broken. A few disoriented sailors came running to his aid. One of the sailors looked around the area in confusion. "Where did he come from?"

Another green faced sailor stood in disbelief. "I think he came from… the upper level. I saw him falling during the…." Before he could finish, he turned his head and threw up.

Back with the president, the look of horror covered everyone's face as they listened to the reports coming from the USS Eldridge. The president picked up his head from being buried in his hands. "What have we done?"

Albert sensed the president's tone. He closed his eyes in an attempt to find an answer to the tragedy. "The principles of physics in this matter are sound. Unfortunately, the variables of human physiology and psyche are far more difficult to predict and manage."

Admiral King also sensed the tone. He put on a stern face. "Sir, what happened is a tragedy just as any incident that happens. Tragedy happens even with basic routine maintenance. What we and every serviceman have signed up do is dangerous. I cringe at every incident that I hear about. What I also do is keep moving forward. I know that if I don't, the sacrifices that those service men made are for nothing. We have seen some incredible success mixed with incredible failures in this trial. We must ..."

The president interrupted the Admiral. "Admiral King, thank you for your inspiring words. I know where you are going with this. However, I don't dare take the same path that you are willing to go down. Tragedies happen and we do everything we can to prevent them, even go to war if needs be. We have seen horrible things happen to a lot of good people as a result. We cannot add to this horror any more than we absolutely have to. This technology is extremely impressive. It can change the world." He looked sympathetically at Albert. "Unfortunately, in the wrong hands, it can lead to the downfall of us all. That is why the Manhattan project exists." President Roosevelt punched his fists on the desk and painfully stood up out of his wheelchair. "We will not make any more of our boys' lab rats! We are going dark with this. From now on, this project will be in the hands of the OAPC." He looked at the sixth man at the table, who had been sitting quietly this whole time. "I trust that you can handle it properly."

The sixth man grinned while trying to maintain an empathetic look on his face. "Yes sir, we absolutely can. I will need full control and resistance-free cooperation to make this completely secure sir."

President Roosevelt looked boldly at Admiral Leahy. "I don't think that will be a problem. Isn't that right Admiral?"

Admiral Leahy kept a serious face and looked back at the president. "It will not be a problem at all with the Navy sir. I will personally see to the complete secrecy and cooperation with my men sir."

The President looked back at the sixth man. "There you go. Full control and resistance-free cooperation. I better not hear of any more horror stories like the one that just took place. Albert, if you will stay on, please see to that."

Albert looked at the President and let out a sigh. "I will stay on to advise the crew. You know my feelings about weaponizing technology. We will only succeed in advancing human kind by using our discoveries for the good of men, not for the destruction of them."

The sixth man gave Albert a warm gaze. "I think that we will get along just fine." His warmth turned cold and serious as he looked at the Admirals. "Gentlemen. I will need everything that has to do with, connected to, and recorded about this project on trucks and taken to the Nevada facility. All records of the Eldridge and the men on the ship that have faced unfortunate tragedy will need to be changed to being stationed somewhere else."

Admiral Leahy had a puzzled look on his face. "Nevada? I didn't know we had a facility in Nevada."

The sixth man stared straight into Admiral Leahy's eyes and leaned slightly forward. "And let's keep it that way."

Admiral King briefly clenched his eyes shut and locked his jaw. His hopes of a quick turn-around from a long stretch of defeat at sea vanished. "And what of our men that still have to face the enemy out at sea?"

The sixth man looked at Admiral King with a slight grin. "Maybe we can help with that. We have been working on a machine that is meant to repel enemy mines away from a ship's hull. It's no teleporter and it won't make you invisible to U-boats, but it will give you an advantage. It will also fill in the void that will be left on the Eldridge from us removing the machinery. Any "rumors" of top-secret projects linked to the Eldridge will be diverted to the development of that."

The President sat back down in his chair. "It seems like the OAPC have things taken care of on their side." He turned towards the Admirals. "I have confidence that the Navy will too. I wish things would have turned out differently. God knows that it's been a rough year. Nevertheless, even without this technology, I have faith that the two of you will overcome the challenges that we have and will be faced with." The president pounded his fist on the table. "We will prevail! Gentlemen, let's get to work!"

The two Admirals stood up sharply in perfect synchronization and saluted the President. Together they said, "Yes sir!" They both turned at the same time and marched toward the door.

President Roosevelt looked down on the desk as he sank back down on his chair, deeply reflecting on the event that just took place. A heavy weight from his chest pulled him down as he said with a crack in his voice, "May God have mercy on our souls."

Chapter 1

Rachael's spine slammed against the side of the Orion space capsule. Amy's eyes stayed glued to her laptop, scanning for any sign of corrupted code while pinned next to Rachael. Adam's grip slipped from the maintenance panel, slamming him hard against the opposite side of the ship. George's knuckles whitened as he clung to the control screen. As the ship spun faster, Rachael's breath hitched as her crew blurred into darkness.

Twenty-Four Hours Earlier...

The bleachers facing launch pad 39B were full of excited NASA employees, families, and friends, all anxiously awaiting the explosive roar of rockets at the Kennedy Space Center's Observation Gantry in Florida. Beads of sweat covered their faces as they sipped drinks, fighting the humid eighty-eight-degree heat. The breeze was scarce and the sky lacked clouds for shade. Everyone knew the true cause of their perspiration came from the fear that the launch of this SLS rocket might be the last.

At the bleachers' base, a news reporter positioned herself strategically with the rocket in the background. To her left stood a man in a tucked-in yellow short-sleeved shirt, brown slacks, and glasses. On her right was a taller man with three young kids next to him. Two eight-year-old twin boys stood as patiently as they could, occasionally kicking the grass beneath them. A six-year-old little girl clenched tightly to her father's leg, trying desperately to hide her face while her father wrapped his arm around her to comfort her.

The reporter straightened in her red dress, smiling into the camera with a heavily powdered face. "I'm standing at the Observation Gantry at the Kennedy Space Center with NASA Engineer Max Carter and Sam Williams, husband of astronaut Amy Williams, along with his three kids. Thank you all for joining me. Behind us is the Artemis V mission rocket that will be carrying our four astronauts to the moon: Head programmer Amy Williams, former military fighter pilot George Hinderman, the talented engineer Adam Caller, and mission commander, acclaimed scientist Rachael Miller. In just a few moments these four individuals will be blasting off into space." The reporter turned to the man in the yellow short-sleeved shirt. "Max, can you tell us a little about this rocket?"

Max pushed his glasses closer to his face as he proceeded to explain the functionality of the rocket as if he was explaining his purpose in life. A bead of sweat dripped down his cheek as he explained in detail the different stages of the rocket.

She struggled to mirror his genuine enthusiasm. "Wow. That is amazing!"

A twinkle in Max's eyes appeared as he grinned. "Yes, everyone at NASA is very thrilled about the launch."

The reporter tilted her head with her plastic smile. "I'm glad that there is so much excitement, especially with the rumors of more cutbacks. Private companies like SpaceX have dominated the industry at a far lower cost. They say the only reason the SLS made it this far is because of Congress protecting the program. Is it true that this could be the last Artemis mission and that NASA is considering contracting all further missions to these private companies?"

The twinkle left Max's eyes. "SpaceX is an amazing company, but it serves for a particular purpose. The Artemis program has far more safeguards for space travel to places like the moon and, more importantly, back to Earth. A lot of things can go wrong on such a trip. It's the tried-and-true method, which is important when dealing with human lives."

The reporter quickly fired back. "That's not what SpaceX is claiming. They claim that their design is just as capable and safe and can take up more people for far less than the SLS rocket, which D.O.G.E. has shown to have hemorrhaged billions of taxpayers' dollars. With the massive cutbacks not too long ago, the word is that a lot is riding on this launch to go perfectly. Is that why NASA switched to sending up four individuals that have never been in space? To up the ante on the SLS rocket being the safest bet when it comes to trips like this?"

Max's grin left his face. "I know that there are a lot of conspiracy theories out there, a lot of rumors and hearsay. What I can tell you is that a trip like this will always be risky and there is nothing better than proven experience, no matter what SpaceX claims. The four individuals who are sitting on top of that rocket right now are highly experienced, highly qualified, even highly decorated individuals. It gives me great comfort that they are the ones on this mission right now. Are things changing? Of course. Is NASA disappearing? Never. In fact, we are working with SpaceX to build a space port where we can launch nuclear powered spacecraft from space. There is a lot that needs to happen, a lot of building. Until then, this rocket is the best thing we have for a little while longer. We are all still very eager about these missions."

"Well, the people at NASA are not alone in excitement, I can assure you. I have heard a lot of great things about these astronauts. Speaking of the astronauts." The reporter turned to Sam and his kids. "Amy, your wife, is sitting right now at the top of the rocket behind us, patiently waiting with her three other crew members to go into space and head to the moon. Sam, only a few short moments until take off. How are you feeling right now?"

Sam smiled at the plastic reporter. "We are all very proud and excited for Amy. We've been excited ever since she was chosen for this mission. She's been working hard preparing for this for a while now. It's hard to believe that this moment is finally here."

"These missions are fully automated from launch to splash down. Amy was the one in charge of the actual programming that will basically run this whole mission, is that correct?" The reporter seemed genuinely interested.

"Yes, that's correct." Sam felt his daughter's grip tighten on his leg as they spoke. "She played a big role in this mission. One thing that she kept telling me was how grateful she was that she had such a great team of programmers that spent countless hours creating and checking the programs over and over again. They are the ones who made it possible."

"I'm sure they are. They aren't the only ones that should claim credit, though. I'm sure that she has great support from her family as well." The reporter looked down at the kids with a bright gaze.

"Yeah, she definitely has all of us cheering for her." Sam looked at his kids with a warm sense of pride.

"I'm sure it comes with some sacrifices. I hear that you own your own architectural firm. With both of you in demanding positions, does that make things difficult for your family?" The reporter's tone became more serious as she directed her questioning toward Sam.

Sam sensed the change of tone. "Well, yes and no. It definitely keeps me busy, but since it's my firm, I can work from home and control my schedule. That makes it very convenient when Amy is away."

The reporter's smile dissipated as she continued to question Sam. "I also hear that you have been getting a lot of resistance from environmentalists. They say that because you specialize in designing cabins in the woods, the damage caused by building roads, utility lines, and construction have been wreaking havoc on nature."

Sam put away his smile as well. His voice became less upbeat. "Those claims have been grossly exaggerated and a lot of straight out lies. All guidelines and regulations are always adhered to."

The reporter continued to dig into Sam. "The environmentalists even filed lawsuits against your company claiming that you weren't. Is that correct?"

Sam shook his head as his lip curled up in disgust. "Yeah, all those lawsuits were immediately dismissed and those so-called environmentalists have done a lot of damage to not only my equipment, but to the nature they claim to protect. I thought we were talking about Amy and the moon mission."

The reporter's demeanor instantly shifted as she put on her plastic smile again and turned to the kids. She bent down so that she was at eye level to the boys. "And how are you three feeling? Are you excited to see your mom go into space?"

Jumping up with excitement, the two boys threw their hands up in the air. "Yeah!" The youngest daughter clenched tighter to her father's leg as she continued to hide her face.

Letting out a small laugh, the reporter kept her attention on the boys. "Are you proud of what your mom is able to accomplish?"

The boys were happy to get attention. They jumped up again. "Yeah!"

The reporter stood back up and looked at the camera. "Well, there you have it. The support team for Amy Williams anxiously waiting for Artemis V to get under way."

As the reporter said her final comments, Sam picked up his daughter and motioned to his boys to follow him toward the bleachers. He looked up to see many familiar faces. Geniuses in their profession. Most of them had families who were counting on them to provide. The rude reporter's words to Max echoed in Sam's brain as he walked closer to them. Was this the last mission for this crowd? If it was, did they know that their sustenance was about to be yanked away? With all that brain power, they had to know. As Sam sat down with his children, he wondered how at risk the people around him really were.

Back on top of the SLS rocket sat the four Astronauts who were strapped tightly into their seats. They all had their personally fitted bright orange Orion Crew Survival System suit and helmet on, which, for the most part, were relatively comfortable. Their noise-reducing helmets each came equipped with communications systems that they used to communicate with each other as well as mission control.

The seats backs were attached to the floor of the capsule, positioning each astronaut on their back, facing the top of the rocket. George occupied the pilot's seat, Rachael the commanders. They had access to four windows, though currently covered by the launch abort system, blocking any outside view during launched. In front of them sat the control console which consisted of three large touch screens surrounded by knobs, dials, and switches. Below sat the other two astronauts, with Amy on the left and Adam on the right. Their heads were positioned just below the feet of the first two. The capsule's interior offered about as much space as two minivans.

George and Rachael looked over the screens to verify that everything was in good shape for launch. George flipped a switch to communicate with mission control. "All systems looking good from here. We are go for launch."

A voice from mission control echoed back. "Roger that. T-minus six minutes and counting." Adam flinched, pulse spiking, as he heard the mobile launcher access arm swing away from the rocket, taking away their access to escape by foot if they needed to.

George flipped the switch to end communication with mission control while maintaining communication with his crewmates. "And just like that, my job is done. I think I'll take a nap. Wake me up when we're in space."

Adam's muscles tightened as he grabbed onto the handles on the seat. He was not in the mood for George's corny comments. "I get that this isn't as exciting as your many secret military missions you supposedly were on, but I swear if I hear you snoring, I will personally disconnect that helmet of yours to slap you awake."

George grinned. "I don't know what the problem is. Rachael is perfectly capable of taking control if something were to happen. Are … are you saying that she's not? That's pretty messed up. Don't you have faith in your commander?"

Adam's grip on the seat loosened a little from George's jab and poor attempt at humor. "Oh, I absolutely trust Rachael. I'm just a little tired of her constantly carrying you while you slack off on your duties. You need to do something to earn your moon walk."

George let out a small laugh. "I do plenty. Besides, everything on this mission is automated. Everything that I need to do for the launch is done. The system's program is going to do the rest of the work for this trip. I'm just an eighth string backup. Isn't that right Amy?"

Amy attempted to look up at George but quickly remembered that she couldn't see him from where she was sitting. "That's right, George. You are a just in case to the just in case to the just in case. The system's program will do everything. In fact, I still don't even know why you're up here. I'm still holding to the claim that you have something on someone."

Adam closed his eyes and shook his head. "Yeah, but there's always that possibility that something could glitch." He nervously looked to his right at the hatch that was securely shut.

Amy laughed heartily. "Alright Adam. Here are some facts for you to help calm the nerves. I have personally overseen the flight software development and testing that has been proven successful on multiple missions already. That software includes resolution to well over three hundred thousand different mission scenarios that we may face during this mission. The software is also constantly monitored by many, many teams of program engineers. Not only that, but to help you to not have to use your built-in bathroom system in your suit, the software is updated to account for current weather factors right up to the time that we launch to ensure that we have a smooth ride. Does that help Adam?"

Adam took a deep breath. "No." He tilted his head up to look in George's direction. "My earlier statement stands. One hint of snoring and I'll be on you like a pimp trying to collect money from one of his girls that is holding out on him."

"Adam, that was quite a descriptive and slightly inappropriate scenario you just gave." Rachael said, chuckling despite a hint of disgust.

George immediately jumped in. "If you want, I'll switch the auto pilot off and grab the stick. It will give me something to do and you won't have to worry about any computer glitches."

Adam waved his hands in rejection to George's suggestion. "Just like you did in that simulator? No thanks."

A slight grin appeared on George's face. "Are you still mad about that?"

Adam raised the tone of his voice. "We spent three hours in that simulator and you had to purposely crash us to, quote, see what would happen. We had to re-do the simulation! I missed my wedding anniversary dinner! My wife was pissed!"

George laughed. "Yeah, but don't you remember? I took care of your wife for you."

Adam's eyebrow rose on his face. "What's that supposed to mean!?"

Catching Adam's tone, George spoke in a slow, bold voice. "I treated both of you to a really expensive restaurant. Quit being so paranoid."

Remembering the meal, Adam calmed down and quickly changed his tone from angry to friendly. "Oh yeah. That was a good meal. Thanks again for that."

"No problem," George said with a smirk.

Adam's muscles tensed up again. He rose his hand up to George. "Still, if you mess with our flight, I'll have my pimp hand ready for you."

Rachael jumped in the conversation between what she perceived to be two children. "I'm sure that George will be fully engaged with his duties and follow all the protocols when we start to blast off. We all are a little anxious right now. Let's all just try to stay focused."

George raised his eyebrows and slightly tilted his head. "Eh."

Rachael crinkled her nose at George's comment. "Come on. You must be a little anxious. We are about to be blasted up into space by a huge controlled explosion and you don't feel anything?"

George shrugged his shoulders. "Honestly, not really. Maybe it's because I'm used to having jet engines behind me from flying fighter planes, I don't know. In all honesty, right now, I'm a little bored."

Rachael rolled her eyes. "Wow. You must be dead inside."

At the same time, Adam and Amy replied, "Yep."

They all broke into laughter. As they were laughing, the electronics and fuel were cut off from the four umbilical's that were attached to the outside of the rocket.

Over at the Observation Gantry, the viewers anxiously awaited as they continually glanced at the large display showing the countdown. Amy's daughter, now sitting on her father's lap, was clenched onto her father's side as she peaked at the rocket. Their two boys were standing at the rails jumping up and down as they looked back and forth between the display and the rocket.

As the countdown hit twenty seconds, the crowd joined in, shouting the final numbers aloud. At "fifteen," water nozzles beneath the rocket activated, unleashing thousands of gallons to suppress the impending engine roar. The crowd pressed on: "Fourteen, thirteen, twelve, eleven, ten, nine…" The four engines and two boosters ignited, spewing fire past the water into the flame trenches, exhaust barreling from side openings. Power built as two stabilizers on the forward skirt held firm. "Five, four, three, two, one, blastoff!" The crowd roared as the four umbilicals and two stabilizers released simultaneously. Eight-point-eight million pounds of thrust propelled the craft skyward, its roar washing over the cheering spectators. The rocket ascended straight from its pad, clearing the tower that had cradled it moments before.

The announcer over the loudspeakers at the observation gantry proclaimed, "Artemis five cleared the tower and is headed towards the moon!" The crowd continued to clap and cheer as the two boys jumped higher and threw their hands up in the air. The daughter looked up at the rocket as it started its ascent up into space. A tear rolled down her cheek. She raised up her hand and waved to the rocket while saying, "Bye Mommy," in a soft innocent voice.

Inside the Orion capsule the four astronauts were pushed back into their seats as they gained speed. The rockets roar, though muffled by their helmets, still dominated their senses. As they gained altitude, the sound started to fade. It continued to fade until it was just a soft background white noise. George took that opportunity to let out a loud fake snore for all the crew members to hear. Adam shook his head in disgust as the vibrations rattled his bones.

"Houston, we have max Q at one minute, thirty seconds." George announced on his communication link after making the observation on his screen.

As they continued to rise into space, the sound of the rockets began to return. Rachael looked at the screen and noticed that they were approaching the two-minute mark. At two minutes, the two side boosters that were attached to the main rocket exhausted all of their fuel. Connections that held them in place disconnected from the main rocket. Adam gripped his chair tighter as he heard the Side blasts from the two side boosters, which caused them to push away from the main rocket, back down to earth and eventually into the ocean below. On the screen, Rachael noticed that the boosters were disconnected and cleared. "Houston, we have a clean separation from the two side boosters." She proclaimed.

"Copy that. We are seeing the same down here." A voice came back to them.

Rachael and George continued to watch the screen, waiting for the three-minute mark to hit. When it hit, they heard the three panels that were protecting the Orion service module disconnect and eject off of the craft. Thirty seconds after, the Launch Abort System that was covering the windows of their capsule disconnected. Rockets positioned on the side of the tower of the Launch Abort System ignited, causing the tower to separate and lift away from the Orion capsule. "Houston, we have tower jettison." George announced.

"Roger that. Tower clear." The voice from the ground confirmed.

The four windows that were once covered by the Launch Abort System were now clear. Rachael and George could now see outside. They both looked out the windows in amazement. This was the first time any of them traveled outside of earth's atmosphere. They only knew what to expect from training videos, pictures and simulators. They never expected it to be so astounding in real life. Through the window, Earth appeared flawless, surpassing any high-definition screen. The details were stunning. They could see multiple continents and multiple oceans at the same time. The atmosphere's glow hugged the planet's curve brightly. On the distant continents where the sun didn't reach, city lights outlined the coasts like houses during Christmas. The cloud formations on the different parts of the earth were mesmerizing. Even George, who had seen amazing views from inside the cockpit of planes, was awed by the sheer beauty of the planet that they just escaped from.

George glanced over at Rachael and saw she was in the same trance that he was in. He shook it off and diverted his attention back onto the control panels, carefully monitoring the stats as they constantly updated on the screen. It was only a couple minutes before Rachael escaped her trance and joined George in monitoring the screens as they continued to rise into orbit.

At the eight-minute mark, the screens indicated that they had reached orbit. The SLS core stage engines shut down. "Houston, we have obtained Earth orbit. We have SLS core stage shut down and commencing on SLS ICPS separation." Rachael announced.

"Roger that. ICPS separation is a go." The voice from Houston replied.

Seconds later, the Interim Cryogenic Propulsion Stage (ICPS) – the Artemis V's upper section - detached from the large orange tank that housed the fuel that blasted them to space. The ICPS carrying the crew slowly moved forward and away from the orange tank. As they crept further away, the large tank slowly began to lose altitude and toward its descent to the Pacific Ocean.

"Houston, separation complete. ICPS is stable. All systems nominal." George proclaimed.

"Roger that. That's a good deal. Systems confirmed stable." The voice from the ground confirmed.

"Houston, the crew is in good shape and high spirits. We are going to unbuckle and resituate the capsule for travel."

Rachael informed the ground crew as she proceeded to detach her seatbelts.

"Sounds good commander. Approximately forty-three minutes till ICPS engine ignition." The ground team responded.

"Alright guys, let's get out of these suits and stow the seats before we hit another burn. How you feeling down there?" Rachael finished unbuckling her seatbelt and glanced over at her crewmates.

Closing his eyes, Adam took slow, deep breaths in his helmet. "Nauseous."

Amy was playing with the weightlessness of her limbs in wonder as she was still buckled into her seat. Her attention, however, was quickly diverted to Adam. "Yeah, you look pretty green Adam. Let me get you some nausea pills. I have some in my leg pocket."

Quickly taking off her seatbelt and gloves, Amy reached in her pocket for the pills. After taking off his helmet and seatbelt, George looked at Adam and grinned. "Adam, why don't you keep that helmet on. Keep the chunks in your own space."

With a very green face, Adam grinned back. "Was planning on something like that. Just make sure to check for gifts in your sleeping bag later."

Now freed from her seat, Amy floated over to Adam with a curled lip and pills in her hand. "Gross." She placed the pills in Adam's glove and helped him take his helmet off. She let go of his helmet as if she were placing it on an invisible shelf. It floated right next to his head, very slowly spinning counter clockwise.

Adam carefully put the pills into his mouth and swallowed them. "Thanks Amy." He closed his eyes again and continued to take deep, slow breaths. "Just give me a minute and I'll be good."

"No problem. Just, please, no gross pranks. I deal with little boys back on earth. I don't want to have to deal with that while we're up here." As Amy took her helmet off, she started to feel a little nauseous herself. Tightly closing her eyes and taking a deep breath, she was able to temporarily shake it off. She grabbed nausea pills out of her pocket and threw them into her mouth. Feeling a little better, she folded up her seat to shed her survival suit.

By this time both George and Rachael had taken off their suits and balled them up. Underneath their suits, they had on white t-shirts with NASA logos on their left breast that were tucked into their blue light weight track pants and white socks. Methodically, they detached their already folded up seats from the capsule wall so they could stow it away. Behind the now detached seats were lockers used for storage. Carefully, they slid the seats and survival suits in the lockers.

Rachael checked the screens once again to make sure that everything was functioning properly. Once she was confident that all was well, her curiosity fueled, science-driven mind started teasing her like an itch. She began experimenting with her movements in micro gravity, tucking her knees into her chest, forming a ball, and spinning as much as the limited room would allow her to. George was in a similar mode. He would slightly push himself back and forth, seeing how much force it took to move around. As he was experimenting with his movements, George noticed that Adam was still buckled up in his seat.

George raised his eyebrows as he looked down at his struggling crewmate. "You alive over there Adam?"

"Yeah, I'm alive. The nausea is fading. Give me a few more seconds and I'll be good." Adam's eyes were still closed but the heavy breathing stopped. He could feel the medication start to kick in.

George flipped around and slapped Adam in the arm. "Good. Your rotting corpse would stink up this place pretty good. Give it a couple days and you'll get used to it… hopefully."

Adam shook his head at George's comment. He slowly opened his eyes as he took one more deep breath. The urge of throwing up had faded him, but he still was very careful with his movements. Slowly, he started the process of unbuckling from his seat. Rachael noticed Adam's slow movements and pushed her way over to help him out.

Amy finished balling up her survival suit and pushed it over to George who was waiting to catch it. He grabbed it out of the air as it floated over to him and carefully placed it in the open locker with the other suits. She successfully removed the seat and pushed it over as well. George grabbed and stored it with the others.

Adam was finally out of his seat and proceeded to strip out of his survival suit. As he took off his gloves, shoes, and other layers, Amy collected it. While this was going on, Rachael disconnected Adam's seat and pushed it over to George who stored it away with the other three seats.

Finally, Adam was out of his survival suit and was exposing his white t-shirt, blue pants outfit like the other three. Amy rolled up the suit and tossed it to George. Rachael looked over at Adam with a raised brow. "Feeling better?"

Adam blinked hard a couple of times, then looked up at Rachael with a nod. "I'm feeling better than I was. I'm not going to be spinning myself for fun in this zero G environment anytime soon, but yes, much better, thanks."

"That's good to hear." Rachael glanced warmly between Adam and Amy. "If you want something to take your mind off of possibly losing your lunch, go check out the view."

Both Adam and Amy looked toward the window on the other side of the capsule. George positioned his body where he was floating above Amy so that they could switch places. Rachael did the same with Adam. As they got closer to the windows, their jaws dropped at the amazing view.

Time flew by quickly for the crew as they repositioned the inside of their module and gazed down on the Earth. A voice over the radio from ground control announced, "Ten seconds until solar array deployment."

Rachael was shocked how fast a half an hour went. "Roger that Houston. Deployment on schedule."

Outside of the craft, four solar panels retracted from their neatly folded state. A few seconds later, the solar arrays were fully extended to form an X, with the space capsule in the middle.

George looked at the computer as it cycled through the program of the trip. He sighed at the mundane task of babysitting an automated system. "Houston, solar panels fully extended. We are on track for the orbital raise maneuver in T-minus one minute." After announcing the status of the ship, George looked out the window again at the Earth. It instantly made him grin.

"Copy that. Looks good from down here." Ground control replied.

Rachael leaned forward as she looked at her crew. "Brace yourselves for this burn. Once we reach a higher orbit, we will only have a short time before another burn to put us on a path towards the moon. Enjoy this view of the Earth while you can."

The crew put their hands against the walls of the capsule right before the engine fired up again, bringing the capsule farther away from the Earth. The roar of the engines went silent. The crew continued to Earth gaze between tasks as they prepared for their last burn to escape Earth's orbit.

Again, half an hour went by quickly. The voice from ground control sounded again. "Thirty seconds until trans-lunar injection burn. How you looking up there?"

Rachael grabbed onto the side of the controls to stabilize herself, then flipped a switch. "We are looking good Houston. Both crew and capsule are ready for the burn."

Rachael and George continued with their tasks with firm and precise movements as they prepared themselves for another burn. Adam looked around the capsule intensely, triple checking that everything was in place. As Amy prepared herself, the view of Earth outside the window captured her attention. Her body drooped as she looked at her home where her family was.

Ground control's voice announced over the radio, "Trans-lunar injection burn in three, two, one, ignition." The ICPS engine fired up again, slightly displacing the crew inside the ship as it escaped Earth's orbit and repositioned the craft on a new trajectory to the moon. Excitement filled the emotions of both the team on the ground and in the ship as the rocket's explosion continued to push them in their desired direction. Twenty minutes later, the engines turned off.

George looked at the computer screens and closely examined the numbers presented. "Houston, we have ICPS engine shutdown. Looks like our trajectory is on the mark. All systems are nominal. ICPS separation is a go on this side."

Ground control replied, "We are reading the same. That is a good deal, George. We will allow the program to run its course."

"Copy that, Houston. Service module – ICPS separation in T-minus thirty seconds." George continued to monitor the data on the screens. Rachael did the same. Amy pulled out a tablet from one of the storage bins and plugged it into the back of the ship's screens with a cord. She pulled up the program that the mission was currently running to make sure that everything was running correctly. Adam aggressively put his ear against the ships wall to hear that the carbon dioxide filter was rotating properly. Everyone was inspecting the ship as if they were medical doctors doing a thorough medical exam on a patient.

Ground control announced, "ICPS separation in three, two, one."

The service module carrying the Orion capsule detached from the Spacecraft adaptor that was holding it to the interim cryogenic propulsion stage of the rocket, exposing a large main engine on the bottom of the service module. The main engine was also surrounded by eight smaller auxiliary thrusters. The thrusters fired small bursts, slowly pulling the module away from the ICPS. Bursts from the ICPS own thrusters fired, positioning itself in a slightly different direction but within visual distance of the Orion capsules windows.

Rachael confirmed to Houston, "Houston we have successful separation from the ICPS and are in position for visual confirmation of CubeSat extraction."

Ground control replied, "Copy that. CubeSat launch in three, two, one, launch."

Rachael looked out the window to see five shoebox-sized packages spring out of the inside of the adaptor attached to the ICPS. Each package went in various directions to monitor some part of space.

"Looks like five successful extractions Houston. CubeSats are launched and cleared of the ICPS." Rachael announced as she squinted her eyes out the window.

The voice from ground control replied, "Good to hear. We will continue to monitor and keep you updated on its journey to Mars. Now is a good time for you all to get settled in and get something to eat."

"I was thinking the same thing. We will keep you updated on our status." Rachael replied with a grin.

"Sounds good. Have a safe journey." The voice on the radio said sincerely.

George joined Rachael in looking out the windows at the ICPS. It had made quite some distance from the Orion capsule by now. They watched with wide eyes as the main engine ignited again, pushing it towards Mars to deliver the communications satellite that it was carrying. While watching the ICPS George asked, "There goes the overpriced multi-billion-dollar delivery vehicle. Do you really think that this will be the last Orion mission? The private industry has NASA beat when it comes to this stuff."

With an uncertain tilt of her head, Rachael replied, "I honestly don't know. Worried about job security?"

Nodding his head, George turned to Rachael. "Well, yeah. I could get used to stuff like this. Don't know if I'd be ready to give it up. You think SpaceX is hiring?"

Rachael laughed. "Probably. But I hear you have to have a certain number of followers on X to qualify and your resume is your past posts."

Looking down, George murmured under his breath, "Crap."

Once the ICPS was nothing more than a dot, Rachael turned her attention away from the window and towards the rest of the crew. She clapped and rubbed both of her hands together. "I don't know about you guys but I'm pretty hungry. Let's crack open tonight's dinner."

George quickly pushed himself towards one of the storage cabinets on the floor of the ship. "I'm all over it. I think we could all use something to eat… well, maybe all except for Mr. Green over there." George smirked as he nodded his head in Adam's direction.

Adam caught George's criticism and curled his lip. "Ha, Ha, I get it. Mr. Green because I got a little nauseous after blasting up at incredible speeds out of the Earth's atmosphere in to an environment where there is no real up or down orientation. Well for your information I am a little hungry! And thanks again Amy for the pills!"

Everyone cracked a smile as George opened the food cabinet and handed out that night's food rations. After the crew finished their meal, they continued to monitor the ship as well as perform minor experiments of various topics that they brought along with them for a few hours.

"I think it's about that time to get some sleep." Rachael turned toward the crew and looked at her watch. Digital time was now the only thing that they could rely on to know when it was time to sleep, considering that there were no sunsets or sunrises from where they were. "Do what you need to do and let's strap into our sleeping sacks."

Each of them took turns using the small but fully enclosed bathroom, which was located on the floor of the ship, right next to the door where they entered the capsule. After, they pulled out their sleeping bags, they strapped them to the walls of the ship so that they wouldn't float around while they were sleeping. They each got in their bags and wished each other a good night before Adam flipped the light switch off.

Chapter 2

An alarm pierced the capsule with a relentless chirp. Adam reluctantly squinted at a digital clock that he mounted on the wall next to him with half-open eyes. Eight and a half hours ticked by since they first climbed into their sleeping sacks. The crew's first night in space was a haze. Slipping from sacks, they drifted to the window, eyes wide, hearts pounding at the Earth's glow. They each got about four hours of broken sleep, except for George. He never climbed out of his bag and slept almost the whole time.

Adam flicked on the capsule's lights as the crew slowly crawled out of their sacks. After stretching their limbs in the limited space, they stuffed their sacs back into their storage cabinet. Adam rubbed his face. "I don't know about you guys, but I'm definitely going to tap into that supply of sleeping pills tonight."

Rachael nodded in agreement. "Yeah, I think the first night is always the toughest one."

George, alert and smug, tilted his chin at Rachael. "I don't know what you're talking about. I slept great. Zero G is better than any mattress that I've ever slept on."

Rachael chuckled while rubbing an eye. "That's because you're dead inside. Since you're fully awake, why don't you get our breakfast while we attempt to wake ourselves up."

"No problem." George quickly moved toward one of the cabinets. "I'll get out some of that freeze-dried coffee to help you out."

"Thanks, George." Rachael smiled as she turned and pushed her way over to the control panel to check the data on the screens.

After breakfast, the crew continued to get ready for the day in their small space that they shared. They each had an outlined schedule that consisted of monitoring the ship, conducting experiments, and working out.

Hours later, video call time neared. Rachael sighed. There was no family or love interest waiting for her call. She never made time for it, always focused on her career. She turned to George, who was exercising on the ROCKY, or the resistive overload combined with kinetic yo-yo device. "George, it's time for video calls. Have anyone that you want to say hi to?"

George braced both feet on a shoebox-sized device under the side hatch. He had a bar on his shoulders with cables on both sides that connected to the ROCKY device to simulate squats. His face strained as he stood straight from squatting. "No, I have no one I want to call."

Amy looked at him with a raised eyebrow. "What about that girl that you took out the other day. I think her name was Mindy. Won't she be disappointed?"

George finished his set and grabbed a towel floating next to him. He wiped his forehead as he looked over at Amy with a straight face. "No. She knows of the family-only policy."

Rachael tilted her head. "NASA doesn't have a family-only policy."

The corner of George's lip rose. "I didn't say it was a NASA policy. You guys can use my time."

Rachael rolled her eyes, then looked over at Adam and Amy. "Alright, who wants to call first?"

Amy looked at Adam and lifted her chin. "Why don't you go first. I'll probably take a lot of time and I don't want to hold you up."

Adam nodded. "Alright. I'll call home, then Ashley at college."

"Go for it," Amy said, waving casually. "I just talked to Ashley two weeks ago about her programming project. She's sharp."

Adam nodded with a smirk on his face. "Yeah, I know. I have a feeling that she'll end up talking to you more than she will to me. She really looks up to you."

Amy rolled her eyes and placed her hand on Adam's arm. "She looks up to you too."

Adam's eyebrows lifted. "Really, she said that huh?"

Amy wrinkled her nose and briefly looked away. "Well, no, but you can absolutely tell. It's obvious."

"Thanks." He grabbed one of the tablets and dialed his home. It took a second to connect, then rang. A couple of rings later, Adam's smiling wife appeared on the screen. His wife's face was a breath of fresh air. "Hi honey. It's good to see you."

"Hi Adam! It's good to see you too and that you're still in one piece." His wife's face beamed with excitement and relief.

"Yeah, I'm still in one piece, although if you ask my crewmates, they'd tell you something different, bunch of jerks." He made sure to say that loud enough for everyone in the ship to hear. "Where's Dillan?"

His wife looked behind her and yelled, "Dillan! Put away your VR and come see your father in space!" She walked over to their living room with the camera showing every step where Dillan, their sixteen-year-old son, was taking off his head set. He put it down on a chair and walked over to the tablet that his mother was holding.

"Hi, Dad." Dillan spoke with a casual voice, as if his father never left Earth. "How's space?"

"It's amazing! Moving around in zero gravity is a blast. And you should see the view of the Earth from up here. It's unbelievable!" Adam smiled with raised eyebrows.

Dillan's voice elevated in excitement. "Yeah, I've seen it! I just downloaded this awesome game on the VR that takes you into space on Starship. You can look out the windows and see the earth in photo realistic images. It's pretty cool."

Adam's head tilted at his son's excitement of his virtual world. "Nice? It sounds like you're enjoying your time off from school. You know, it's good to get out and see the non-virtual world. Why don't you spend time hanging out with your friends?"

Dillan rolled his eyes and said with a smart aleck voice, "I am Dad. They have the game too and we are all in the same ship."

Adam's wife playfully pushed on Dillan's head. "I wish Ashley could join in on the call at the same time. Are you sure we can't do that?"

Adam looked down and slowly nodded his head. "Yeah, I'm sure. I wish she could too. Unfortunately, these calls are going through NASA and being heavily filtered and screened for any corrupt data and viruses. It's a quick, seamless process, but it can only handle one source at a time. I was going to call her after I called you guys." Adam looked at the faces of his wife and son, enjoying every second of the moment. "It's really good to see you two. I miss you."

Adam's wife squeezed her son with her arm as she radiated a warm glare on the screen. "We miss you too."

After another thirty minutes of talking about their experiences both at home and in space, Adam noticed that his time was running out. "Hun, it looks like my time is almost up and I still need to call Ashley."

Adam's wife looked down for a second. She lifted her head wearing a fake, awkward grin. Her eyes began to water. "I know. It was nice being able to see you."

Adam could see right through her. "It is really nice seeing you guys too. I'll see you again tomorrow."

A tear crawled down Adam's wife's cheek. "I know. You know. Space. Gets me worried."

"We'll be fine. Remember, I'm an awesome engineer." Adam put on a smug smirk. "Love you guys."

Both Dillan and Adam's wife replied at the same time, "Love you too."

Adam tapped the tablet and the video of his family vanished. Tears welled, floating in zero-G. He rubbed his eyes, took a deep breath, and dialed Ashley. After a couple of rings, an enthusiastic picture of his daughter appeared on the screen.

"Hi Dad!" Ashley had a big smile on her face that mimicked her mother.

"Hey Ashley! It's good to see you." Adam returned the smile.

"How was the launch? Everything go smooth? Did you get sick?" Ashley fired questions with wide eyes, knowing her dad's queasy streak.

In the background, George shouted, "Yes! He almost threw up everywhere!"

Adam looked over at George and shouted back, "That's not true!" He turned his attention back to his daughter on the screen shaking his head. "That's not true. Yes, I did get a little dizzy and disoriented, but I didn't almost throw up everywhere."

Ashley let out a little laugh. "It's ok Dad. I'm sure it was a really intense and disorienting event. Remember that time a couple of years ago when we went on that rollercoaster and you…"

Adam cut her off. "Yes, I remember. I just ate too much before we went on, that's all."

Ashley laughed again. "I'm sure you did, Dad. I bet it's amazing up there in zero gravity, looking out the window into space."

Adam grinned. "You know; besides the tight space, it is pretty amazing. I have to adjust how I do everything, but it's an incredible experience. The view of Earth is amazing. Way better than any VR set your brother has."

Ashley gave him a weird look. "I'm sure reality does beat virtual reality. So, how's the ship doing. Did you ever figure out the problem with your exercise machine?"

"Yea, I did." Adam put his head down, then looked up only with his eyes and a grin. "Problem was I was using it wrong. I fixed it. Turns out that if I don't do that exercise, it works just fine, so I don't."

Ashley shook her head and gave him a condescending grin. "Master engineer at work."

"Ha, ha. Very funny. So, how's MIT going for you?"

Ashley shrugged her shoulders. "It's going ok. Acing all my classes. It's almost too easy."

Adam's eyes twinkled. "That's great to hear! Did you finish your big programming project that you were working on?"

Ashley crunched her face. "Almost. I got stuck on one part of it. I was kind of hoping I could talk to Amy about it."

He dropped his head, but quickly picked it back up, hoping that his daughter didn't notice. Adam was proud of Ashley and wanted to be supportive in any way that he could. He reluctantly replied, "I'm sure she'd be happy to help you out. Let me float you over to her."

Ashley shrugged her head into her shoulders as she grinned. "Thanks Dad."

Adam pushed the tablet over to Amy who was half laughing, half empathetic towards Adam. Amy caught the tablet and started talking to Ashley. They spoke back and forth, working out the programming problem that Ashley was having. After a few minutes, Amy pushed the tablet back over to Adam.

"Did you figure it out?" Adam's lip half rose in a poor attempt to hide his frustration.

"Yes. It should all line up now. Thanks Dad!" Ashley tried to manipulate him with a large grin and tilted head in an attempt to fix any annoyance he might have.

It worked. Adam instantly perked up. "I'm glad it's all figured out." They talked for another ten minutes. Adam reluctantly looked at his watch and frowned. "It looks like I'm out of time."

Ashley returned the frown. "Really, already?"

"Yeah, unfortunately. It's ok, I'll call you tomorrow and we can talk some more then." Adam put on his fake smile.

"Ok. Stay safe up there. Love you." Ashley matched his fake smile.

"Love you too sweety." Adam ended the call. He closed his eyes and put his head down.

Raising his head back up, he turned toward Amy. "Well, that's a good way to distract me from the fact that I'm stuck in here with George." He pushed the tablet back over to Amy.

George raised his hand and started to speak. He stopped himself, thought about it for a second, then nodded in agreement.

Amy snagged the floating tablet, tapped the screen, and dialed home. Her three kids answered immediately, waving and shouting, "Hi Mom!" Her two boys bounced with excitement, Sam standing behind them.

Amy's face lit up and tears floated out of her eyes. "Hi my babies!" she exclaimed as she watched the show. She continued to engage with her kids as they asked questions like what space was like and how did she eat and go to the bathroom in space. She gave them a tour of the inside of the capsule and continued to talk to them for another thirty minutes. "It's so good to see all of you. Why don't you go play in the living room for a second while I talk to your father for a little bit."

The kids all out of sync replied, "Ok!" They ran off into the living room, shoving and jumping as they went.

Sam took a short breath and smiled, finally able to talk. "How are you doing dear?"

Amy tried to hold off the tears. "Seeing them so eager and happy. I wish I were there. It makes me feel so guil…"

Before Amy could finish, Sam quickly jumped in. "Don't. We are all so proud of you. You are up there with all of us. Besides, you video chat with them so often, it's like you're always at home. Don't worry. I got it covered."

Amy gave him a wet, tearful smile. "Thank you." After a short pause she asked, "How's work?"

"Well, you know." Sam rolled his eyes.

Amy crunched her nose. "Are the so-called environmentalist protesters still at it?"

Sam took another short breath. "You mean the terrorists? Yeah, they are still at it. Costing us a fortune in time and money. The media definitely isn't helping."

Amy shook her head. "I'm sorry. I wish I could help."

"Don't worry about it. Just focus on your mission. How's it going up there?" Sam tried to change the subject.

The two talked for another ten minutes about Amy's experiences up in space before Sam got their kids back on from the other room. They joyfully continued to talk together for another ten minutes. Unfortunately, it was time to say goodbye. The kids didn't think much about saying goodbye to their mom once again over video chat. They were used to it. They happily waved their hands in the air, blowing kisses like they always did when she was training. Sam kept high spirits and continued to confirm that everything was good at home and she shouldn't worry. After sharing an emotional good bye for the day, she disconnected. Inside, Amy still felt some guilt, despite her husband's reaffirming their decisions were more than justified. More tears floated off in front of her as she blinked. Rachael noticed and gave her a hug.

After a short moment, Amy rubbed her face with the palms of her hands and looked up at Rachael. "Thanks Rachael, I'm ok now." She pushed over to her laptop that was plugged into the main computer. She took a deep breath and resumed her duties. While looking through the system, her laptop screen went blank for half a second, then back to normal. She quickly checked the cables, suspecting a glitch or a loose connection. Though she dismissed it, unease lingered.

A minute later, George saw all three control panel screens went blank for a second, then restored back to normal. "Huh, that was weird." George banged on the side of the screen.

Amy looked over at George. "What's weird?"

George inspected the back of the screens. "The screens went blank for a second. Haven't seen that before."

Amy squinted her eyes at George, then looked down at her laptop with suspicion. "The same thing happened a moment ago with my laptop. I didn't think much about it at the time, but now…"

Rachael's ears perked as she overheard what was going on. "I'm sure it's nothing, but we should double check all the systems anyway. Adam, make sure that all the connections and hardware is good. Amy, look over the program and see if there is anything that shouldn't be there." Rachael pushed on the radio to communicate to Houston. "Houston, we had a split second where the screens on our equipment went blank. I'm sure it's nothing, but I'm having Adam and Amy are checking out the systems to make sure."

A voice over the radio replied, "Copy that, Rachael. All systems look good from down here, but we'll keep our eyes open for anything."

"Thanks Houston. We'll keep you updated if we find anything." Rachael flipped the open mic off.

Adam and Amy quickly went to work. Adam started opening panels and testing connections and voltage while Amy hacked away at her laptop. After about thirty minutes, Adam came up empty.

"Everything looks good on my end." Adam concluded while putting panels back into place.

"So far so good here too. Not seeing any…" Amy froze. Her heart skipped a beat. Digging deeper into the files, she noticed weird code she hadn't notice before. "Wait a second. There's something here that shouldn't be." As she continued to explore, the code disappeared. "That's weird. There was some mysterious code in the system that just disappeared."

Rachael raised an eyebrow as she looked over at Amy. "That's strange. I'll notify Houston." She flipped the switch to comms. "Houston, Amy found some mysterious code that suddenly disappeared. We'd like some further assistance in identifying it."

No answer.

"Houston, did you copy?" Rachael's eyebrows sank as she looked to see if the mic was on.

Still, no answer.

Rachael's voice rose. "Houston, did you copy?"

George went over to one of the ship's screens, and looked at the communications status. It was offline. He flipped a few switches to reconnect, but nothing was responding. "Yeah, comms are offline and not turning back on."

Adam frantically pushed himself over to the controls and tried to reconnect. "Nothing's responding. Maybe it's the circuits." Adam looked down in thought for a second, then pushed himself over to a panel that he just checked minutes ago. He opened it up and thoroughly started reexamining everything.

Twenty tense minutes later, Adam still found nothing, rechecking every panel. Rachael and George continued to monitor the ship, looking for any signs of other systems glitching. Amy dug through the ship's vast programming for signs of the mysterious code with no luck. Suddenly, the cabin lights flickered. Seconds later, the reaction control system's side thrusters fired in bursts, glowing on-screen. George lunged for the controls, trying to shut them off. Nothing worked. The ship started to slowly spin. George tried to fire the other thrusters to compensate, but nothing was responding. The capsule began to spin.

"Adam, shut us down and reset the system!" George yelled out as he gripped the screen and controls.

Adam crawled to the top of the module, fighting the centrifugal force from the spinning ship. He clawed at a panel, but the spin ripped his grip free, slamming him against the module's side. Rachael and Amy were pinned on the opposite side, Amy clutching her laptop to see the screen. She scoured the code desperately as alarms blared and darkness crept in. Rachael and Adam felt the cold touch of unconsciousness moments later.

George lost his grip on the screen and crashed against a window. Held against the window by the accelerating spin, he swore he saw a light outside in space which blurred into a streak. Everything started to darken as he too slipped into unconsciousness.

Chapter 3

George suddenly awoke, jerking his head up instinctively. He jolted upright, finding himself on a firm, white mattress the size of a hospital bed. He rubbed his eyes, confused as to where he was. As his mind cleared the fog it was in, he noticed that his whole body felt numb. No pain, no warmth, no cold. His senses were gone. He scanned a white fifty-by-fifty-foot room that lacked any windows or other furniture. There was just a flight of stairs next to another bed-like table that Rachael was on.

Rachael stirred, sitting up slowly, her face etched with confusion. She glanced at George, who scratched the back of his head as he returned the glance. "What happened?" Rachael examined the room once again. "Where are we?"

George looked around again. He thought about what happened to their ship. After glaring at his hands and feet, he looked back up at Rachael with wide eyes. "Are we dead?"

Rachael paused, then pinched her arm. "I can't feel anything. It's weird. I have full function of all of my extremities, yet it's almost as if it's not there." She looked down for a second. Her eyes widened at the possibility that the answer to George's question could be yes. "We might be dead." For a brief second, a slight sense of terror entered her mind to that conclusion. The sense of terror was quickly taken over by curiosity. Raising an eyebrow, she stared back at George. "If we are dead, then we no longer have our physical bodies. Is this what our spirits are like? Are our bodies really gone?" She carefully got off her bed-like table and examined her arms and legs. There was no feeling in any part of her body. She stretched out in an attempt to get circulation to her limbs. She cautiously jumped into the air. "Well, seems we're not in space anymore. And if these are our spirit bodies, gravity seems to affect us the same way."

George just watched her perform experiments on herself for a moment with his jaw slightly open. After abruptly shaking his head, he started to examine his own limbs. As he did, he noticed a scar on his right forearm that he received on an earlier military mission. His brow wrinkled as he raised his eyebrows. "I guess scars are more than skin deep." He raised his arm and pointed to his scar with his other hand. Rachael walked over to George to examine his arm. George carefully slid off his bed-like table. Looking over himself, he noticed that he was no longer wearing his NASA clothing. Instead, he had on grey sweat pants, a plain white t-shirt and athletic running shoes. Rachael was wearing the same thing. "Guess the whole white robe thing and wings is nonsense too. Don't see any fire or horned red creatures with pitchforks ready to stab us, so we got that going for us." He nodded his head over to the stairs. "How about we go and see if there are pearly gates or brimstone waiting for us."

Rachael looked over her attire. She couldn't believe that she didn't notice the change in her wardrobe. After glancing at her new clothes, she looked over to the stairs. They seemed to disappear into the ceiling. She froze for a second, looked over at her bed-like table, looked over to the stairs again, then looked down in thought. After a moment, she looked up at George, nodding in agreement. "I think we should. We won't learn much from just sitting around in this room."

George carefully moved over to the stairs. He positioned himself to the side of the steps so that if someone were looking down from the top, they wouldn't be able to see him. He glanced up to see if he could see anything. The only thing he could see was the ceiling at the top of the stairs. He motioned to Rachael to come over. She cautiously made her way over to George. They carefully started to walk up the stairs, George in the lead. Reaching the top, they entered a warm, inviting room resembling an American living room. Light-colored hardwood covered the floors, adorned with nature scenes spaced along the walls. In the center of the room was a very cushy beige leather couch with a recliner on each side. In front of the couch was a large wooden coffee table with a rolled-up newspaper in the middle. A hint of baked cookies filled the air. On the far wall was a small bar with four bar stools and many different bottles on shelves behind it. On the wall in front of the couch was a large mounted TV. In between the tv and the bar was a single door.

George examined the room with his mouth slightly open. "If we are dead, my preacher is full of crap."

Rachael gave a slight grin, then noticed the rolled-up newspaper on the table. Cautiously, she picked it up and opened it. Her grin vanished, eyes widened, and jaw dropped.

George walked over to look at the paper she was holding. "What does it say?" He realized why she seemed terrified. On the front page of the paper was a picture taken from a telescope. It was a picture of debris floating in space. The headline read "Disaster on the way to the moon!"

As they started to read the article, the door to the room opened. A man in a dark blue two-button suit walked in. He had kind eyes but wore no expression on his face. "Yes, you two are dead - at least to the world, you are dead." His voice was soft, yet clear.

Rachael and George dropped the paper and stepped back, eyeing the man. They stared at him for a second with squinting eyes. Once the shock wore off, they took a couple of steps toward him and started launching questions at the same time. George jabbed a finger at the man, voice rising. "Who are you and what in the world are you talking about? Where are we? What are we doing here?

Rachael was not as brazen with her tone. Her head was slightly tilted to the side and her eyes were laser focused on the man. "What do you mean at least to the world? Why can't I feel anything? Did you drug us?"

The man raised both hands, palms out, urging them to calm down. "I know you have a lot of questions, and you deserve answers. If you will calm down a bit, I will explain." He motioned his head toward the direction of the bar. "Why don't we discuss this over a drink?" After he walked over to the bar, he pulled out three medium-sized glasses. The two slowly walked over to the bar, staring at the man as they went.

The man grabbed an ice ball with metal tongs from a mini-icebox under the bar, dropping one in each glass. He turned around and grabbed one of the bottles sitting on the shelf, then carefully poured the liquid from within the bottle into each of the glasses, filling it to the top. "I know you want immediate answers. Please be patient and you will get them. Just know that you are not in any danger. At least not anymore. In fact, we saved you."

George slammed both hands on the bar. "Who is 'we' and why can't I feel anything?"

"Like I said, please let me explain. You will get answers. Just relax, take a deep breath, have a drink." The man kept a mellow voice. He gently put the bottle back on the shelf behind him.

They both looked down at their drinks. They looked up at the man with distrust as they pushed their glasses slightly away from them.

The man in the suit turned back around to see their glares. "No? It's pretty good. It tastes and goes down like rum, but doesn't have any of the negative effects since there's no alcohol in it. However, it still does have a warm and calming effect to it. Very useful in stressful and high-tension situations. As a bonus, it contains a lot of vitamins, especially vitamin C, so it's good for you. We nicknamed it "Liquid Gold." Well, if you won't have a drink, at least have a seat on a stool." He grabbed the third glass and took a sip.

Rachael and George pulled up a stool and sat down, keeping their eyes locked on the stranger.

The man had a bright smile as he began to speak. "Let me introduce myself. My name is Isaiah. Believe it or not, we are a secret organization that doesn't officially exist anymore. We possess technology the world can barely imagine. With this technology, we pulled you out of your predicament that you were in before your space ship blew up."

Rachael sneered at his explanation. "A secret organization with advanced technology? Sounds kind of cliché to me."

George continued to stare in the man's eyes with a wrinkled brow. "If you saved us, where are the other two. Did you save them too?"

Isaiah continued to keep a calm voice. "Yes, this seems a little too outrageous to believe but I assure you that this is real. Your other two crewmates are just fine. They are in another room and will awaken shortly. The reason that you feel nothing, not hot or cold or any pain or other physical feelings is because we made it that way."

"What? So, you did drug us." Rachael elevated her voice slightly as she leaned in.

Isaiah put down his glass and calmly put both hands flat on the bar. "To put it bluntly, yes. Don't worry, you are perfectly fine."

George slammed both hands on the bar, spilling some of the liquid from the glasses in front of them. "Of course, why should we worry? We only woke up in the twilight zone where, come to find out, our captors have drugged us!"

Isaiah briefly closed his eyes and nodded his head. "I can understand your frustration. Please keep in mind that you have just been through a very traumatic ordeal. We have found that dulling one's senses helps with the immediate trauma of the situation both mentally and physically. The effects will wear off shortly."

Rachael sat up as her eyebrows lifted. "Helps many? So, you do this sort of thing regularly?"

"Let's just say we have had quite a bit of experience. We are, however, speeding you through this process rather quickly. With some, it takes a day or two of easing them into where we are at now." Isaiah grabbed his glass and took another drink. "We looked up your backgrounds and put you two together on purpose. You both have had focused careers most of your adult lives, which involved problem solving and acting on your solutions. Both of you also have had no real intimate attachments to anyone on Earth, giving you a sense of having nothing to lose. We figured you were both the type that would take caution to the wind to find out what was going on. The fact that both of you charged up those stairs with not a lot of hesitation proves that we were right on our judgment with you."

"I don't know if I should be insulted or honored." George had lowered his tone.

"I would say honored." Isaiah gave them an encouraging smile.

George leaned in again. "You still haven't told us where we are."

Isaiah grabbed a small towel from underneath the bar, wiping the spilled liquid. "Believe it or not, you are back on earth in a facility deep beneath the Ocean."

Rachael clenched her eyes shut briefly and shook her head. "Hold on. Why don't you start from the beginning? What is this secret organization and how did you come to exist?"

"I'd be happy to. Let's start the history lesson." Isaiah stowed the towel under the bar, pulled out a remote, aimed it at the TV, turning it on. Images of soldiers in World War 1 trenches cycled across the screen. "July of 1914 started the beginning of World War 1. It was a terrible time of raiding, killing, and conquering. With that conquering came the spoils." The TV flashed to pictures of soldiers standing in well decorated lavish German homes holding paintings and other property. "To avoid the appearance of thievery and establish trust with other nations, the United States Department of Justice created the Office of Alien Property Custodian or OAPC in the year 1917."

"Wait a sec. The government had an alien property task force in 1917? Really?" George rested both forearms on the table as he leaned in. He picked up his glass. After a quick examination he took a sip, then nodded with approval.

Isaiah shook his head. "It's not that type of alien. When they referred to aliens in this case, they simply referred to people from another country as alien, not the little green creatures from outer space type. Originally its main function was to seize any property gained through war or similar events. They dealt with such property, organized it, and put it in the hands of those who it rightfully belonged to. But just like many things, its purpose started to evolve. As World War 1 ended, so did the confidence of the U.S. in its ability to fend off all threats foreign. That's when OAPC became something more. To the public, OAPC did not change its purpose. Behind the scenes it became an intelligence and technology gathering and developing organization. The intent was for the U.S. to always be ahead of their enemies. It secretly sent spies all around the world and cyphered through any database to advance its knowledge."

The screen changed to a picture of Nikola Tesla. "Which brings us to this man. Nikola Tesla. He was a brilliant individual. A man ahead of his time, yet didn't get much recognition for it. Because of that, his brilliance was, for most of his life, underfunded. That didn't stop him from pushing forward. In 1928 he filed a patent for an aircraft." The screen flashed to a picture of Tesla's aircraft design. It looked like a typical sci-fi alien flying saucer. "It was quite a unique concept at the time. Unfortunately for him, he didn't have the funding to construct it. OAPC saw the patent, and became very interested in his work. They took his design and studied it. In the process of going through his design, they discovered a big problem with it. There was not a strong enough power source to get it properly working. So, they started to look for a solution to solve that problem." On the screen appeared a picture of Albert Einstein. "OAPC recognized the work of another brilliant man who lived in Germany. To help advance the technology, they decided to recruit him. In 1933 Albert Einstein came over to the states and secretly started working with OAPC to create a power source to get the "Tesla aircraft" to work. Three years later he was successful with his task. A picture of a round looking large metal flying saucer appeared on the screen. "Many years later, they got the craft to work. It was the greatest technological advancement in the history of man that few ever got to know about."

Isaiah took another sip of his drink. "Unfortunately, Germany had spies of its own. They kept a close eye on Einstein after he defected to the United States. As a result, some of his work on the newly created energy source got into the hands of German scientists. They sought to weaponize it. This news of German scientists discovering a powerful source of destruction got out to the world. The U.S. reacted by forming the Manhattan Project in 1939." Pictures of the Hiroshima A-bomb as well as its explosion popped on the screen.

"Many people understand the Manhattan Project to be the birth of the atomic bomb that ended the war. What people don't know is that it came about because of the leaked technology that came from OAPC. Tensions were high in the world. The US government could not risk such a thing to happen again. When Tesla died in 1943, to protect Tesla's brilliance from getting in the wrong hands, OAPC seized all documents and designs from Tesla's room. The documents held a flood of ideas the organization had never dreamed of. One of these documents contained Tesla's "dynamic theory of gravity" letter. This was a letter about anti-gravity that Tesla claimed to write in 1937 that the world never got to see. Nobody could find it. People assumed that he was making it up so that his theories could be recognized. Einstein was not only excited to see that it actually existed but that it unlocked the secrets to gravity. That knowledge helped him greatly advance other projects that were being worked on, including the advancement of the Tesla aircraft. Technology kept evolving out of OAPC over time. What we have today, the facility that you are in now, is the result of that development."

George raised his hand. "Wait a second. Are you saying that the thousands of UFO sightings that happened over the years came from this organization?"

Isaiah nodded his head. "Well, to put it simply, yes."

Rachael rubbed her eyes with her hand, then looked up at Isaiah. "So alien beings visiting us from other planets is fake news?"

Isaiah looked at Rachael and gave her a slight grin, "I can confidently say that there are no little green men from another planet that are visiting the Earth."

George jumped off of his stool and pointed his finger at Isaiah. "You didn't answer her question. Just tell me this." He pointed his finger toward the door. "If I walk through that door, am I going to see people in black suits and dark sunglasses ready to erase my mind with a flash of a light?"

Isaiah chuckled a little. "I understand your excitement. This is a lot to take in. Understand that there are calculus levels of information that are yet to be explained. I am giving you the basic one plus one information. I know that you want it all right now. It will come over time." He kept a calm voice.

"You understand my excitement?" Rachael exclaimed in a loud voice. "You abducted my crew and I from our capsule, drugged us, and dumped an extraordinary story on us leaving an unbelievable number of questions floating around with the promise that it will come over time. I think excitement is an understatement!"

"See that article on the table?" Isaiah pointed to the paper on the table. "Please understand that if I weren't for us, you would be part of that debris. We saved you. As far as abducting you, I would call this more of an induction into the group. There are a lot of unanswered questions as to how your ship was destroyed and you and your crew are the best source for those answers. Unfortunately given the circumstance, time is not on our side. I am really sorry about the circumstance, I really am."

Isaiah realized that both of them were unsatisfied with his explanation. "You know what, why don't I show you around. It might help bring some perspective for you. Go ahead and take your drinks. You might need it." Isaiah grabbed the bottle from the shelf again and topped off George's glass.

George took his drink and took another sip. "Agreed."

Rachael's eyes shot like daggers at Isaiah. She thought that he was crazy to think she would willingly drink it. Isaiah understandingly nodded and grabbed both his and her drinks. He took a sip out of her cup to help ensure her that there was nothing wrong with it. He carried both cups with him, placing one cup between the side of his chest and his arm and held the other cup in that same arms hand, freeing up his right arm. He turned and walked over to the door where he originally entered the room. George immediately jumped off his seat and started to follow him. Rachael cautiously followed George's lead.

As they followed, Rachael turned to George and whispered, "How can you be so trusting?"

George looked at Rachael. "Don't get me wrong, I'm very skeptical. Right now, we don't have many options, so I figure just go with it and see where it takes us."

Rachael pierced her eyes at the glass he was carrying. "And the drink? You just trust that there's nothing wrong with it?"

George smirked as he shrugged his shoulders. "I was thirsty." Rachael gripped her forehead and shook it in disapproval.

As George and Rachael were conversing, Isaiah opened the door and walked through to a short hallway. The two followed behind him. At the end of the hallway was a metal door with no handle. Isaiah placed his hand on the wall to the right of the door and the door slid open. Walking through they found themselves in the middle of a much longer hallway. Doors lined one side while the other side had an inwardly curved metallic wall that extended the whole length of the hallway. The floor and ceiling looked as though it were concrete, but had a unique shine to it.

Isaiah turned to the right, and started walking down the hallway. "As I said before, it is my goal to explain your situation as quickly as possible. We determined that you would be able to absorb the reality of your situation relatively quickly. Please understand that your other two co-workers probably won't be so quick to accept. They will respond better with your assistance. But before you can help them, you need to get some sort of grip on it yourselves."

Rachael scratched her head while raising an eyebrow as she gazed at Isaiah. "So, wait, you want us to know and accept what's going on quickly so that we can explain to our crewmates what is going on and help them accept the situation, even though we barely know ourselves what is going on."

Isaiah kept his eyes straight ahead. "Correct."

Shaking her head, Rachael expressed her doubts. "That's a pretty big assumption. Don't know how I feel about that."

They walked to the end of the hallway and turned left. Ten feet from the turn was another metal door with no handle.

George took another sip of his drink. "So, what's in this, what did you call it? Liquid Gold?"

Isaiah again put his hand on the wall and the door slid open. "The secret ingredient? It's no secret. It's in its name. Gold. Prepared just like back in the days of Moses, when he prepared it for his people."

"Wait, what did…" Before Rachael could finish her thought, her attention was immediately diverted. They stepped into a much wider hallway that extended both ways, twisting and turning far beyond where they could see. The layout was similar to the hallway that they were just in. But instead of one side of the hallway having a concave dome shaped wall, both sides had it. The only exception was where there were doors. The top and bottom of the doors extended from the floor to the ceiling and were straight, not curved. On both sides of the door the wall ramped fluidly down to the rest of the dome wall.

Waiting for them on the side of the hallway was a vehicle that looked like a cross of an ATV and a golf cart. Sitting in the driver's seat was a friendly looking guy patiently waiting for them to arrive. Beside him was an empty passenger seat. Behind him were two rows of three bucket seats. Both George and Rachael stood wide-eyed and open-mouthed as they stared at the machine. The vehicle had no wheels. It hovered about a foot off the ground.

George walked up to the vehicle to confirm what he was seeing. Putting his drink on the ground, he laid down in a half push-up beside it to look underneath the vehicle, fully expecting to find some sort of object that was holding it up. There was nothing. "This is crazy." He pushed up off the ground, picked up his drink, and turned to Isaiah like a kid to his parent in a candy store. "If I quickly adapt to this place, when is the soonest I can get one of these vehicles?"

Isaiah pointed in the driver's direction. "I'd like you to meet Teancom."

Teancom gave a friendly smile and gestured a quick friendly wave. Rachael rose half her lip as she waved back.

George's eyebrows rose. "That's kind of a crazy name, Teancom. Fitting for this place." Teancom nodded in agreement.

Walking to the back row door of the vehicle, Isaiah opened it for George and Rachael to get in. George did not hesitate to get in. Rachael followed, but much slower. As they got in, George noticed that the vehicle did not rock to the side like any other vehicle would from the displacement of extra weight. In fact, it didn't move at all. Isaiah stepped in, careful not to spill the drinks that he was still holding, and closed the door. He looked over at Rachael and George as they studied the inside of the vehicle. "Are you ready?"

Restraining himself from shaking the front seat to get the driver to move the vehicle, George bit down hard and grinned. "Yes sir."

Rachael took a deep breath as she looked back at Isaiah. "Why not."

Isaiah rose his voice so that Teancom could hear him. "We're good." The vehicle silently pulled forward. As they picked up speed Isaiah turned to Rachael who was fidgeting with her hands. "Rachael, how are you holding up?"

Rachael caught herself fidgeting, and made tight fists to stop. "I'm still trying to take it all in. I'll be fine."

Isaiah rose one of the glasses. "I still have your drink for you if you'd like."

"I think I'll manage without it." Rachael gave Isaiah a sincere friendly smile.

As they traveled down the long hallway, George leaned forward to talk to the driver. "So, what do you call these vehicles?"

Teancom cocked his head back while still looking ahead. "What, these things? We just call them golf carts."

"So, wait a sec." George's brows wrinkled as he leaned forward a little more. "You have a name like Teancom and all you can come up with for a vehicle like this is golf cart?"

Teancom straightened his head and gave a simple nod. "Something like that. They say it helps when you associate equipment to objects that people are most familiar with. Besides, I didn't name it." Leaning back in his chair, George watched as the doors in the hallway buzzed by.

The vehicle picked up speed as they went down the slightly widening hallway. George leaned forward to see Isaiah around Rachael who was sitting in the middle seat. "How big is this place?"

Isaiah leaned forward as well. "This facility is only about 10 miles long. The width varies depending on where you're at."

Rachael rose a hand. "Speaking of where we are at, where are we again?"

Isaiah sat up straight again. "We are in one of our underwater, underground facilities several hundred miles off the coast of Massachusetts."

Rachael slouched her shoulders. "Why underwater? What happened to the so called 'Area 51?'"

Isaiah tuned his body toward Rachael. "We used to be there decades ago, but we moved because it became too well known to the public, too "cliché" as you put it earlier. For a short time, the organization relocated inside the Rocky Mountains. Unfortunately for us outside technology became better. Drones and the ability to take high-definition video is now technology that a little kid has access to. We needed a more secure location where hardly anybody had access to."

George put his hand on his leg as he continued to lean toward Isaiah. "Think you need a better location. Haven't you seen those on-line videos of UFOs traveling in and out of the water and up into the skies?"

Isaiah nodded his head. "Yes, we have. That has been the challenge, but we've come up with a solution that has worked so far."

"Yeah, what solution is that?" George tilted his head slightly.

"Conspiracy theories." Isaiah took another sip of his drink.

"Conspiracy Theories?" George sat up slightly as he raised an eyebrow.

"Yes, conspiracy theories. People have wild imaginations and use it to fill the void of unknown phenomena that occur. We encourage that. It's no coincidence that as soon as I mentioned the name Office of Alien Property Custodian you immediately thought of beings from outer space. I bet in your mind they were bald, green, and big eyed too."

George looked down and lowered his voice. "Maybe."

A small grin appeared on Isaiah's face. "That's half the battle for us. Magicians call it misdirection. A "look over here" approach. We encourage and a lot of times create conspiracy theories for the public to jump on. We then do things to support those theories."

Rachael tilted her head. "What do you mean?"

"Let me give you an example. You actually might have heard this one. In 1975 there was a crew in one of our "tesla aircrafts" testing some equipment near the mountains of Arizona. As they were performing their tests, issues arose within their craft and they were unable to move. So, there they were hovering slightly above the ground trying to get the craft going again when they noticed a pickup truck full of men that started to approach them. One of the men in the truck actually got out and started walking closer to the craft. Luckily, the crew was able to fix the craft rather quickly. Unfortunately, by the time they fixed the problem the curious gentleman who got out of the truck made his way underneath the craft and stared up at it. At that point the crew had to enact what we call protocol alien abductee. You see, we have technology that not only repels objects, but acts like a tractor beam as well. The crew shown a spotlight on him. At the same time, they hit him with the repelling beam, which caused him to fly back. Just before he hit the ground, they reversed the beam and pulled him up to the craft. They were hoping the jolt would render him unconscious. It worked. The crew pulled him aboard the craft. By that time the truck with the other men fled. The crew brought him back to the base. Once there they took him to the medical ward and injected an IV in his arm to keep him asleep. For five days they kept him unconscious while a team went to find out who the other men in the truck were. Turns out they were just a group of loggers working late that night."

Rachael looked intensely at Isaiah. "So, what did you do, capture them too?"

Isaiah continued, "No, but it did turn out that the loggers were being accused of murdering the man that was brought up to the ship. So, the organization continued to play out the alien conspiracy. They laid the man whom they abducted on a surgical table and "attached" many different tubes, cords, and other surgical material to him. Finding three of the shortest people that they had in the facility, they put them in alien costumes with medical lab coats over those costumes. The three "aliens" went in with the unconscious man and woke him up, keeping him in somewhat of a drowsy state. The man became ecstatic, ripping off all the things that they attached to him. After the "Aliens" left the room, the man followed them out the door. He staggered down a hallway to find another room that was empty. The organization sent another person in, this time wearing an astronaut's suit. The man in the suit took the man, who seemed somewhat relieved to see a "human", and lead him to a hangar where they kept all the other tesla crafts. The point was of course to sell the idea that they were all alien space craft. The man in the space suit continued to lead him into another room where there were three more men wearing space suits as well. They restrained him and gassed him until he was unconscious again. Shortly after, they dropped him off on a road near the town where he was from. The rest is history."

George chuckled. "I remember that story. They made a movie out of it."

Rachael was a little less amused. "So, you dress up and pretend to be aliens after abducting people, and you think this will bring less attention to your organization?"

With a straight face, Isaiah looked at Rachael. "Yes. Think about it. A few years ago, there was a congressional hearing about actual footage of our high-tech craft. No one really paid attention to it. Many people didn't even take it seriously. Why? Because the world doesn't take what they believe to be conspiracy theories seriously. That's what we've become. We're just a crazy story that 'crazy conspiracy nuts' follow."

George quickly jumped in. "So, if you are the source of all the crazy stories that everyone has had in relation to being abducted, I have to ask; what's with the anal probes?"

A swift punch in the arm came from Rachael. "What is wrong with you?"

The golf cart started to slow down as they turned a corner. They traveled a few hundred feet before they arrived at a large bay door, which lifted as they approached it. As they went through, Teancom announced, "Ladies and Gentlemen, welcome to the hangar!" He swung the vehicle 90 degrees to the left. In front of them was an enormous room.

George and Rachael's eyes widened at the massive hangar. The room had to be at least three football fields in width and a few hundred feet tall. Looking forward, they couldn't even see the end of it. They started to pick up speed again as they traveled down the middle of this gigantic room. To the right and to the left were small groups of ships hovering together.

George pointed to the groups of ships. "Are those..."

Teancom jumped in before he could finish asking. "Yes, they are. If you look to the right, you can see our classic Tesla Alpha 15F models." Teancom waved his hand to the right toward a group of saucer-shaped craft in a tourist guide type voice. He motioned with his other hand similarly in the other direction. "To the left you will see our more upgraded Delta class models." On the left was a group of ships, each slightly bigger than the ships in the first group. Each craft seemed to be in the shape of triangles.

Rachael rubbed her forehead as she gazed upon the craft in disbelief. "What… I mean where, or who is in charge of this? Who knows about this? Does NASA, the Congress, the President...?"

Teancom laughed heartily. "Could you imagine…"

Isaiah quickly interrupted. "Very few people outside this organization know about this. It used to be more government centralized a long time ago. Unfortunately, politics got in the way of judgment."

"Define a long time ago." Rachael questioned as she unknowingly scratched at her leg.

"The last President that knew about the organization was President Johnson. He, in fact, was the one that officially shut down the Office of Alien Property. After that, it was funded in secret, pulling funds from other government projects until the organization became self-sufficient." Isaiah noticed Rachael scratching at her leg. He offered her the drink that he was holding for her. She politely shook her head to decline.

George's focus returned to Isaiah. "Why would Johnson shut it down?"

Teancom quickly glanced back at the crew. "Because he didn't want to be JFK'd."

An icy stare resonated from Isaiah towards Teancom. "If you don't mind Teancom, I'll finish the story." Teancom faced forward again. "There was a lot of controversy going on at that time of Kennedy as to what to do with the technology that had been kept a secret. The United States was in a cold war with the USSR and tensions were high, especially after the Cuban missile crisis. Kennedy, who was bearing the most weight of the situation, wanted to show all our cards. He wanted to show the world that they could not compete with us. He wanted the US to never again be threatened by foreign influence. Many people disagreed with him, including most of the people in the organization."

"So, they killed him." Rachael Barked. Small beads of sweat formed on her forehead.

"Not exactly." Isaiah said, maintaining a clam voice. "They just didn't stop those that did. President Johnson blamed the organization for his death. He saw such an organization with advanced technology as too dangerous for the world to handle and ordered it to be shut down and buried, or so he thought."

"That's the problem with having politics involved." Teancom explained while still looking ahead. "They don't see it as a great advancement to human kind, but as a means of leverage to advance their own cause, push their narratives."

Isaiah looked over at Rachael and noticed that she was rubbing her head. "Are you ok Rachael?"

"I'm fine." Rachael snapped back. She closed her eyes while looking down and took a deep breath. "I'm sorry, I just have a slight head ache. Whatever you gave us must be wearing off."

"I still have your drink if you want it. It helps. I promise." Isaiah rose the glass again.

Rachael took another deep breath. "No thanks. I'll...I'll be ok."

"Yeah, I'm feeling kind of tingly myself." George put the glass to his mouth and finished off his drink.

"Maybe we should head to your quarters that we have prepared for you. You've both had a lot of information thrown at you already." Isaiah looked at both of them with concern in his eyes.

"I'm good. Really, I'm ok." Rachael insisted as she sat up straight and at attention. She continued to look intensely at the craft as they passed them.

Isaiah rose his eyebrows. "We can continue a little lat..."

Rachael looked over at Isaiah as she cut him off with a slightly elevated voice. "You said it yourself. We need to be brought up to speed so that we can help our companions, which we have yet to see. Besides, my mind doesn't work like that. I still have a ton of questions that I need answered."

Teancom glanced back with a cheerful grin. "How about I show you a little bit more, then we can go get something to eat and you can continue to ask whatever you want."

George looked at Rachael with concern. He shook his head in agreement. "That sounds like a great idea. I am getting pretty hungry."

Rachael gave a nod as she continued to scan the area. She noticed that her hands were trembling a little and quickly folded her arms in an attempt to control herself as well as hide it from others.

Teancom slowed the golf cart to a stop and got out. "You're going to want to check this out." The others followed his lead and got out of the cart as well. Teancom pulled out of his pocket what looked like an ordinary smart phone and made a few swipes at the screen. He briefly had a ten-second conversation with someone on the other end, then looked up. The others noticed him looking up and did the same. On the ceiling were three closed bay doors, one next to another. Each bay door was about four hundred feet long by four hundred feet wide. The group was standing underneath the middle of the three bay doors. The door that they were under started to open from the middle. Each side slid into the roof until the middle bay was fully opened. All they could see was an eerie void of darkness. Teancom spoke into his phone again. Lights turned on to reveal what was on the other side of the door.

There was a huge glassless dome holding back an enormous amount of water from pouring in on top of them. As they gazed upon the scene with their mouths open, they could see fish swimming around as though they were looking at a gigantic aquarium. On the sides where the bay doors disappeared into, they could see rock like structures to compliment the whole scene. As they looked with amazement, a large school of fish swam by. A lot of the fish seemed to break the glassless dome barrier for a split second just to get pushed back into the vast body of water.

Rachael's brow lowered as she noticed the fish breaking the barrier. "That's not glass up there holding back the fish and all that water. How is this possible?

Isaiah looked over at Rachael. "Remember how I told you earlier that they figured out Tesla's "dynamic theory of gravity" letter? Well, that is how. When you can control gravity to your will, it opens the door to all sorts of possibilities."

As they were gazing at the amazing view, a triangle shaped craft pulled over them hovering about fifteen feet off the ground. The only sound that it made was a low and very quiet hum. The once observers of the ceiling aquarium diverted their attention toward the large craft. It was about one hundred fifty feet on all sides and was made of a strange metal material that, despite seeming to have a shine, did not reflect light or images off its surface. The bottom wasn't flat but very slightly bowled, having a convex shape. On top, it shared a similar same shape but more protruding. The whole thing was very smooth with no windows, openings, or signs of any type of object that would give it thrust like a jet or propeller. Because of that, there was no push back caused by the exhaust of a jet. It disturbed nothing around it. There were no markings or decals to identify where it was from. It was a strange aerodynamic piece of art. George began slowly walking around the vehicle with his mouth still open. "You can keep your "golf cart." When do I get to claim one of these?"

"The goal is to get you flying in one as soon as you're ready." Teancom looked at George with a grin.

George eyes dropped from the craft and straight at Teancom. "Are you serious? I'm ready. Let's go! Open the hatch, drop the steps, beam me up, or whatever you do to get in." Just then the craft slowly rose up until it got to the opening of the hangar. It slowed down and crept its way towards the water. The bubble that was keeping the water out reshaped to include the craft as it continued to rise. It was as if the craft had its own invisible bubble around it. Not a drop of water was getting close to it. The craft kept rising until it was surrounded by the body of water. As it disappeared into the void, the original bubble of the opened hangar regained its shape, keeping the water from coming in. The outside lights turned off and the large bay doors began to close. The observers kept staring up in amazement until the doors shut completely. "That was amazing!" George shouted. He paused for a second and looked down as though in thought. After a few seconds, he looked up at Isaiah with squinted eyes. "Why are you showing us all of this. This is as top secret as anything out there, yet we didn't take any psychological test, no lie detector tests, no physical tests, no countless contracts to sign sworn to secrecy. I've been through the drill, yet there's none of that. Why?"

"Isn't it obvious?" Rachael jumped in seeming very jittery. "We have no choice. Don't you remember? We're dead!" Rachael started looking around very nervously. "There's nowhere to go. There's no escape. We're trapped in this!"

"That's not exactly true." Teancom brought both hands in front of him to his waist, palms down.

With a shaky voice, Rachael yelled, "Yeah, we can be JFK'd!"

Isaiah gave a cold stare toward Teancom with both eyebrows darting down. He turned to Rachael and started motioning his hands slowly up and down to calm her down while still holding onto their drinks. "I know this is a lot to take in. Why don't you take a deep breath and calm down so we can…"

Rachael saw Isaiah motion to her and mistook it for another attempt to get her to drink. As a result, she knocked one of the glasses out of his hand. "I told you I don't want a drink!" Rachael stumbled back, sweat beading on her face. Slowly, she started to spin around anxiously looking around her. Her vision became very fuzzy, causing her to collapse on the floor. The other's rushed to her aid. At this point she seemed barely conscious.

"She's in shock." Isaiah diagnosed as he put down his other glass on the floor and propped up her head. "Elevate her legs slightly and give her space to breath." George obeyed Isaiah's command and slightly lifted up her legs. Teancom took a step back and called someone on his phone. Thirty seconds later a slightly larger modified "golf cart" pulled up with a driver and passenger. In the back was a larger open section that had bench seats on both of the sides. In the middle was a stretcher. Both the driver and the passenger got out and pulled out the stretcher. It, much like the golf cart, was hovering as they pushed it towards Rachael. They checked her vitals and carefully lifted her on the stretcher. They loaded the stretcher with her on it in the back of the modified golf cart. The passenger got in the back with her. The driver jumped in the driver's seat.

Isaiah looked at George. "You should probably go with her."

George nodded in agreement and jumped in the back of the vehicle with them. The modified golf cart sped off towards the direction that they originally came from. Isaiah shot Teancom a look. "You might want to be careful about how you word things." He turned and walked toward their golf cart. Teancom followed. "Understand, they didn't ask to be here. If you are going to lead them, you might want to attempt to gain some trust."

Teancom said nothing. Instead, he put his head down as though he were in deep thought. They both got into the front seats of the golf cart with Teancom in the driver seat. They too pulled away towards where they came in.

Chapter 4

Rachael's eyes flickered open, the ceiling blurring past. Her head was in a daze as she tried to make sense of her situation. Everything was blurry as she went in and out of consciousness. Her mind reflected back to all that had happened. She started to remember the recent events with distorted twists. She found herself pinned to the Orion's wall, the ship spinning wildly. As she struggled to move, she saw a large four-armed tailless lizard creature jabbing clawed fingers into the console. It screeched at her as she slowly faded into unconsciousness. She woke up in the white room where they first gained consciousness. Alone in the white room, she faced a large mirror. As she looked at her reflection, she noticed wires coming out of the top of her head. After swiping at them frantically, she found herself lying in the back of the golf cart traveling at a fast rate.

As she looked around, she could see that she was not alone. Two figures in trench coats and brimmed hats sat beside her, collars raised, hiding their faces. Glancing over for a better look, she froze. Their skin was green, with large black eyes and nasal slits on long faces. One caught her stare, seized her arms, and pinned her down. Suddenly, she lay on a stretcher, four green aliens shoving her down a hallway. She tried to move but she couldn't. They took her to a room and put her on a surgical table. Her vision became very blurry and could only see faint images of bodies poking and prodding at her. Breathing very heavily, she tried to find the strength to move. Slowly, she started to gain functionality of her limbs and started swatting at those around her. As she gained more control, she stumbled off of the table and moved backwards, still swinging her arms to protect herself from these unknown beings that she was seeing from harming her.

In the treatment room, Rachael pushed herself into a corner, swinging desperately. Her IV tube disconnected, dripping onto the floor with a faint patter. The medical team tried frantically to calm her down. The doctor stepped toward her, kneeling. "Rachael, I need you to take a deep breath and calm down," she repeated softly.

Rachael ceased swinging, rubbing her eyes. Her daze started to fade away. Her surroundings started to become clear. Her reasoning started to click in again. As she looked around, she started to analyze her situation. Her scientific mind clicked, piecing it together. She started to remember what had happened. She started to make sense of the visions she just experienced in her mind. Putting together the pieces, she realized that she just had a panic attack. She understood what she was experiencing was caused by her emotions playing with her mind. She took a deep breath and looked at the doctor in tears. "I'm so sorry. I lost control for a moment. I was hallucinating. I'm so, so sorry."

The doctor looked at her, amazed. "Wow. That was easy. You figured that out pretty quick on your own. Don't worry about what just happened. There is no need to apologize. Everyone in this room understands what you are going through."

Rachael wiped the tears from her face. "Thank you."

The doctor helped Rachael back onto the table. As Rachael got back up, she noticed that her muscles were very stiff and sore. She also had a terrible headache. Rachael turned to the doctor while grabbing her head. "My muscles… they hurt and my head is pounding."

After attaching a heart monitor clip to her finger, the doctor looked at Rachael and gave her a confirming nod. "Yeah, they probably do. It seems like you had a severe case of psychological shock. In your case, your blood rushed to your muscles causing them to stiffen up. It will take a little bit of time for it to go away, but it will."

Rachael felt embarrassed for losing control of herself like she did. "I'm so sorry. I should have reacted better. I lost control of my own reason and freaked out. I should be better than that."

The doctor looked at her with a warm expression. "We tend to be our own worst critic. Don't be so hard on yourself. You came out of your panic attack faster than anyone that I've seen before. You are an amazing individual. Remember that."

The corner of Rachael's mouth rose slightly. "Thanks. I appreciate that." She began to take greater notice of the pain that was piercing threw her skull. "My head hurts so bad."

The doctor grabbed the IV tube that was dangling from its bag. "Let's put this back in. It's just IV fluid to help maintain hydration. It will help."

Rachael looked at the doctor and gave her a nod of approval. The doctor proceeded to put the tube back into her arm. "What would help the most is if I give you something to relax your body. It acts like a sedative and you will more than likely fall asleep. It will make both your muscles and head feel better, I promise."

Rachael dropped her head in thought for a second. "Yeah, I think that's for the best. I need to recover." She smirked and jokingly continued, "Just please don't experiment on me or whatever you do in this place."

The doctor compassionately smiled back. "I promise, I won't do any experiments on you. We have set up a place for you to stay. It's quite nice. We will move you there while you recover, if that's ok with you."

Rachael looked at the doctor and nodded. "Yes, that sounds ok. Thank you." She laid down on the table, gripping her head with both hands. Pain drowned her thoughts.

The doctor grabbed a couple of bottles of medicine, pulled the liquid out with syringes, then slowly injected them into the IV. Gradually closing her eyes, Rachael faded into unconsciousness.

Outside of the treatment room, George sat tapping his foot, waiting for news of the status of Rachael. The waiting room that he was in was built for comfort. It was covered with hard wood floors and had a couple of very cushy leather sectionals that wrap around a large square wood table. Lining the wall were a mixture of leather recliners and sturdy hard chairs. George sat on the edge of one of the hard chairs with his head bowed. He had flown many missions that built up his tolerance and patience. Yet at that moment, he found that his patience was very thin. He was worried about what had happened to his Commander and friend. He was also worried that what happened to her might also happen to him. His curiosity was itching at him as well. He really wanted to continue to check out the facility and ships.

Forty-five minutes later, the doctor entered, facing George. George immediately stood up and walked over to her. The doctor put her hand on his shoulder. "She's going to be ok."

George exhaled in relief. "That's good to hear. What happened to her?"

The doctor put her hands into her white lab coat pockets. "She suffered a severe case of psychological shock but is recovering. Her muscles became extremely tense and she developed a migraine so we gave her some strong muscle relaxers and migraine medication."

"So, she's probably really loopy right now I would think."

"Not exactly. It knocked her out. She'll be asleep for a little while. When she wakes up, she'll feel better. We're prepping her now for release so that she can recover in her bedroom at her place."

"Her place? You're taking her back to her home?" George's eyebrows rose in the hope that they were going to be taken back to the real world.

The doctor put her head down while placing a hand on her forehead, "No, I'm sorry. I forgot for a second that you were pulled early from your tour. You each have been set up with your own place to stay within the facility. They're pretty nice. You'll like it."

"I'm sure it will be fine. Can we go elsewhere, or are we confined to our quarters?"

"That, I cannot tell you. My job is to make sure you're healthy and occasionally stitch you up." The doctor cracked a grin.

George rolled his eyes. "Wonderful."

The doctor placed her hand on George's arm. "I'm sorry I couldn't give you more answers. If I could give you more information I would."

Nodding his head, George gave a friendly smile. "I know you would. Thank you for taking care of Rachael."

"It's my pleasure." The doctor stepped to the side as a couple of the medical staff came through the door pushing an unconscious Rachael on the floating stretcher. "Here they are. They'll take you to your place. I hope things go a little better for you. I know this can be a confusing time right now."

George reached out and shook the doctors' hand. "Thanks doc."

Looking into George's eyes, the doctor gave him a gentle glance of sincere empathy. "Not a problem. Good luck."

George nodded his head. He followed the medical staff who continued to push Rachael through the entrance of the clinic. They were back in the main hallway which led to the hangar. The emergency golf cart that carried them to the clinic was waiting for them. The staff loaded the stretcher with Rachael into the back of the vehicle. After George and a staff member jumped in with her, they took off down the hall.

Chapter 5

The door slid open to Teancom's dark, silent underwater home. Teancom swiped a hand up the wall by the door. Immediately the lights turned on and classic 90s alternative rock started playing softly in the background. He stepped into a small entryway, kicking off his shoes. He moved into his living room. His bachelor pad was furnished with a leather couch and matching leather recliner facing a cardboard thin eighty-five-inch TV dominating the wall. On the other walls were pictures of different places around the world. In the middle of the room was a solid wooden coffee table situated in front of the couch as well as some small side tables on both sides of the couch. Some small fake tropical plants stood next to a large tiki located in one of the corners.

The hardwood floor of the large room was softened by a grey shag rug beneath the couch. To his left was the kitchen entrance. Next to the entrance was a bar table that connected the rooms together. The bar made a 90 degree turn and extended into another room which had a pool table in the middle. The only thing that separated this room from the living room was a small step that stretched across the floor.

Beyond the kitchen and the pool table room was a hallway. The hallway extended to other doors leading to other rooms. Four bar stools lined the bar that connected the pool table room to the kitchen. Across from the bar stool on the other side of the room was a wall with a large glass sliding door. On the other side of the glass door was a wooden balcony that was engulfed in darkness.

He walked over to the large kitchen which has an island counter top in the middle. He went over to the cabinet and pulled out some liquid gold. Opening one of the cupboards, he pulled out a glass cup and filled it. He grabbed the cup full of liquid gold and walked back around the bar and across the pool table room where the sliding glass door was.

Sliding the glass door open, he walked onto the wooden deck. The decent-sized deck stretched to another sliding door, leading to his bedroom. On the wall between the two sliding doors was a button. He pushed it and said, "Maui beach at sunset with a slight breeze. Pause time of day."

The darkness beyond the deck morphed into a stunning beach, the sun poised to dip below the ocean. The sound of seagulls and waves crashing could be heard in what seemed to be the distance. A slight breeze carried the smell of salt water and sand, filling the air. Teancom faced the artificial sun, eyes closed, soaking in its radiant heat with a deep breath.

After a moment's reflection, he sank into a chair near the deck's center. The chair looked like a cross of an office chair and an outside resort chair that was made of cloth. In front of the chair was a rectangle shaped table which had a top made of marble. The rest of the table was made of a material that resembled bamboo. On top of the table was a closed laptop. Attached to the laptop was a cord that extended to the wall with the button that he just pushed. The cord fed directly into the wall, bypassing a typical outlet. The cord itself was slightly thicker than a normal power cord.

Teancom leaned back on his chair and dug deep into his thoughts. After a short moment he took a drink and set the glass down on the table. He opened the laptop and turned it on. Typing in his password, he clicked into a program labeled communications. Once the program opened up, he clicked into a subfolder labeled contacts. He scrolled down to a contact labeled "Parents" and clicked on the option that said video connect. A message appeared on the laptop that said "Establishing link. Please wait."

An older Teancom look-alike appeared onscreen. "Son! It's been a while. Everything OK?"

Teancom smiled as he sat up. "Hey Dad. Everything's fine. How's you and Mom?"

"You just missed your mom. She just left for the spa. She's going to be mad at me that she missed you."

Teancom laughed. "Why would she be mad at you?"

Teancom's dad shrugged. "I don't know. It's just how it works. Maybe if you and your brother would call more often it wouldn't be so bad."

"I know for a fact that I call more than he does."

"Well, you got that." His dad nodded. "Have you heard from him lately?"

"No, not lately. It's completely understandable though. You know how Skinwalker Ranch can be. It sucks the time out of you." Teancom explained, trying to defend his brother.

"That it does. Studying refined matter will do that. Your Mom tries to convince them to have a kid so that they can get transferred out of there." Teancom's Dad grinned.

"Yeah, well he likes it there. I think that's why they are holding off on having a kid. Besides, Mom just wants grandkids." Teancom grinned back.

His father nodded his head again. "Yes, she does. You're lucky she isn't here or you would get the interrogation. Then I would be in the background nodding my head and saying "listen to your mother."

Teancom rolled his eyes. "I bet that would happen. Too bad she's at the spa. Those calculus missions that you two are on seem really brutal. I don't know how you bear it."

Teancom's Dad chuckled. "It can be. What about you? I heard you were assigned your own crew. How's that going?"

Teancom lowered his head. "Well, one passed out in shock, which I'm pretty sure I had a hand in. The other is ex-military - acts like a child, but internally, I'm pretty sure he's plotting my demise the moment he feels threatened. I still haven't met the others. To tell you the truth, my confidence is a little shaken."

"I wouldn't be too hard on yourself Son. Lots of people have gone into shock, even without the time restraint which I hear your team is on. Not to mention they were placed in this situation by not the best means. You didn't get to pick them. The good news however is that your crew is NASA astronauts so you have a lot to work with."

"I know. I think that's part of the problem." Teancom explained.

Teancom's Dad rose an eyebrow. "What do you mean?"

Teancom took a deep breath. "If you think about it, "my team" have been picked out of a big group of very talented people because they are the best of what they do. They are highly skilled, extremely smart, and highly accomplished. That's a little intimidating. Not only that, they had a lot to lose. They have a lot that they are now forced to leave behind. How am I supposed to compensate for that? I mean the two without families, they won't be as hard to deal with as opposed to the two that do have families. Even then, I already put one in the med bay."

His father gazed at him, eyes warm with empathy. "Teancom, why do you think you were chosen for this assignment?"

Teancom looked back at him for a second, then looked away. "I don't know. I've been questioning that myself. Maybe because of family connections I guess."

His father let out a little laugh. "You're too modest. You have been on mission after mission and have made great decisions on difficult situations. Your experience and success in the field are well known."

Teancom looked back at the screen. "Yeah, well taking orders and giving them are a little different."

His father laughed a little more. "When have you willingly taken an order. You're the person that commanders really love and at the same time really hate."

Teancom snapped, "And now I'm one of them. I'm the person who I always questioned."

"Except you're not them. You're you. You are the reason you were chosen to lead them." Teancom's Dad paused for a second to let it sink in. "Look, you are the most "down to earth" person I know in this organization. You say things as they are. You're relatable. That's what they need. They don't need someone just to tell them what to do. You know personally how well that works. They need someone to point them in the right direction. Someone to coach, counsel, mentor them through how the system works. A good leader isn't someone who is the best at everything and dictates. A good leader surrounds themselves with others that are the best and if they aren't they make them the best they can be. That's your job and I can't think of a better person to do it." Teancom looked down, absorbing the words his dad just gave him. "Look son, just do what you do. More important, let them do what they do. You will do great. I know you will."

Teancom looked up at the screen with a little more confidence in his face. "Thanks Dad. That helped." A lighter demeanor came back on his face. "I guess one good thing that comes from this is that I get to make the call when to clear out a section of the mountains for practice."

His father let out a hearty laugh. "That's right. You always loved using the BFR's."

"They are called BFA's now." Teancom corrected his father with a playful smirk.

"Robots, Avatars, doesn't matter. What matters is scaring the crap out of unsuspecting campers." They both laughed.

"Look Dad, I better go. They don't like it when we take up too much air time. It was great talking to you. Tell Mom I said hi."

"No, you call back later and tell her that yourself. Love you, Son. Stay safe out there."

"Love you too Dad."

Teancom tapped the screen and disconnected the call with his father. He took a deep breath, with a smile still on his face, and stared at the still setting sun. He took a moment to reflect on the words his father said to him. Satisfied, he grabbed his glass and finished it off. Getting up out of his chair with the glass still in one hand, he turned and walked to the wall next to the sliding door. He held the wall button for a couple of seconds. The beach, breeze, and sunset vanished, seagull cries fading into silence.

He returned inside, rinsed his glass in the kitchen, and stowed it away. At the front door, he put his hand on the wall. Swiping down, he turned everything off as he walked out the door.

Chapter 6

The golf cart carrying George and Rachael stopped at an unlabeled hallway door. George had noticed none of the doors bore markings. He wondered how the driver knew what door to stop at. George raised a hand to the staff member beside him. "How did the driver know where to stop? There are no markings on these doors and the hallway all looks the same."

The person with him motioned his head and hand to come closer to him. George obeyed and knelt next to him. The person pointed toward the driver. George eyed the driver's gauges. Right behind the steering wheel was a screen built into the dash, which led to a larger center screen, perfectly blending with the contour of the vehicle itself. The screens displayed a plethora of information, including a facility map with a dot marking their location. Next to the map was a zoomed in view of their location, giving more details of their surroundings. The facility itself looked like a long stick with the bay at its core. The hallway that they were in surrounded the bay on all sides. In front of the driver was a heads-up display that showed information on the door that they stopped at.

As George studied the drivers displays, the staff member moved the stretcher with Rachael on it out toward the back of the vehicle. George noticed and promptly followed. As they moved out of the vehicle, a lady driving another golf cart pulled behind them.

She stepped from her vehicle, grabbing a small duffel bag, and approached in a tan suit and white blouse. Smiling warmly, she extended a hand to George. With a bright voice she exclaimed, "You must be George. It is a pleasure to meet you. My name is Nancy. I'm here to show you where you are going to stay." Her voice was very perky.

George shook her hand and returned the smile. "Ma'am."

"It's so good to have you with us! I'm sure that you're still adjusting with everything. It's a lot to take in all at once, especially how fast you have been introduced to everything." Nancy seemed to have a lot of energy in her voice.

George looked down at Rachael, who was still asleep on the stretcher, and nodded his head in agreement. "Yes, it is."

Nancy looked at Rachael with a big frown. "Oh, poor thing. I know I would be the same way, if not worse if I were in her position. I can only imagine how she must have felt, how you must have felt. One moment you're floating around in space and the next moment you're in a secret facility where there are flying saucers! It's like you're part of a movie or something. I mean, I've been around these things for quite a while so I'm completely used to it, but I've seen a couple of movies where people are thrown in a completely foreign space and they seemed pretty freaked out. Even those who have been slowly introduced to this place are really shook up at first. You seem different from everyone else though. You seem pretty calm. How are you feeling?"

George could tell that Nancy liked to talk and knew that if they were going to get anywhere, he would have to initiate the movement. "I'm feeling ok. I've been in the military as a pilot for almost all my adult life. I'm used to being displaced." He started to walk to the door. "So, this is where we are going to stay?"

"Yes and no. This will be Rachael's place. Your place will be a few steps that way." Nancy spoke quickly as she pointed down the hall to a door in the distance. "You are free to visit each other as often as you want. I know experiences like this can bring people closer together. Not that I'm saying that you weren't already close. You worked together on missions and shared a tight space together in space. If that doesn't bring people close together, I don't know what will."

George interrupted, "So I noticed that there are no door knobs. How do you get in?" George already knew the answer from observing Isaiah and Teancom but wanted to move things along.

"That's a great question!" Nancy's eyebrows rose and a bigger grin appeared on her face. "Most everything here works by placing your hand on the wall next to the thing that you want to operate. In this case, if Rachael wanted to open the door, she would put her hand on the wall and it would open. If you were to put your hand on the wall, it will notify Rachael that you are at the door and then she could let you in. I find it so much more convenient to do things this way than to have to carry keys around everywhere you go. Not only carrying them around, but having to pull them out, find the right one, insert it in the door. What a giant waste of time. This is so much better. You and Rachael are already in the system so these rooms are set up so that they respond to each of you in your own way. Here, let me show you." Nancy gently pushed the stretcher that was carrying Rachael next to the door. "Now if you would ever so kindly lift Rachael's hand up and place her palm on the wall next to the door, the door will open."

George lifted Rachael's limp hand, pressing her palm to the wall. With a soft hum, the door slid open.

"See, it worked." Nancy said as she cheerfully showed her teeth. She turned to the two helpers from the hospital. "You're all set. Go do your thing. You're both awesome!" She turned quickly back to George. "They are going to push her over to her bedroom and carefully place her on her bed while she recovers from the medicine that they gave her. It must have been a strong dose. She really looks like she's in a deep sleep. Hopefully she'll feel so much better when she wakes up. That's what medicine is supposed to do, right?"

The two helpers pushed Rachael in the stretcher into Rachael's place. Nancy briefly watched them as they went. "So, while they are taking care of Rachael, let me show you around. All these rooms are almost identical so if I show you around here, you will know about your place. Now, if you would walk with me, we can start the tour." Nancy walked through the door, turned around and waited for George to follow. George stepped inside. She pointed to the wall next to the door on the inside. "Now, if you would, please put your hand on the wall and hold it there for a few seconds. Remember what I said, almost everything is activated this way." George complied and put his right hand against the wall. Five seconds later, a crisp twelve-by-twelve-inch hologram bloomed, framed by colorful flowers. Geroge jerked his hand back, eyes wide. In the middle were the words "Hello. Please pick your preferences".

Nancy watched George's reaction to the hologram. She was extremely excited as she watched him. "Here is what

I call your welcome options. When you enter your place, all you have to do is swipe your hand up where you just put your hand. It will not only turn on the lights to however bright or shade of light that you set it to, but it can also do things like turn on music, turn the air conditioner on to your set temperature, and even give you a pre-programmed welcome announcement. For example, I have mine set up where when I walk in at night it says "Good evening, Nancy." If I have been gone all day, it will add "I hope you had a good day." When I leave in the morning and I turn it off it says "I hope that you have a good day." You can change the voice, the volume of the voice, the volume of the music, what type of music, and even turn voice control on or off after you swipe it on. Go ahead and try it. All you have to do is swipe the hologram with your finger to move from screen to screen and make your choices."

George swiped the hologram with his finger. The next hologram appeared with a few options. It said, "General Controls" and "User Specific Controls." Nancy continued to explain. "Here, you have the option of setting up the general controls where if anyone swipes it on, it will default to these settings unless you have set up a user specific control. If you did, it will read your hand print and use the settings that you set up for yourself."

George was amazed at this. He grinned as he clicked on the "User Specific Controls" option. The hologram showed a bunch of other options. He looked and found the option that said Greeting phrases and selected it. A handful of other options appeared which included "Volume," "Voice Type," "Pre-selected phrases," and "Manually enter phrase." George chose the manually enter phrase option. A keyboard appeared in front of him, as if it were floating in the air. He slowly pushed the letter W to try it out. His finger met no resistance, but touching the hologram summoned the letter *w* in its display. His grin increased as he typed "Welcome to my home King George. I am so grateful that you are here. You make everything so much better." He hit the enter button and more options appeared on the screen. He chose an option that said "Announce when you enter." He hit the "Voice Type" option. This group offered options like "Male," "Female," "Tone Up," "Tone Down," "High," "Low," as well as many other options to customize the voice. He tweaked the settings for a minute, mimicking Rachael's voice. He hit the playback button and in Rachael's voice it said, "Welcome to my home King George. I am so grateful that you are here. You make everything so much better." He was pleased with himself.

George turned around to see how Nancy was reacting. She was typing a message on her phone. With her big smile, she looked back up at George. "That is very creative of you. I'm sure Rachael will appreciate the message, or get mad at you. I know that if someone programmed that into my place, I would find it pretty funny. Did you still want to explore the options?"

George shook his head. "No, that's good for now. I might revisit it later though." He turned back to the hologram, hit the "Save" option, then hit "Exit". The hologram disappeared.

"Please follow me and I'll show you the rest of the place." Nancy walked further inside. It was very similar to how Teancom's place was set up, except slightly smaller in dimensions. From the living room when they walked in to the kitchen with a bar attached to the pool table room, the layout was the same. Except in this room instead of a pool table, there was a rectangle shaped dining table with chairs surrounding it. The walls were bare except for a mounted sixty-five-inch TV. The furniture consisted of a brown cloth covered couch, coffee table, and recliner. Beyond the kitchen and dining room was a hallway that connected to a decent sized bathroom and bedroom where they laid Rachael. Nancy introduced George to each room, explaining everything in detail, plus her added commentary. George tried his best to listen but was half distracted by his efforts to push her along. In the midst of the tour, the two helpers left with the stretcher. The last area that they explored was the deck, which, like Teancom's place, connected to the bedroom and the dining room. Everything was dark when they walked onto it.

Nancy held down the button next to the door with her thumb and said, "Iguazu Falls, Argentina on a sunny afternoon, low breeze, turn sound to very low." The deck morphed into a platform over countless waterfalls, rainforest stretching miles, mist faintly shimmering. In the distance, birds flew through the mist-filled air as a faint sound of water crashing echoed down below. A breeze carrying fresh water and wet vegetation brushed their skin. The sun that manifested radiated heat as if they were actually standing outside.

George's jaw dropped. He couldn't believe what he was experiencing. It was as if they were transported to another part of the world. After walking over to the railing of the deck, he looked down to see a very detailed body of water that the falls were crashing into. Squinting his eyes toward a riverbank, he could see a jaguar laying on the grass under a tree. He turned to Nancy with wide eyes. "This is incredible! How is this possible?"

Nancy diverted her attention from the view back to George. "What you see is holographic video of one of my favorite places in the world. Isn't it beautiful? I go there for real at least once a year. You can go on boat tours and see all sorts of nature. I have a friend there named Cinthia. She works on one of the boats. I love to talk to her about the people that she meets. They all have really interesting life stories."

George interrupted her. "Wait, this is a hologram? How can a hologram produce wind, smells, sound, the sun? This seems way too real."

Nancy maintained her big smile. "Yes, you're right. It isn't just a hologram. There are fans and artificial smells that help the illusion. The sounds are recorded from the actual locations. The sun is actually more like a heat lamp that gives off similar rays that the actual sun gives off. The artificial rays actually help your body produce vitamin D and, if you want, can give you a sun tan as well. I like to lay on the deck of my place and sun bathe every once in a while. It's a nice escape when you're cramped up in this underwater base for long periods of time. In the past, people would go stir crazy. That's why they developed this. It helps to take the pressure of life off your shoulders."

George froze, jaw slack. "So, engineers built this tech just to ease emotional stress?"

Nancy tilted her head. "Well, they don't come up with it themselves. Our engineers here are really smart, but they have help. They have full access to all sorts of data collected through things like the patent office, laboratories, and R & D from many different businesses."

George stared at Nancy. "And everyone is ok that you steal intellectual property from them." He closed his eyes as he immediately remembered where he was at.

"No one knows we exist silly. It makes it really easy. Besides, we aren't going to steal their ideas and run them out of business by selling it first. Most of these ideas are incomplete anyway because of a lack of funding or interest. We simply finish the research and combine it with research from other places. It's amazing what you can come up with when you put everyone's ideas together." Nancy tilted her head back and forth, still smiling.

"I suppose so." George continued to gaze out into the incredibly scenic and vast display of waterfalls and rainforest.

Nancy pointed to the button on the wall. "If you want to change the scenery, all you have to do is push this button and describe where you want to be, the time of day, and any other details that you want to include. For example..." She held down the button. "The Sahara Desert at sunset." The waterfalls and rainforest disappeared into darkness for a second, then a vast scene of sand dunes appeared with the sun setting in the distance. The cool breeze and smell of wet vegetation was replaced with very dry wind and the smell of sand. Nancy let go of the button, and then pushed it again, "Svalbard, Norway in November." The sand dunes disappeared into darkness just like before. A vast view of frozen mountain ranges appeared near a body of water that housed very small islands of snow-covered ice. The sky became covered by rich strips of color created by the northern lights. The dry wind turned into an icy chill.

George looked around with his jaw open as the scenes changed. He walked over to Nancy. "Can I try?"

Nancy gripped her hands with excitement. "Of course you can. Just hold your thumb on this button and name your destination."

George pushed his thumb on the button. "Pinnacle Peak, Washington, in August, no clouds, sunny afternoon." The display of the northern lights disappeared into darkness only to be replaced by a blue sky with the sun shining from above. Looking out from the balcony was a vast region of pine trees and mountain ridges that stretched for miles. In the background stood a mountain halve covered in snow. George let go of the button and walked slowly toward the railing of the balcony to observe.

"This is such a beautiful place." Nancy pointed at the mountain. "What mountain is that?"

George kept staring at the scenery. "That is Mount Rainier."

Nancy looked around at the scene. "That is such a lovely view of that mountain. Is this someplace that you went to a lot?"

George looked down for a moment, then over to Nancy. "Only once. I grew up an orphan, bouncing between foster homes, never settling with any family for very long. The only family that ever took me anywhere was a younger couple. She was unable to have children and he was in the Army. They took me up to this spot. I loved being able to look down from above, even though we weren't extremely high up. It was here, in the back of my mind, that I decided I was going to join the military and become a pilot." George continued to glance around while his mind took him back to that moment.

His thoughts were quickly interrupted by Nancy. "Wow, what a touching story. Thank you for sharing that with me. I bet you were extremely grateful to that couple for taking you there. They changed the direction of your whole life. Can you imagine if they didn't take you there? Who knows where you would be right now? I would be talking to a completely different person."

George shook his head as his mind jumped back into reality. "Yeah, imagine that. Thank you for showing me how this works."

Nancy placed her hand compassionately on his shoulder. "You are so welcome. It is my pleasure. I've pretty much shown you everything in this place."

"Then would you mind showing me where my place is?" George inquired.

"Of course. If you would please follow me." Nancy started walking to the door, then stopped. She pulled out a phone from her bag. "I almost forgot. This is for Rachael. Let me put it on her night stand so she will have it when she wakes up. It has a welcome note programmed on it so that she can call me when she wakes up. I'll be right back." She walked over to Rachael's room and disappeared for a second, then came right back. "Ok, let's go."

George followed Nancy out the door. Nancy continued to talk but George phased her out. He thought she mentioned something about a cat. It didn't matter to him. There was a mixture of thoughts that was going through his head. It made it difficult to focus on the endless small talk that Nancy produced. They walked out of Rachael's place and back in the hallway. They continued to walk to a distant door which Nancy identified earlier as George's place. As they arrived Nancy concluded, "…and finally, here we are."

George began to raise his hand to the door when Nancy said to him, "When you put your hand against the wall, swipe to the right."

George nodded his head. "Copy that." He obeyed and swiped to the right. The curved wall slid up to reveal a space that resembled a home garage. In the middle of the space was a backed-in "golf cart."

Nancy threw both hands up in the air. "Ta da! Your very own golf cart. Teancom said that you would want one to get around. He must really trust you."

George grinned at the sight of his own issued golf cart and walked over to the driver's seat. He held back his excitement as he looked it over. Not just for the golf cart, but for the mode of transportation that would take him to the ships that he saw not too long ago. He looked over at Nancy. "He trusts me, huh?"

"He must trust you a lot." Nancy grinned as she tilted her head to the side. "Most people don't get their own golf cart the first day of orientation but Teancom insisted that you have one. He only asks that you stay here until you hear from him."

George saw through it. It wasn't Teancom's trust in him, but Teancom's bid for his trust.

"Want me to show you how it works?" Nancy pointed to the controls.

George quickly shook his hands. "No, no. I… I watched how the others drove it and it seems pretty simple to operate." He knew that was a lie but figured that it would be quicker to figure it out rather than get the full narration from Nancy.

"Awesome! If you want to close this door all you have to do is swipe down with your hand on the wall next to it and it will close. One last thing, let me give you your phone. It has a map of the area as well as phone numbers for your companions, when they get their phones. If you are hungry, instead of going over to the dining hall, you can just order it on your phone and they will send it over through a transport tube like the one I showed you earlier in the kitchen. It also has my number on there in case you have any questions about anything. I will be more than happy to help you. Feel free to call." Nancy handed George the phone.

George gave a warm smile as he took the phone. "Thank you. I will."

Nancy enthusiastically shook George's hand, "It has been a pleasure to get to show you around. I hope you have a great rest of the day."

George nodded his head. "Thank you. You too ma'am."

Nancy gave George one last friendly glance before she turned around and went back to her vehicle. George wanted to blow off his instruction to stay at his newly assigned place and jump in the golf cart to go exploring. Tempted to explore, he hesitated, then exited the garage. With a downward swipe of his hand, the door closed. After walking over to the door of the entrance to his place, he placed his hand on the wall. The door immediately opened.

Chapter 7

George entered his quarters, swiping his hand on the wall to ignite the lights. He roamed, opening cabinets and doors to see what was available to him. He found utensils, cleaning supplies, writing materials, and basic household items. The refrigerator was completely empty, except for ice stored in the ice machine. While he was looking through one of the kitchen drawers, he came across a flashlight. He thought for a second, then grabbed it and walked over to the balcony.

As he stepped on the deck, all he could see was darkness. He turned the flashlight on and walked over to the railing. His flashlight illuminated a giant dome screen, twenty feet across at its farthest point. Thousands of pinholes speckled its surface. As he pointed his flashlight directly beneath him, he noticed the light reflected onto the ceiling above. He leaned over the side of the railing and looked down. Right below the railing of the balcony was a giant mirror that covered the entire area. George was tempted to hop the railing but doubted the screen's strength. He decided against it. Instead, he turned the flashlight off and walked over to the button on the wall.

Pushing the button he said, "Niagara Falls." The room blazed to life seconds later. He was immersed in the atmosphere of the New York and Canadian border. The sound of crashing water echoed in the background while a slight updraft rose from the railing, along with the smell of damp air. He glanced over the scene dumbfounded. "Unbelievable." Crossing his arms, he stared at the sight for several minutes. After taking a deep breath, he walked back into his new place, leaving the projection on.

Walking over to the living room area, George noticed that there was a remote on the table. He picked it up and turned the television mounted on the wall turned on. As he played with the options, he noticed that every streaming service as well as every cable channel that you could get was available. He went through the channels to see the latest sports updates. Pleasantly surprised with his entertainment options, he switched the television off and continued to explore.

Making his way into the bedroom, he reflected on his outfit that they dressed him in. Even though he was in fresh clothes, they did not attempt to bathe him in any way. Although relieved that they didn't wipe his unconscious body down, he felt stale from the lack of a shower while in space.

George walked out of the bedroom and into the bathroom. It was a decent-sized bathroom that had the luxuries of a fancy hotel. The sink, vanity, and bathtub were very large, accompanied by a granite countertop. After placing his phone on the counter, he went over to the bathtub and opened the glass sliding door. The large tub had water jets built in with shower heads mounted on both sides of the wall as well as on the ceiling. Built into the side wall was two different dispensers labeled "Soap" and "Shampoo."

George turned on the shower, stripped, and stepped in. Warm water cascaded, easing his tension for the first time in days. His thoughts went blank as the water pressure from the showerheads acted like a masseuse. After a long while, the reality of his situation creeped back into his thoughts. The curiosity of the unknown of that facility began pecking at his brain again. His hard-earned patience, honed by years as a pilot, slipped away. Curiosity demanded action. In his mind, the decision was made, no matter the consequence. He quickly finished his shower, grabbed a towel, dried himself off, then wrapped it around his waist. Grabbing his phone, he walked out the door to the bedroom.

Locating the dresser, he discovered that there were many different articles of clothing, all in his size. He grabbed underwear, cargo pants, T-shirt, and socks and threw them on the bed along with his phone. Throwing open the door of the walk-in closet, he glanced around to see what was available. There were several dress shirts, polo shirts, suits of different colors and fabrics, ties, and many other decorative articles of clothing. On the floor were several different pairs of shoes for every occasion that he could think of. They all looked like his size. He grabbed a pair of running shoes and walked back out of the closet. After throwing the shoes on the floor next to the bed, he quickly put on his newly found outfit. He grabbed his phone and turned it on. It looked like an ordinary smart phone with a very basic operating system. On the screen was an icon that said facility map. Tapping on the icon, an app opened up to reveal a hallway with the location of Rachael's place, his place, a place for Amy, a place for Adam, a gym, and a dining hall. There were no other details. George sighed. "Of course."

He debated whether or not to take the phone with him, knowing that it was a way they track his location.

Figuring that they would know where he was in the facility with or without the phone, he put it in his pocket and walked out the front door. He put his hand next to the outside of the door to close it, then swiped sideways to open the garage door, revealing the golf cart. Jumping in the driver's seat, he scanned the layout.

George looked at the dash of the vehicle and noticed that it looked similar to the dash of the vehicle that took them to the med bay. He looked around for an on-switch or button, but found none. No gas or brake pedals at his feet like a normal car. Glancing to the right, he noticed a handle that looked like he could push forward or backward, much like the throttle on a fighter jet. He tried doing both but it would not move. As he continued to scan the controls, he noticed the large center screen. Looking at his hand, he commented, "Makes sense." He placed the palm of his hand on the center screen. The vehicle came to life. On the windshield in front of him read the words "Welcome George." As he glanced at the warm welcome, he noticed that in place of a rear-view mirror was a long thin screen that displayed a panoramic view of what was behind him. George grinned as he put his seat belt on.

Once again, he tried pushing the handle to his right very slightly. This time it moved, along with the rest of the vehicle. He crept out, turning left toward their origin. As he started to move, he noticed that the map for the facility appeared just as it did on the other vehicle. Slowly moving forward, he noticed that the Heads-Up Display labeled Rachael's name on her door as he passed it. The center of the screen started blinking and the words "Close Door?" appeared along with the two options "Yes" and "Dismiss." George selected yes and noticed the garage door close in the rear display. With a grin on his face, he pushed the center lever forward. As he inched it forward, the lever stopped at a certain point. He looked down on it and noticed that it could go a lot farther forward but something was causing it to stop. He looked over at the Heads-Up Display to see that he was only going 15 MPH.

He took a deep breath. "Yeah, that's about right." He knew they put a governor on his vehicle, only allowing him to go a certain speed. Shaking off the slight frustration, he continued down the hallway. As he drove down the hall, he noticed that the vehicle handled extremely well for it having no traction on the ground. As he turned to the right and left, the vehicle responded as if the front of the vehicle turned while the rear of the vehicle followed, just as if handling a normal car with the front wheels turning.

Glancing back at the center screen, he noticed a round icon on the lower right corner. He touched it. A bunch of other icons appeared. Among the many icons, there was one labeled "Handling". Pushing it revealed five other options which were labeled "Ground control," "Flight control," "Aquatic Surface control," "Submerged control," and "Zero G control." All of the options were faded except for "Ground control." He tried to push the faded icons but it didn't do anything. Finally, he pushed "Ground control." A whole new set of icons appeared.

Among the many icons were "Traditional," "Rear Traditional," "Center Turn," and "Side Pivot" to name a few. The "Traditional" icon was highlighted in green. George figured that was the mode he was in now. He looked at the "Rear Traditional" icon and knew that must mean that it controlled the vehicle as if the "back wheels" turned instead of the "front wheels." He didn't bother with that. The "Center Turn" icon did pique his curiosity. He touched it. Icons labeled "Sensitivity," "Immediate," and "Delayed" appeared. He touched the "Delayed" icon and the words "How many seconds?" as well as the number "1" with a two-sided arrow beside it. George, not knowing what any of this really meant kept it at "1." On the bottom of the screen, it said "Confirm Changes" with the options "Yes" and "Cancel" below it.

After looking at it for a second, he shrugged his shoulders. "Sure, why not." He pushed "Yes." He turned the steering wheel slightly left. The vehicle pivoted from its center, drifting sideways before aligning with the new direction a second later. George was headed toward the curved wall. He quickly turned the vehicle away from the wall, but because of the second delay the golf cart went half way up the curved wall before it started moving in the direction that he wanted. He was now heading toward the other wall. He quickly pulled back on the center handle and stopped the vehicle before climbing the opposite wall.

George's brow wrinkled as he stared at the controls. "Why would you ever want to control this vehicle like that?" He shook his head in disgust and turned his attention back to the screen. There, he spotted the "Side Pivot" option and selected it. He confirmed the selection. A voice came from the vehicle that said, "Steering wheel released."

He noticed that he was able to not only turn the steering wheel, but push the sides of the steering wheel away from him. As he pushed the right side of the steering wheel away, the left side moved toward him and vice versa. Also, when he pushed the right side, the vehicle spun to the right. When he pushed the left side, the vehicle spun to the left. When he turned the steering wheel to the right, the vehicle moved sideways to the right. Same with the left. George liked this option. To him it was a familiar way to control. It reminded him of controlling an airplane with foot rutters. He continued forward, swaying back and forth as he went to get the feel of the steering. It was a little awkward that the vehicle stayed level and did not lean with the turns like an airplane would, but he got used to it. In fact, he preferred it to the traditional steering.

George continued to drive for several minutes until he came to the left-hand turn at the end of the long hallway. On his map he could see that he was at the end of the facility. Taking a left, he continued down the hall until he came to the entrance of the hangar. As he approached the entrance an icon that said "open bay doors" appeared on the center screen. Unfortunately, the icon was faded. George pushed the icon. As soon as he did the words "Access Restricted" appeared in big red letters. He banged on his steering wheel with the bottom of his fists. As he came up to the doors, he slowed the vehicle to a stop. "Well, so much for "He trusts you."

Shaking his head with a frown, he was about to turn the vehicle around when he noticed another icon on the center screen. It said "Access Bridge." He looked at it for a second, then pressed on the icon. Above him the ceiling opened and the golf cart started to rise straight up. As soon as the vehicle was above where the ceiling use to be, it closed back up. George was now staring down the continuation of the hallway. The big difference was that instead of curved walls on either side of him, there was large glass windows. To the right was a gigantic aquarium with a rock background. Few fish swam among sparse decorations—just rocks. On the left was a view of the giant bay where they were earlier. George pulled forward to the center of the stretch of hallway, stopped the vehicle, unbuckled, and got out. He walked to the window that showed the bay and looked around. He could tell that he was about half way from the floor of the bay to the top of it. It gave him a great view of the area. He could see both the round and triangle shaped craft in the distance.

Staring out the window with his mouth open, he was amazed at the scale of the facility. He couldn't believe that something like this existed in the ocean floor. As he continued to look out, he noticed very little activity going on. The signs of life he could see was a couple of people going in and out of what Teancom called earlier the Delta class model. It looked like they were inspecting them. George wished he could be down there with them, inspecting the craft.

A thought came to him. He took out his phone that Nancy gave him, turned it on, and looked for the camera icon. Once he found it, he opened the app and activated the camera. He pointed it at the Delta class craft that was being inspected and zoomed in. He was amazed on how remarkable the pixilation was. He zoomed in on a worker, spotting the pores on his face. He zoomed back out to get the whole craft in the picture. When he tried to snap a picture, a 'Feature locked' message appeared. At this point he was not surprised. Nevertheless, he continued to use the camera zoom feature to look at the different craft in the bay. He studied the curves of each one and tried to make out any defining features. They were all plain on the outside. There were no signs of air intakes, propulsion systems, or anything that a standard jet would have.

After several minutes of looking, George decided to keep exploring. He got back in his vehicle and buckled up. The displays in the vehicle were still on. He looked at the map on the dash and noticed that the hallway kept going and eventually took a ninety degree turn to the left. He continued down the raised hallway until he got to a wall at the end. As he pulled up to the end, an icon appeared on the center screen that said "Exit Bridge." When he pushed it, the floor opened up and the golf cart hovered down to the continuing hallway. Immediately behind him was another large door which no doubt led to the giant bay area. George noticed the large door in the rear display and shook his head in dismay, knowing that it would never open for him. He reluctantly proceeded down the hall.

As George turned the corner, he noticed that things were a little different. The doors that he passed were no longer mystery doors. They were labeled for everyone to see, not just on the Heads-Up Display. He passed several doors that were labeled "Storage 1," Storage 2," and so on. A door labeled "BFA" left him scratching his head. It was clear to him that this half of the facility was meant for regular personnel while the other half was meant for "new recruits." He was tempted to stop to see what was behind the "BFA" door but knew that it would just be a lost cause.

As he continued, he noticed a dot on the enlarged section of the map that was coming closer. As the dot became visible to his sight, he realized that it was another golf cart heading his way. A couple of people that occupied the front seat were in it. They drove by without paying much attention to him. A couple of other vehicles passed him shortly after. Occasionally there would be a golf cart parked next to a door with no one in it.

He eventually came up to a door that said "Gym" on it. Next to the door were three Golf carts parked on the side of the hallway. As he passed, someone came out of the door and walked toward one of the golf carts. George looked over to him and immediately stopped. It was Teancom. George looked over to him and yelled, "Hey, you going to finish my tour?"

Teancom looked over with a smirk on his face. "I thought the military was better at following orders?"

"Yeah, well I'm an astronaut now. It's my job to explore. Really, I blame you for leaving me with the means to do so." George playfully replied, hoping that he read Teancom's personality correctly.

Teancom grinned. "How about we get something to eat. I'm hungry."

The thought of food had escaped George's mind until Teancom mentioned it. He now realized how hungry he was. "Come to think of it, that sounds like a good idea. I'm driving."

Teancom laughed. "Sounds good." He walked around to the front passenger's seat and got in. George continued to drive on, assuming that they would eventually run into a dining hall. "How are you liking your new ride?"

George shrugged his shoulders. "It's nice. A little slow for my taste and doesn't get to the places where I want but other than that, not bad."

Teancom nodded his head in agreement. "Yeah, I know. Remember, this is your first day. You don't know the conversations I had to have to get you one this early."

George grinned. "Much appreciated. I would say that it's quite a coincidence running into you, but I doubt that's the case."

Teancom pulled out his phone and showed George the screen that had a map of the facility with a dot at their location labeled "George."

"So, you seem to be adjusting to all of this extremely well. I mean, you were just on your way to the moon." Teancom observed.

Staring down the hallway, George replied, "Yeah, I served in the military long enough. I'm used to being thrown into complicated situations. Not much shakes me anymore. That's probably what made me so attractive to NASA."

"I can imagine being dead inside has its advantages." Teancom looked at George and laughed.

George smiled at the familiar words. "You aren't the first one that's said that to me. And yes, it does. But that doesn't mean my curiosity is dead. Believe me, I still have a ton of questions."

"I can only imagine. Hopefully I can have some answers for you." Teancom pointed ahead toward a door in the distance. "The dining hall is coming up to the left. Just pull behind one of those carts on the side there."

There were four other carts parked to the side of the hallway next to the door labeled "Dining Hall." George stopped the golf cart in the middle of the hallway, just shy of the farthest vehicle parked on the side. He spun the steering wheel to the left, sliding the golf cart sideways until it was positioned right behind the already parked vehicle. Teancom looked over to George. "Yeah, I prefer the Side Pivot steering option too."

As they got out and started to walk towards the door, George asked, "So why are there so many different steering options? Are they all necessary?"

"Not really. Pair sharp engineers with creative programmers, give them free rein, and you get wild results."

George laughed. "Imagine where we would be as a species if that were always the case. Too bad money and politics get in the way."

When they reached the door, Teancom his hand on the wall next to it and it slid open. As they walked in George looked around with an approving nod. It didn't look like he thought it would. In his mind he pictured it to be a bunch of lined up park benches like a military mess hall. Instead, it looked more like an upscale large diner but not too fancy.

The aroma of smoked hickory wood filled the air. The lighting was slightly dimmed, but not too much. A mixture of booths and tables surrounded by very well made wooden padded chairs filled the room. The floors were still made of the same material that the hallway was made of, but the walls were decorated with various types of art. There was a bar in the background where a couple of people were sitting. The tables were all made of dark wood that looked to be coated with a thick layer of high gloss sealer. They were all different shapes and sizes and all had a very thick stand in the middle to hold them up.

No host greeted them, unlike a traditional restaurant. Teancom picked a small side booth and sat. George sat across from him. Teancom put his hand flat on the table and a menu appeared on the wood surface. He looked up at George and motioned with his head to follow suit. George put his hand on the table and a menu appeared as well. George looked up and saw Teancom scrolling up and down with his finger to reveal more of the menu. He did the same. There was a large selection for him to choose from. George picked a ribeye from the steak section. It gave him options of size and cooking preference. He selected 16 oz and medium rare. Words appeared next to the menu asking if he wanted any sides with it and gave him a large selection of sides. He chose asparagus and garlic mashed potatoes. It asked him if he wanted anything to drink and gave him a large number of options. He chose a large ice water and hit the "Finished" option on the lower right-hand corner. The menu disappeared and the words "Thank You" appeared on the table top. Below it appeared the numbers 10:00, which started counting down indicating how long before his food would be ready.

George's eyebrows rose as he saw the timer. "Wow. Efficient. The cooks must be rushing to get that food ready before the timer gets to zero."

Teancom grinned. "Yeah, there are no cooks. It's all automated. Machines are making the food. When the timer hits zero, your food appears."

"That's incredible! And you can order anything at any time?"

Teancom nodded. "Yep."

"There must be a lot of fat people wandering around here." George looked around the restaurant.

Teancom shook his head. "Actually, everyone that is here are all highly self-motivated. They either have a pretty good exercise routine or are so involved in what they do that food isn't the first thing on their mind. You will find that most people here are in pretty good shape, with a few exceptions."

"Speaking of the devil, what is this place, this organization called?" George leaned in on the table.

"This place is called facility C. This organization has no official name. It avoids names to stay untraceable. Now, as for what I call this organization, I call it the CTC or Conspiracy Theory Corps."

George gave a slight grin. "CTC huh? Catchy."

"I like it." Teancom nodded. "I wish I could claim it as mine, but I can't. I heard it from someone else. It explains the backbone of how we operate from the rest of the world. Just be careful where you mention that name. They hate it when you put a name to this organization."

George rose an eyebrow. "So, who are they? Is there someone in charge that governs and regulates everything?"

"Not exactly. There isn't one person that is in charge of everything. Instead, there are four main division heads that are in charge of specific areas. There's Internal Affairs, World

Oversight, Refined Matter, and Calculus. Each division head is in charge of a specific area within the organization. Their job is to make sure that their area is running as effectively as possible. If there are concerns on how things are running, the Calculus division acts as sort of an oversight to guide it back in the right direction through the division heads."

"And you don't worry about corruption?" George questioned.

"There's some of that but it's rare. The division heads follow and use strict AI protocols which have proven to be extremely trustworthy. It also helps that the CTC gives you everything you would ever need and allows extravagant vacations with an unbeatable retirement when you choose to retire. Corruption for monetary gains is worthless. Radical ideology is really the only motivation and that is evaluated and isolated through recruitment. Sound minds dominate and when there's signs of extreme agenda's, they are caught pretty quickly." Teancom explained.

George threw up his hands and said with a smirk on his face, "Oh, so you're communist. Everything is given to you as long as you think the right way."

Teancom grinned. "Some might interpret it that way. Just leave out the poverty, mass killings, suppression of religious beliefs, and power-hungry leaders. I like to think of it as a branch of the military, only no political influences. You can relate to that."

"Yeah, I get it." George nodded his head. "Hence the Corps. in the unofficial nickname Conspiracy Theory Corps. Only, how do you know that there aren't power-hungry people? Can you read people's minds? Even in the military there are plenty of people that want to rank up and will do anything to do it."

"Yeah, there are those types of people everywhere. I've accused many, although, looking back on it, they might have just been making poor decisions, not grasping for power. And no, we can't read minds. Look, I get the fact that you are skeptical about people. You have to be, especially here. It's just there is far less here than in what you would call the normal world. In the normal world, there are more things to influence people in the wrong direction. They do things that would jeopardize their "moral compass" in order to better their life situation. If you took a decent person and backed them into a financial or legal corner they don't want to be in, they might compromise their decency to get out of that corner. Ideology floats around that try to convince them that their status is based on the way they look. I'll tell you; it can be a jacked-up world. But you know the difference here George?" Teancom wagged his finger.

"What's that?" George listened intently.

"Here we understand that culture and motivation drive society. The "normal world" tries to hide that fact so that they can blame everyone else for their short comings. They'll say that they don't succeed because other people are holding them back. They don't want to hear that their personal choices in life caused their lack of success. That would be offensive. Here, we make it pretty clear that personal decisions have consequence. The culture here is driven by the motivation to make things better, whether that comes by developing new tech, or improving some equipment, or even sometimes saving the world from a disaster. It doesn't mean that corruption can't creep up, but it definitely helps the cause." Teancom explained.

"I guess it helps that you seemingly have an enormous number of resources. How do you get that, by the way? Extravagant vacations, killer retirement, endless amounts of tech. All of this cost money, no matter where you live. How is all of this funded? Wait, let me guess. Government funding. There is no way they would fund millions to see if shrimp could run on tread mills." George placed his arm on the table, leaning in a little more.

"No, we have been detached from the U.S. government for quite some time now." Teancom replied.

George threw up his hands. "So then, how is this place funded?"

Teancom sat up in his chair. "Have you ever heard of the Psyche Asteroid?"

George thought for a second. "Sounds familiar."

"Well, it's an asteroid located somewhere between Mars and Jupiter that holds massive amounts of precious metals. We've been mining it. It gives us all the funding that we could possibly need." Teancom explained.

"Huh… must be nice." George nodded with approval while thinking of the possibilities that unlimited money could bring.

"It definitely eliminated a lot of issues." Teancom added.

George replied, "But not all issues, I'm sure. You said that you monitor extreme agenda. How do you interpret what's extreme? To me, right now, this whole place seems awesome, yet extreme."

"Like I mentioned earlier, moral compass. Just to make things clear, we aren't here to overthrow governments that we don't agree with or destroy entire nations. We intervene when something bad is about to happen. For example, we could have taken out North Korea a long time ago. We haven't, although we've sabotaged a lot of their missile developments. Remember 911 and the four planes that were taken over, two of which crashed into the world trade center?" Teancom asked.

"Yes." George leaned in again.

"Well, what you don't know was that there were actually supposed to be fifty. We were able to prevent forty-six of them from being taken over. Unfortunately, we missed four." Teancom continued. "Now, to answer your question as to what an extreme agenda is. Let me give you an example. Back in 1967 a few members of the organization were sick of the world tension caused by the cold war. So, they thought that it would be a good idea to shut down the worlds stash of nuclear weapons. They were successful in doing so at sights in the Soviet Union, Brittan, and the U.S. Unfortunately for them, all three nations were able to get their weapons operational again. All they did was stir the pot of an already tense world. It was an innocent idea to establish world peace which led to an extreme agenda of trying to control all the world's existing nuclear arsenal without thinking of the consequences. This was a year after the U.S. government officially shut the organization down. That's when the organization itself had to define what its purpose was going to be when it came to world intervention."

As they were talking, the countdown on the table reached zero. Replacing the timer appeared the words "Order Ready." Teancom touched the words that were in front of him with his finger. Two circles on the table opened up. One was a small circle and the other was a larger circle. In the larger circle rose a plate with a metal cover on top of it. Out of the smaller circle appeared a covered glass with Teancom's drink in it. After witnessing what happened, George immediately pushed his "Order Ready" message. His order appeared in front of him.

George lifted the cover off of his plate. Steam and the aroma of a well-prepared steak escaped from the prison of the cover. On the plate sat a well displayed placement of food. The smell almost caused him to drool. Catching himself almost salivating all over the place, he figured that he must be hungrier than he thought. He was ready to attack the meal in front of him, but noticed that there were no forks or knives to eat with. He looked over at Teancom to ask him about the missing utensils but noticed Teancom flipping the plate cover over. Attached to the inside roof of the cover were two forks, two spoons, a butter knife, a steak knife, and a tightly folded napkin that was in a flattened ring. George flipped his cover over to reveal the same setup. The utensils looked like nothing was holding them to the cover. George figured that they had to be magnetically held. He reached for one of the forks. As soon as he touched the fork, the force that was holding it to the cover let go and the fork fell into his hand. Unfortunately, George also accidentally touched the other fork as well. That fork came falling down onto his steak. Teancom noticed George's error and grinned as he went to work on his salmon and mashed potatoes. George didn't care. At this point he was fully aware of his hunger. He put the lid on the table beside him with the open side up, grabbed the steak knife, put the extra fallen fork on the table beside his plate, and dug into his steak.

"How's your food?" Teancom asked as he watched George devour his meal.

George quickly finished chewing and swallowing the mouthful of food he had. "Really good. I didn't realize how hungry I was. And you said machines made this? My compliments to the engineers."

Teancom rose his fork in the air with a piece of salmon on it. "Yeah, they do a good job, most of the time. If you want, you can go back into the menu and tweak the way that the food was prepared. It will remember your adjustments for the next time that you order it."

"That's good to know." George glanced at Teancom's cup with a questionable look. "Chocolate milk?"

Teancom quickly swallowed the mouthful of salmon. "Kind of. Protein drink. I did just come from the gym."

"Makes sense." George cut another piece of steak. "So how long have you been with the CTC?" He devoured the steak that he just cut.

"All my life. My parents met in the organization. They married and had my brother and I. We grew up in the CTC." Teancom explained.

George swallowed his steak. "Didn't think they would allow kids in such a place."

Teancom took a drink before he replied. "It's actually a pretty family friendly organization. Mind you they don't let kids run around in facilities like this, but there are a lot of options on raising a family."

George questioned, "Do you resent not growing up in a normal environment?"

Teancom shook his fork. "Absolutely not. Don't get me wrong, I've kept myself updated to the "normal world." As a teenager there was some desire to break off, but that quickly faded. Seeing how things are, I don't have any desire or even imagine wanting to grow up in what you call a normal environment. I don't even know if that term "normal environment" even should exist. Ideologies have such vast ranges of normality now a days. Looking back, it was nice to grow up in a stable environment such as the CTC."

George thought about it for a second, then nodded his head in understanding and continued to finish of his meal.

Once finished, he felt the urge to go to the bathroom. "Is there a bathroom around here?"

Teancom still working on his food looked up at George and pointed behind him with his fork toward the back of the dining hall. "Yeah, it's in the back."

George grabbed the napkin in the lid, pulled it out of the ring, wiped his mouth, put the napkin down on his plate, got up, and headed to the back of the room. In the back was an opening that said "Restroom." To the right of the opening was a door that said "Women." To the left was a door that said "Men." He began to put his hand on the wall next to the "Men" labeled door. Before he could put his hand on the wall completely, the door opened. He figured that there must be a sensor on the wall so that you didn't need to touch it to open the door. Walking in, he hoped to see some high-tech type of facility. Instead, he discovered that the bathroom looked like a typical public restroom with four stalls, four urinals, four sinks, soap dispensers, a large mirror on the wall in front of the sinks, and a paper towel dispenser.

George walked over to one of the urinals. Once he was done, he went over to wash his hands. As he was washing his hands, he noticed that one of the walls opened up. Out of the wall came a squared shaped robot hovering slightly above the floor that was slightly larger than one of the urinals. Behind it came a smaller robot that begin cleaning the floors. The larger robot moved over to the urinal that George just used. The urinal disappeared into the robot as the robot attached itself to the wall. George heard sounds much like a dishwasher would make. A few moments later the large square robot detached itself from the wall and headed back to where it came from. The Urinal that he just used looked sparkling clean. George nodded his head. "Huh. Neat." He turned to the door and headed back out to the restaurant.

As he walked back to the table to sit back down, Teancom was just finishing his meal. George slid into his seat while motioning his head toward the exit of the restaurant. "So, can we finish that tour that we started earlier?"

"We will, once we get the others up to speed." Teancom wiped his mouth and put his napkin and utensils on his plate.

George tried again. "Is there any way we could check out…"

Teancom interrupted George. "Look, I get it. There are a lot of new toys to play with. Just be patient with it. There are bigger fish to fry right now."

George's brow dropped. "Tell me."

Teancom's voice hardened. "We have strong reason to believe that your "accident" in space was intentional. Someone wanted you dead and the window to find out who is closing on us."

George dropped his head in thought for a moment. With all that was happening, it seemed like forever since he was in space. The possibility that there might have been sabotage evaded his mind. He lifted his head and looked at Teancom. "What's the play?"

"Like I said, we need to bring the others up to speed. Once that is done, we can brief you all on the details." Teancom explained.

George slapped his hands on the table. "So, get Isaiah in there with the other two to give his presentation and move forward with it."

"Actually, we are going with another approach. Instead of Isaiah bringing your remaining crewmates up to speed, we are going to have you and Rachael do it. It might soften the blow coming from a familiar face." Teancom finished his drink.

George rubbed his hands together. "Ok, then point me to where they are at and let's do this."

Teancom rose his brow at George's response. "You know, I'm starting to question this strategy. I need you to remember that they will be emotionally compromised. The things that you say to them could lead to serious breakdowns."

"Ok, I get it. Be tactful, not overbearing. Be sensitive to the fact that their whole world has just changed and their love ones think that they are dead." George smirked. "Don't say things like you might get JFK'd."

Teancom playfully nodded his head at the jab. "Yeah, don't say things like that. Only an idiot would do that."

George laughed as he stood up. "Sounds good. Let's go."

Teancom looked at him with raised eyebrows. "Wait, aren't you going to pay your bill?"

George stopped and tilted his head. He started to pat his pockets as if he were looking for his wallet. "Wait. I thought that this was…"

Teancom grinned as he stood up. "Just kidding." He put the lid back on top of his plate and put his hand next to it. The word "Finished" appeared on the table. He pushed it and the plate disappeared into the table. As he started to walk away, he patted George's shoulder with his hand. "Clean up and let's go."

Lowering his head, George let out a quick chuckle. He quickly put everything on his plate, put the lid on top, and put his hand next to it. The word "Finished" appeared just as it did when Teancom did it. After he touched "Finished", the plate sank into the table as well. He turned around and quickly jogged toward the exit to catch up with Teancom.

As both men were walking to the golf cart, Teancom said, "Why don't you drop me off at my golf cart and then follow me. We'll head over to Rachael's place and see how she's doing. From there we can discuss our strategy."

George nodded. "Agreed."

They both got into George's vehicle. With a few movements of the wheel, George moved the vehicle sideways and out from their parked position. He pulled forward and swung around to go back the way they came from. Teancom noticed the move. "Remind me to show you some tricks on this thing. There's a way to pull a stationary one-eighty with a touch of the screen."

"Sounds good. While you're at it, why don't you lift the governor off this thing so I can go faster than fifteen miles an hour."

Teancom shrugged his shoulders. "Ok." He went onto his phone and messed with some settings. The golf cart sped up from fifteen miles an hour to twenty miles an hour.

George noticed the slight difference in speed and said with a very sarcastic voice, "Gee, thanks."

With a serious voice, Teancom replied, "You're welcome." A slight grin appeared as he looked over to a slightly annoyed driver. "If I was in your position and you were in my position, how much control would you give me?"

Without even thinking about it, George immediately replied, "Honestly? You wouldn't be given a golf cart. The phone would be questionable. I don't know that you would be even allowed out of the room." He looked over at Teancom and said with a sincere yet firm voice, "Thank you."

Teancom grinned. "Given your answer, I think you need a little more faith in humanity."

George shook his head. "I think you have too much faith. I guess it's the price you pay when you live in a bubble."

Teancom turned his upper body to face George. With a stern voice he replied, "I've seen the disgusting nature of mankind across the globe. I've had to deal up close and personally with my share of scum bags. I wouldn't mistake my kindness with ignorance to the twisted and disturbing acts of humankind."

George sensed Teancom's change of tone and tweaked his approach. He calmly explained, "Look, I'm not saying that you don't know what's going on in the world. All I'm saying is that there is a lot of advanced technology in this organization. In the wrong hands it can be a serious problem. I don't know your culture or protocols. I'm sure they're solid. I'm just saying with a place like this, it seems that even a small percent of a possibility could do some serious damage."

"Yea, I'll keep that in mind." Teancom replied in a slightly sarcastic voice. He looked out the window in thought.

They arrived at the gym where Teancom's golf cart was parked. George pulled up to it. Teancom got out then turned back to George through the window. "Alright, follow me and we'll head over to Rachael's." He turned around, walked over to his vehicle and got in. His vehicle was facing the direction of the dining hall where they just came from.

George watched as Teancom got in his golf cart. It pulled out sideways from the side of the hallway, did a one hundred eighty-degree spin, and took off. George followed, maintaining a distance of about fifty feet behind.

As they got closer to the turn which led to the entrance to the hangar, Teancom reached out with his right hand and placed it on the center screen. He announced, "Security access for George Hinderman."

A female voice came from the speakers of the golf cart replied, "Security profile for George Hinderman open."

Teancom continued, "Grant access to this facilities hangar."

The voice replied, "Access granted. Profile updated."

Teancom added, "Send me an alert when we are not together and he accesses the hangar."

The voice replied, "Notification added to your device."

Teancom took his hand off the screen and reached for his phone. After clicking on a few icons, he reached a screen that controlled George's golf cart. In the center of the screen was an icon that said "Emergency Stop." He kept it on that screen and placed the phone on the seat next to him.

They approached the hanger's turn. George followed Teancom around the corner, the hangar door sliding opened for them. George looked to his right down the hangar. He noticed the different craft in the distant. George's hands gripped the steering wheel a little harder. The temptation to break off to go exploring hit him like a severe itch. In his mind, the different scenarios played out. One optimistic scenario was where Teancom allowed him to break off to go exploring, putting off the current task. Given their recent discussion, that was highly unlikely. Another scenario played in his head where his golf cart blew up as he made his way down toward the craft. In reality he knew that it would play out somewhere in the middle. He also knew that any trust that he gained would be lost. As he contemplated the scenarios, he unconsciously slowed down, increasing the distance from Teancom's vehicle.

Teancom noticed George's increasing distance. He picked up his phone, ready to push the emergency stop icon. As he came closer to the other side of the hangar, George sped up again and closed the distance. As they approached the other side of the hangar the door opened. They both exited and continued towards Rachael's place.

Chapter 8

Teancom glanced at the HUD, names flashing on the windshield as doors passed. Nearing Rachael's door, he slowed and pulled aside. George pulled up right behind him. They both got out and walked over to her door. Teancom swiped his right hand on the wall beside the door and waited. After a minute, he swiped again. Moments later, the door slid opened, revealing Rachael, groggy yet refreshed.

Furrowing her brow, Rachael stepped aside. "Come in." George and Teancom entered.

After George entered, he turned to Rachael and asked with concern in his voice, "Feeling better?"

Rachael rubbed her temple. "Better is a relative term. Physically, I'm fine. My headache is gone and my muscles don't hurt anymore. Mentally, I'm all over the place. I'm assuming that this is my assigned place to stay."

Teancom nodded his head. "It is. How do you like it?"

Rachael's eyes were half open. "It seems nice, thanks. I just woke up a few minutes ago so I barely have had the opportunity to look around." She glanced around the room.

George smirked, "Maybe Nancy can give you the grand tour. Life story included."

Teancom grinned. "Nancy is a very nice person. Be nice."

George pulled out his phone. "I agree. She is a very nice person. Let me call her. She gave me her number, begging me to call anytime. I wouldn't want to disappoint her."

Teancom lowered George's hand holding the cell phone. "I'm sure we are more than capable of showing Rachael around."

Rachael looked at both of them with a blank stare. "I don't know what you geniuses are talking about but please stop." Rachael's stomach started to growl from hunger. "Is there anything to eat around here. I'm feeling pretty hungry."

Teancom nodded. "Why don't you go and freshen up while I get you something to eat. There are fresh clothes in the bedroom and the bathroom is right over there. It will help you feel better, I promise."

Rachael nodded. "That sounds good. As long as you don't drug me again or try to give me anymore of that mystery drink."

Teancom grinned. "I won't, even though I think that you'd like it. What do you feel like eating? If you want it, we probably have it."

Rachael looked down for a second, then looked back up at Teancom. "Do you have a large chicken salad with ranch dressing? Also, a large glass of ice water."

"Yes, we do. It will be ready for you when you get back." Teancom pointed to the bedroom.

"Thanks." She turned around and went to the bedroom. After pulling out some clothes, she disappeared into the bathroom.

Forty minutes later, Rachael emerged from the steamy bathroom, brushing damp hair, dressed in black leggings, a white t-shirt, and a grey hoodie. As she walked out to the living room, she noticed a large bowl filled with salad and a tall glass of water sitting on the bar. George and Teancom were sharing war stories with each other while sitting in the living room. Teancom noticed Rachael and turned toward her. "Feeling better?"

Still brushing her wet hair, she grinned. "Much better, thanks. That shower really felt good."

"I told you that it would." Teancom pointed to the salad. "Eat, relax a bit."

"Yeah, that salad really looks good." Rachael sat down on the bar stool. She picked up the fork that was sitting next to the bowl and started to inspect the meal.

Teancom noticed and laughed. "I think I can find you a Bunsen burner somewhere. You can try to get the chemical makeup of the lettuce if it'll make you feel better."

Rachael gave Teancom a grimace glance as she nodded her head. "I'll survive." She reluctantly shoveled in a fork full of food into her mouth. As soon as she did, her suspicion melted away from how good it tasted. Hunger drove her to shovel the salad in. After a few mouthfuls and a large gulp of ice-cold water she turned to Teancom. "So, you have us here. Why? What comes next? And more importantly, what happened to Adam and Amy?"

"Adam and Amy are fine. They are isolated in their own separate rooms, much like this one. We just slapped NASA logos everywhere and sealed the patio." Teancom replied.

Rachael finished off another bite. "Why put NASA logos on everything, and what's wrong with the patio?"

George jumped in. "The patio is a deck that is surrounded by a holographic system that can make it seem like you're anywhere in the world. It's pretty amazing."

Rachael looked at George with a puzzled face. "There's a holographic deck in their rooms. It sounds like a rip off from an old sci-fi T.V. show that I know of."

Teancom rolled his eyes. "Yeah, engineers here get inspiration from a lot of different places."

"That still didn't answer my question. Why would you block it off and what's with the NASA logos?" Rachael asked again as she looked at Teancom with an icy stare.

As she asked, Isaiah entered the room. "To give them the temporary illusion that they were rescued and back in NASA's care. As I explained earlier, you two are unique. It was easier to explain the reality of the situation to both of you based off of your background and emotional makeup, absent the panic attack. Even then, you recovered very quickly. Your crew mates are different. They both have a greater connection to the lives that they left behind when they took off into space. They both have kids and spouses. It would be a lot more complex if we were to introduce them to this place like we did with you. We have determined that the fastest and most effective way to inform them of their situation is by letting you tell them."

Rachael rose an eyebrow. "Fastest and most effective? Why the rush?"

"As mentioned before, our window of opportunity of gathering relevant information of the explosion is depleting. We would like to gather data from everyone as soon as possible." Isaiah explained with a straight face.

"Window of opportunity is depleting? What is that supposed to mean?" Rachael questioned again, now staring down Isaiah.

George quickly stood up. "It means that they don't think that the explosion was an accident."

Tension built up in the room. Teancom knew he had to relieve it. He stood up and spoke in a nice, calm voice. "Look, we're not saying that this was done on purpose. We just aren't ruling out the possibility that it was. If that is the case, then we'd like to know why. That's why we're trying to get everyone in the boat as quickly as possible so that we can put the pieces together."

George stroked his chin with his hand. "What pieces do you have so far?"

Teancom looked back and forth between both George and Rachael. "We have the ships computer. Analysts have been going through it and compiling as much data as they can. Once they're done, they'll brief all of us and we can go from there. What we need to do now is get the other two up to speed so that they can be part of that debriefing and we don't miss any details."

"Ok. Then point us the way so that we can break the news to them." George was done with the formalities and the agendas. He just wanted to get to it.

Isaiah gently rose the palms of both hands towards George. "Hold on. It would not be the best tactic to charge into their room and overload them with information. You need to build a foundation of understanding, then build upon it. First let them know that they are not in a NASA facility. Then explain what happened to the ship. Continue with your experience here and fill in the details that you know. The most important thing that you can do is show empathy and assurance that things will work out."

"How are we supposed to do that when we don't even know that ourselves?" Rachael put down her fork and quickly jumped to her feet. Her brow was down and jaw was locked. Noticing her state of mind, she closed her eyes and took a deep breath. "We still don't know what's in store for us. You said it earlier; the world thinks we are dead. What is to become of us?"

Isaiah looked at Rachael with kind eyes. "Those are very valid questions. You have the right to be frustrated right now. A lot has happened in a very short amount of time, and I must say, you've dealt with the stress of the situation quite impressively according to your tending physician. Now, to answer your question, you and your team have a few options that you can choose from. Your first option is one that we all hope you choose. That is, you continue on with us in this organization. Here you will continue to learn about what we do and become involved in the inner processes which make everything work. There are many branches in which you may choose to explore within the organization. Your families will believe you are gone and move on. The next option is that you can bring your immediate family members within the organization with us, pending approval. They too will have the same opportunities that you would have."

Rachael interrupted. "Wait. Pending approval? First, who decides that. Next, what about Amy's younger kids. What kind of environment is this to grow up in?"

"Very valid questions." Isaiah nodded. "There is a screening process that they must go through in order to prevent any future incidents that might occur from unstable individuals. As for Amy's younger kids, there are programs built for those that have chosen to raise families within the organization. They will receive a solid education and social interaction with other kids will thrive. Teancom grew up within the organization. I'm sure that he would be happy to share his experience with you. There is, however, another option where you and your family live outside the workings of the organization in an isolated environment. You will be monitored to ensure that the knowledge of this place does not go public. The upside to this is that you will be provided everything that you will ever need to live. Those that choose this option often times act as a consultant when needed."

"Monitored, huh. Like with those infamous bird cameras?" George smirked.

"Usually. We sometimes use the orbs. It helps drive the conspiracy narrative."

"And what if we choose not to be involved with this place at all? Is that an option?" Rachael's icy stare returned.

"Yes, that is an option." Isaiah replied, keeping his smile intact. "You could return to the outside world. It just will not be the life that you had before. Sadly, the world must always think you are dead. If you choose not to be part of this organization at all, we would have to erase your memory. You would not know who you were or where you came from. All of your functional and educational knowledge will remain, but that is all. We would alter your appearance and set you up with the appropriate accommodations to live a lavish life."

Rachael raised an eyebrow. "Seems a little extreme."

George quickly replied, "Extreme is the definition of everything here. Are you surprised?"

Rachael winched her face. "No, good point."

Isaiah added, "There are also variants of options that can be worked out if it makes sense. What matters is that the integrity of the organization remain intact."

George slapped his hands together. "Well, I'm satisfied. Let's go educate Amy and Adam."

Isaiah's eyebrows rose. He wasn't sure how he felt about George's gung-ho attitude to the situation and internally questioned his ability to successfully inform his crewmates without causing them to fall into hysteria. He took a long blink of his eyes as he turned to Rachael. "Rachael, do you have any other questions?"

Rachael almost laughed. "Oh, so many. Unfortunately, it sounds like we are on a strict timeline so I'll hold off for now. I think it might be best to proceed with getting the others into the loop first."

"I think so too." Isaiah replied.

Teancom looked around the room for any other comments. "Awesome. Then let's get down to business. As mentioned earlier, Adam and Amy are in their own separate quarters. George will drop off Rachael at Amy's quarters, then proceed to Adam's place. There you will be on standby. We will do this one at a time so that if something were to happen, we can respond to an individual event and not multiple at the same time. Once we are confident that Amy is ok, we will notify you George to proceed with Adam. Any Questions?"

George quickly replied, "No Sir. Let's do this."

Isaiah held back rolling his eyes and instead, took another long blink. "Well, seems that George is confident in the situation. How about you Rachael?"

Rachael took a deep breath. "I've had to brief my crew many times before. Although this situation is weighing heavily on the extreme side, I'm confident that I will be able to handle it. Hopefully Amy will be able to take it."

Isaiah nodded his head. "I know that you are the best person for the job. I am sure that she is in good hands. We will be monitoring the situation in a separate room. If there is need of extra assistance, we will be on standby to help."

"Sounds good." Teancom grabbed George's shoulder. "I know that George is ready to go. Rachael, do you need some time to digest your food and prepare or are you good to go?"

"No, I'm good. Let me just dry my hair and get some shoes on, then I'll be good to go." Rachael turned to the bathroom to blow-dry her hair. As she did, all she could think about was what she would say to Amy. How would she approach the situation without causing her to fall in the same state of mind that she fell into, sending her to the medical brig? By the time she was done putting on her shoes, she had a pretty good idea on her approach. She walked out to the living room to find Teancom, George, and Isaiah in conversation while they were waiting for her. Isaiah was attempting to give George pointers on how to approach Adam. She grinned as she looked at George and recognized the apathetic look on his face as he pretended to listen.

Spotting Rachael, George turned, brow raised. "Ready to go?"

"Yeah, I'm good. Let's go get our friends." Rachael replied with some excitement in her voice. She was not looking forward to the task at hand but was excited to see Amy again after everything that happened.

Teancom clapped his hands together. "Great! George, I sent the directions to the location of both Adam and Amy's place to your golf cart. It's not far. You could easily walk to it, but I'm sure you would rather drive. Isaiah and I will head over to a room where we can monitor the situation. Rachael, you will go first. Wait for us to get into place before you enter. We will notify you on your phone." Teancom pulled two additional phones out of his pocket and handed one to both Rachael and George. "Here are phones for Adam and Amy. They are user-specific – no one else can unlock them, so don't fret if they won't turn on. Remember, if you need assistance, don't hesitate to contact us. Good luck."

Teancom turned and headed toward the door. Isaiah gave a reassuring smile. "I know that you will do just fine.

Thank you for your assistance." He too walked toward the exit. They both disappeared through the door.

George faced Rachael. "Ready?"

She glanced down, then met his eyes. "Yeah, I'm ready." After a slight pause she continued, "George, I'm really sorry for what happened earlier. I should have controlled my emotions better. I… I'm sorry."

"Yeah, you should have. What's wrong with you?" George quipped sarcastically. He tried to say it with a straight face but couldn't help but grin. Rachel caught his sarcasm, punching his arm with a chuckle. George continued with a much more sincere voice. "You're good. You know that."

The corner of Rachael's lip rose. "I know. Thanks." She nodded in the direction of the exit. "Let's go." They both turned and headed out the door.

Chapter 9

Two golf carts pulled up to an unmarked door a quarter of a mile down the hall. Teancom and Isaiah exited their separate carts and walked over to the door. Teancom placed his hand against the wall to open the door. They stepped through a short, narrow hallway into the back corner of a spacious room. Three rows of tables spanned a downward-sloped room. Each table held seven laptops and chairs, evenly spaced. On the front wall three rows of fifteen televisions were mounted. Each television was sixty-five inches in size and equally spread out to cover the whole of the wall. Ten of the televisions closest to the middle of the wall were on. Five screens to the right tracked Amy's rooms, including a shot of right outside the door in the main hallway. The five to the left showed the same thing, except of Adam's place. In the middle of the room sat a fit man with a medium build staring at a laptop.

Teancom and Isaiah walked up behind him. Putting his right hand on the man's left shoulder, Teancom asked, "Josh, how are we looking? Are we all set?"

Josh, eyes fixed on his laptop, replied, "Yes, we're all set." He looked over at Teancom then Isaiah. "You know, it's interesting. They both have very similar patterns of living. They woke up a short time ago, both very confused. They explored, sat briefly on their beds, then showered. They both found clothes, got dressed, shoes included, and walked to their kitchens. I sent them a meal. Both were surprised to see it delivered through their tabletops. Now here they are. Amy is still eating and Adam's done and watching TV."

Isaiah nodded his head. "It's not that surprising to me. Think about it. For several months they have been training together. Going over the same repetitious routines over and over again. They were conditioned to think similarly through the same processes if something were to happen while they were in space. Is it really that surprising that their behaviors to this situation have synced?"

Josh thought about it for a second. "No, I guess that makes sense."

Just then on one of the televisions appeared George's golf cart pull up to Amy's door. Rachael got out and walked up to the door. George called, "Good luck," then drove off. Rachael pulled out her phone and waited.

"Here we go." exclaimed Teancom as he messaged Rachael to proceed. After Rachael read the message, she put the phone back in her pocket and took a deep breath. "Josh, open the front door for Rachael please."

Josh typed some commands on his laptop. On the television the front door opened. Rachael walked inside to find Amy sitting at the bar finishing her meal. Amy noticed Rachael and immediately jumped out of her seat. They both rushed to each other and embraced with a hug. Isaiah, Teancom, and Josh could hear every word that they said, even when they softly spoke as they were hugging. Amy expressed her confusion and the questions started coming. The three of them continued to watch and listen as Rachael and Amy sat on the couch and talked.

Rachael explained that they weren't in a NASA facility but that they were still in a safe place. She told her experience of what happened when she woke up, relaying all the details of the organization as to what she knew. How they explored the facility and how she had an anxiety attack. She also explained that she received medical attention and felt much better. She expressed her desire that the same thing didn't happen to Amy.

Amy sat there and absorbed everything. Isaiah noticed the different expressions on Amy's face as she received the information. He saw her go from shock, to amazement, to scared, to disbelief. It was the expression which came after Rachael finished explaining that Isaiah worried about the most. Amy's brows shot up, eyes wide, lips trembling as she clutched Rachael's arms. "If we're supposed to be dead, what about our families?" Before Rachael could answer, Amy broke down in tears. Rachael immediately hugged Amy and continually assured her that things were going to be ok. She explained to Amy that they would be given many options where she could be together with her family again. Amy questioned whether they could believe them. Rachael assured Amy that they could be trusted, even though inside doubt gnawed at her. They continued to hug as they both shed tears.

As they watched them comfort each other, Isaiah sent a message to Rachael asking if she was ok and if she needed assistance. They watched Rachael break from her embrace to read Isaiah's message. She responded that she was fine and that Amy was going to be ok. Following her message, she went back to hugging and crying with Amy.

Teancom folded his arms and nodded with approval. "Well, besides a few tears, that went better than expected. Shall we proceed with George?"

Isaiah slightly cringed his face. "I suppose."

Teancom grinned. "Alright, sending the go ahead to George." He took out his phone and messaged to George to proceed.

George sat in his golf cart patiently waiting for the green light. His phone buzzed. He quickly grabbed it and read the message from Teancom to proceed. Immediately getting out of the golf cart, he made his way to the front door. As he approached, the door opened by itself. He walked through and noticed Adam sitting on the couch watching T.V. As he glanced around, he noticed that the room had the same setup as Rachael and his room. The only difference was that instead of a door leading to the porch where the holographic room was, there was just a wall.

Adam turned to see George come in. He leapt up, brow furrowed, smile shaky. "Hey! George! How did you get NASA to let you out of isolation? Did they tell you what happened? About how we got back to Earth?"

"Yeah…this isn't a NASA facility." George blurted, striding to where a holographic deck should've been. "It's a front."

Back in the observation room Isaiah looked down and shook his head while rubbing his forehead.

Adam looked at George as he inspected the wall. "What are you talking about this isn't a NASA facility? If this isn't NASA, then what facility is it, and why are you looking at that wall?"

After finding no sign of any existing door on the wall, George turned to Adam. "This is a top-secret facility that is located at the bottom of the ocean. We were rescued by a non-government, self-ran, secret organization."

Adam tilted his head as his smile faded. "Wait, what?! A non-government secret organization. What are you talking about?"

"Look, before our ship blew up, they secretly rescued us and brought us back here to join their organization. And now here we are." George gestured his hands toward the room around them.

Adam stared blankly, mouth agape. "I don't know what medication they gave you, but stop taking it."

George lowered his head as he took a deep breath. He looked up and walked over to Adam, grabbing both his arms. "Adam. I'm not on any medication. I am serious. Think about it. How else would we have survived what happened?"

Adam thought for a second. His eyes moved rapidly as he analyzed the information. He glanced over at George with a raised brow. George nodded his head. Adam pulled away from George and started pacing back and forth, looking down and rubbing his chin. "Wait, if what you are saying is true, then what…are we being held captive? If it's a secret organization, then why did they save us? What do they want from us? Are we are supposed to join this mystery organization? Is there some sort of initiation ceremony or something? And what do you mean our ship blew up?! Does that mean we are dead to the rest of the world?!"

Noticing Adam's reaction, George lowered his head in regret. He thought about Isaiah's suggestions. Placing a hand on Adam's shoulder, he spoke with a calmer tone. "Well, yes. But don't worry, you'll get to see your family again. They gave us ways to work it out."

Adam's eyebrows rose and eyes widened. "Gave us ways to work it out?!" Adam rubbed his eyes with the palm of his hands and sat back down on the couch. His hands went from rubbing his eyes to clenching his head as he hunched over in an overwhelmed state.

Putting his head down, George knew that he blew it. He had to think quick. Picking his head back up, George looked at him with raised eyebrows. "Did I mention that this is an extremely high-tech organization? Adam, they have anti-gravity machines."

Adam stopped clenching his head as his ears perked. He lifted his head and looked at George. "Wait, what? Anti-gravity machines?"

George saw Adam's interest spark. "Yup. They have vehicles with anti-gravity. In fact, I have one right outside that door." George pointed to the exit.

Adam looked at George for a second, then shook his head as he pushed at George's chest. "Shut up. You're lying. You're just making all of this up, aren't you?"

George shook his head as he gripped Adam's arms again. "I am not lying. I can show you right now if you want."

Adam rolled his eyes. He couldn't believe he fell for George's nonsense. Still, in the back of his mind, there was a very small amount of belief that he had to explore. "Alright. Let's go. Let's see this anti-gravity machine that's behind that door."

George threw his hands up in the air. "Fine, let's go." They both walked out towards the door.

As soon as they walked out the door, Adam saw the hovering golf cart. He stopped for a moment and stared at it in disbelief. "No way. You weren't lying! It's real!" Adam crouched to inspect the undercarriage.

George looked at Adam with a grin. "What, you doubted me?"

Adam, still looking for anything that would be holding the vehicle off the ground replied, "Of course."

George wrinkled his chin as he nodded his head. "Fair enough."

"How do you know that it's anti-gravity technology and not magnetic force that's holding this up?" Adam questioned as he picked himself off the floor.

George leaned against the vehicle. "For one, that's what the people from this organization told me. Second, when you step onto it, the vehicle doesn't move from displacement to your weight."

Adam looked at George with narrow eyes. "Really? Even if it were hovering by some sort of anti-gravity, that displacement should still occur. Let me try." He opened the back door and stepped onto the golf cart. The vehicle didn't move. "Huh. Interesting. They must have some sort of fast reacting program to increase the resistance as the weight increases." He continued to step on and off of the vehicle several times. Stepping onto the side again and grabbing the top of the vehicle, Adam started jumping up and down to see if he could get the vehicle to move. It didn't. He looked over at George and waved him over. "Come on, help me out."

"Ok." George opened the front door and jumped in sync with Adam.

Adam stopped for a second and looked over at George. "Wait, wait, wait. You did say that I will get to be with my family again, right?"

George stopped jumping and nodded his head. "Yeah, yeah, yeah. They have a way to work that out."

Adam nodded his head once. "Ok." Both of them proceeded to jump in sync on the side of the golf cart.

Back in the observation room all three men were staring at the screen with their mouths open in disbelief.

Isaiah turned to Teancom. "That worked out better than I thought it would."

Teancom closed his mouth and rubbed his chin in thought. He looked at the television where the women were still hugging and crying. He looked over to the television where the guys were jumping on the side of the golf cart. "You know, this scene forty years ago would be normal." He pointed to the screens. "In the world today, this scenario should totally be cancelled due to sexist cliches."

Isaiah grinned while grabbing Teancom's shoulder. "And that is why you were put on this assignment." Isaiah let go of Teancom's shoulder and turned toward the exit. While walking toward the door, he asked, "Are you going to gather them for debriefing? Sounds like the analysis is ready."

Teancom was still staring at the screen of the two men jumping. "Maybe in a little bit. I want to see how this plays out."

Almost to the door, Isaiah shouted, "You might want to get more people on standby then."

Teancom thought about it for a second, then pulled out his phone and started messaging for more backup, just in case.

Outside of Adam's place, the two men gave up on their efforts to displace the golf cart and got into the vehicle. As they were putting on their seatbelts, Adam glanced over the interior. He marveled at how seamlessly the HUD and screens blended into the dash. Once he secured himself, he started playing with the screen. George slapped his hand and pulled the vehicle forward in the direction of the entrance of the hangar. Adam looked out the window and studied the design of the hallway. He admired the walls' perfect curve to the ceiling. It was as if they were designed for vehicles to drive up them to get to the ceiling.

"How much have you been able to drive this vehicle?" Adam was still staring at the walls.

George glanced over to see Adams strange fascination. "Only a couple of times. Why?"

Looking back at George, Adam pointed to the wall. "You haven't been able to drive on the walls by chance, have you?"

"Only by accident. I was messing with the different control functions and accidentally shot up the side of the wall for a second." George admitted.

"Did the bottom of the vehicle scrape the wall as you did it?"

George wondered where Adam was going with these questions. "No, why?"

"The hovering capability must be based on the surface immediately beneath the vehicle, and not relative to what we perceive to be up and down." Adam tapped his hand on the dash as he stared back at the wall. "Try driving up the wall again, this time on purpose."

George shrugged his shoulders while nodding his head. "Sure, why not." He moved the golf cart near the curved wall and slowly creeped the vehicle up the side. Instead of rolling back down, the vehicle continued to move forward as if it were on the floor. They were now driving sideways on the wall. Gravity, however, still worked normally on the inside of the vehicle. They were leaning to the side, trying to hold themselves in place as best as possible, relying heavily on their seat belts.

Adam was laughing as he clung to the side of the vehicle. "This is incredible!"

George had a huge smile on his face. That, however, changed when he saw a ramp leading to a door quickly approaching them. He jerked the golf cart off of the wall and back on the floor before they reached the doorway. They looked at each other for a second with wide eyes. It was immediately followed by laughter. George continued down the hallway, going up one wall, then swerved to the other wall. George looked at Adam with a wild look in his eyes. "You think we would be able to drive on the ceiling?"

Adam looked down while scratching his head. "I mean… the logic is pointing to yes. The consequence of a wrong conclusion, however, is what I'm worried about."

George's curiosity spiked. "Well, when in Rome." He looked ahead and waited for a space void of any door. When it was clear, he made his way half way up the wall, which was the farthest he went so far. He slowly continued up the wall, inverting them a little more as they went. Finally, he made it to the top of the wall and drove onto the ceiling. They were now completely upside down. Both of them had huge smiles on their faces as the blood flowed into their heads. Only seatbelts kept them from dropping to the cart's ceiling.

Adam looked over on the center screen and noticed a faded flashing icon that said "Interior Gravity Correction." He reached out and touched it. Nothing happened.

George saw Adam's futile attempts. "They locked most functions on this thing. The fact that this function is shut off probably tells me that they don't want us driving on the ceiling."

Suddenly a voice came out of the speakers of the golf cart. "That's right. The ceiling is meant for high-speed emergency vehicles. Please get down and come back. George, pick up Rachael and Amy and meet us at the pinned location on your vehicle's dashboard map for debriefing." George recognized the voice to be Teancom's.

"Who was that?" Adam asked as George pulled off of the ceiling on the way back to the floor of the hallway.

"That was Teancom. He's the one that supposedly granted me access to this vehicle." George frowned, reluctant to stop.

Adam rose his brow. "Teancom, huh. And he trusted you with this vehicle to roam around in the top-secret facility?"

George pulled back onto the regular floor of the hallway and came to a stop. He swung the vehicle around and headed back. "As you can tell, they put a tight leash on me. Also, I don't think it's the fact that they trust me. I'm pretty sure he did that to get me to trust him."

"I just figured that they grossly misjudged your character, but I guess what you said makes sense too." Adam grinned at his verbal jab.

George grinned back. "I thought that at first too."

Chapter 10

George and Adam pulled up as both Rachael and Amy were walking out the door. Their red, puffy eyes were now tearless. Rachael had her arm wrapped around Amy. As she looked up, Amy recognized her crewmates were the ones in the vehicle. She straightened, donning a warm smile. Seeing the team together comforted her like a warm blanket on a cold gloomy day. She was so grateful to see her whole team together again. "It's good to see you guys. Even you, George."

George smiled at the remark. "It's good to see you too. Now get in so we can go figure things out a little bit more."

After the girls got in the back of the golf cart and buckled up, George continued down the hallway. Amy turned to Rachael. "So where are we going now?"

Rachael answered, "They somehow retrieved the hard drive from our spaceship and have been analyzing it. We are going to see what they found. Hopefully they can tell us what went wrong."

A chilling thought struck Amy, guilt icing her spine. She knew that it was corrupt code that caused the ship to malfunction. She was the one that was supposed to make sure that the program running the mission was fully functional. Somehow, she missed it. Guilt began to overwhelm her. "It's my fault." She whispered to herself as she buried her head into her lap.

Rachael heard her whisper and immediately lifted her up. "There's no way that it's your fault! Don't even start to blame this on yourself."

Rachael sought Amy's eyes, but she looked away, tears welling. "I was the one responsible to make sure that the program was clean. There was corruption in the programming. I saw it. It was on the screen right before…"

Rachael cut Amy off. "First, I know that you spent countless hours confirming code that dozens of others already confirmed to be good. There is no way that you missed anything. You are the best programmer at NASA. Everyone knows that. Shoot, Adam's daughter worships you because of it."

Adam's ears perked. He turned around to face Amy. "She's right. She does worship you. She'd much rather have a chance to talk to you than to speak to her old man in space. Thanks for that." Adam said with a smirk on his face.

Amy broke from her self-guilt and chuckled. "That's not true."

George spoke up. "Yes, it is. Everyone here knows it. Hell, I'd rather talk to you than Adam."

Amy laughed again. She felt grateful to have such great partners to cheer her up. The vehicle started to slow down as they pulled up to another unmarked door.

"Well, hopefully they can tell us what happened in this debriefing." Rachael commented as she unbuckled her seatbelt.

The four exited the golf cart and walked over to the door which opened automatically. They stepped through a short hallway into a sleek, high-tech classroom. There were five rows of five chairs facing a podium situated in the front of the room. Behind the podium were three large white screens that were mounted on the wall. The screens were to the right, left, and center of the podium, high enough to be seen without being blocked by the person speaking at the podium. The chairs, sleek and padded, resembled recliners without the tilt. Instead of four legs, it was one solid square. The arms of the chair were made of a hard plastic. Compacted on both sides were mechanical devices that could extend out of the chair and serve as a variety of functions.

Five people stood patiently in front of the room waiting for the group to get settled in. Teancom and Isaiah were among them. Isaiah took a couple of steps forward and greeted them with a smile as they walked in. "Welcome. Glad you made it. Please come in and make yourself comfortable in one of the seats near the front. We have a lot to talk about."

Rachael and Adam claimed front-middle seats like an eager Poindexter. Amy and George sat in the seats right behind them in a less enthusiastic, cognizant manor.

Isaiah addressed the group, "For Amy and Adam, let me introduce myself. My name is Isaiah. I am in charge of what some people would call the human resources department. My purpose is to help those that are new to the organization get acquainted with the organization. Standing beside me are Teancom, Josh, Hannah, and Mark. Teancom has been assigned to lead your team in discovering what transpired during your mission that caused the incident. Josh and Hannah will be joining your team in helping with the investigation. Both skilled and deep in the investigation. Mark is the head of the World Oversight division and will be involved in overseeing the operation. He has a few words that he would like to say to you."

Mark stood up tall and with authority. He had a serious face, yet there was a hint of kindness in his eyes. Taking a step forward, he spoke with a deep, empathetic voice. "Thank you, Isaiah. I want each of you to know that everyone standing here with me is extremely dedicated to helping you find out what happened. I can only imagine what you have gone through. Your lives have been greatly uprooted from reality as you knew it. Know that we will do everything that we can to help reestablish your lives again.

I know that this place, this organization can be extremely overwhelming to someone that never even knew it existed just a few hours ago. If it gives you any comfort, I can tell you through personal experience that there is no better organization on this planet that exists. It will greatly increase any knowledge that you had before. It is a feast for the mind. This is a place where you not only can enhance your knowledge, but are encouraged to put that knowledge to use. It does however come with a price. Unfortunately, that price had been forced upon you. Know that you will be able to be reunited with your families again if you chose. There are ways in which we can make that happen. Know that.

We are all here to help. As we work together, we will find out what happened and make things right. I promise." He smiled at the group. Looking over at Isaiah, he nodded his head for him to take the conversation again. As soon as Isaiah stepped forward, he turned and took a seat that was located to the side of the room.

As Mark took his seat, Isaiah continued, "Mark is a very honorable and dedicated person. I am grateful that he is in charge of the division. Now, why don't we get started. I know that Rachael and George informed you a little bit about this place. Let me give you some more details." Isaiah delivered the same briefing he gave Rachael and George, slides flashing on the central screen. Amy heard much of the information from Rachael and was not too shocked by the repeated information. Adam, however, was blown away.

Adam's jaw fell, eyes wide with disbelief. "Wait a second. Tesla craft? The OAPC? Tesla's dynamic theory of gravity letter? You're talking about the medium being Aether type physics, which, by the way, contradicts some of Einstein's theories."

Josh rose his index finger in the air as he spoke up from behind Teancom. "That can be a misconception in many cases. Einstein never denied the existence of what many call Aether. In fact, his formulas work better with it. He did continue to promote some of his ideas like curved spacetime to help throw people off of the concept. Remember, he worked with the OAPC. Although he craved the idea of scientific advancement, he also knew the dangers of what evil people could do with the technology."

Rubbing his eyes in disbelief, Adam was both shocked and extremely intrigued from the fountain of information that he was absorbing. Questions kept brewing in his mind. "And all of this has been kept a secret since World War two? How is this even possible."

Teancom noticed Adam's curiosity and added to the fuel. "The organization did everything they could to keep information under wraps. Viktor Schauberger, for example, was Germany's version of Tesla during the war. After the war, OAPC quickly restrained him, his team, and any signs of their work before Russia was able to. Those intel gathering missions happened quite a bit. Fortunately, the organization has had many resources to make that happen over the years."

Shaking his head while rubbing his face, Adam's questions kept building up. "Resources? What does that even mean? Do you have a large crew of assassins that take out those that know too much? Also, how are places like this even built? Do you have an army of people at your disposal building underwater facilities like this without anyone knowing what is going on?"

Teancom grinned at Adam's enthusiastic questions. "To answer your first question, no. We don't have a large crew of assassins. People like Viktor were not killed. Instead, him and his team were recruited into the organization. They boosted the organization's tech. As for these facilities, just think of a large and mobile 3-D printer, except a lot more advanced."

Rachael sat up as they explained. This information session was scratching an itch that she fought hard to restrain in order to move things along and get to her friends. She enjoying Adam's curiosity. "All of this innovation and infrastructure. How is this funded?"

Adam took a shot at answering the question. "Let me guess, the government didn't really spend millions on finding out if fish could use a treadmill."

"Actually, it was shrimp, not fish." George corrected Adam.

"No, it wasn't. It was fish." Adam argued back.

"No, shrimp!"

"Fish!"

Teancom waved both men down from their dispute. "Hold on. You are actually both right on this one. There were two separate legislations that actually existed to fund both shrimp and fish on treadmills. And yes, that was a real thing. They actually spent money on that. None of the money from that funding went to this organization."

Adam's brow rose again. "You got to be kidding me. So how is this place funded."

"We mine the Psyche Asteroid." Teancom replied.

Nodding her head, Rachael was satisfied with the answer. "Oh, that makes sense."

Adam's eyebrows rose as he looked over at Rachael. "There's so many things wrong with what you just said." He turned his attention to Teancom. "Is that a normal thing here? You can just blast off and travel millions of miles away to mine an Asteroid? No big deal?"

Teancom looked at Adam with a straight face. "Correct."

Adam was thrown back in his chair as if he were physically punched in the face. He lowered his head for a brief moment as things clicked in his mind. With a more sober demeanor, he looked up at Teancom. "What is the name of this organization again?"

George couldn't help himself. He quickly answered, "The Conspiracy Theory Corps or CTC."

Teancom's face cringed as both Mark and Isaiah stared him down. Both Hannah and Josh couldn't help but crack a smile. Isaiah said softly to Teancom, "Still trying to push that name I see."

Teancom, trying to save face, turned to the group and replied, "As I told George before, there is no name to this organization. It's that way for a reason. We want to stay anonymous. Branding a name to the organization helps to make that more difficult to do. The CTC is an inside nickname that the organization does not attach itself to. Please make sure that you keep it that way."

After absorbing the information from the conversation, Amy finally spoke up. "So how do you supply these facilities? Is there a secret tunnel that you use or a submarine that brings things in and out?"

George enthusiastically added, "And how do you keep the ordering of supplies discrete? These are big facilities that had to require a lot of material. Do you have a front somewhere?"

"Those are both excellent questions." Isaiah complimented in an up-beat and encouraging voice, almost to the point of belittlement if it were anyone else. "You are absolutely right George. It does take a lot of material to not only build these facilities, but keep them going as well. In order to solve that problem while being as discrete as possible, we do have what you call fronts in very low regulated parts of the world. One of our bigger fronts is in Dubai. We have a couple of hotels there right now. When we are ready to build a new facility, we demolish an old hotel and develop a new one, using the demolished building for supplies as well as order a plethora of extra building equipment for the new one. As far as food and living supplies, all the ordering is done through our network of hotels throughout the world."

Adam listened intently as he analyzed Isaiah's explanation. "So, you constantly have supplies coming out of these hotels and feeding these facilities that are underwater. Don't you worry that such traffic will create a lot of attention, or is Amy right about those secret tunnels?"

Teancom let out a slight grin. "Not exactly. Have you ever heard the story of the USS Eldridge?"

Adam froze for a second as his mind processed where he heard that name from. His eye widened when it came to him. In an unbelieving and enthusiastic voice, he proclaimed, "You mean the Philadelphia experiment!? It was real!?"

"Isn't that the movie about time travel?" Amy questioned, slightly confused about how it relates to the subject.

Isaiah answered, "Yes, the Philadelphia Experiment is a movie that they made with time travel in it. That is not what we are talking about, however. During World War two, the Navy was looking for a way to overcome the brutal casualties caused by German U-boats. Albert Einstein had been working on a project known as the unified field theory. It made it possible for an object to be teleported from one location to another instantly. Thanks to Tesla's notes that were gathered when he passed away, Einstein was able to fill in the elements that he was missing to make it work. The Navy instantly set up one of their new ships, the USS Eldridge, to make use of that technology. Although it did successfully teleport the ship, it came with extremely unfortunate consequence to those that were onboard. President Roosevelt deemed it unsafe for use during the war and turned the technology over to the OAPC. Over the years, the organization has greatly improved the technology."

George slapped his hands on the arms of the chair. "Wait, are you talking about beam me up type stuff? You can teleport people around?"

Teancom nodded his head. "Something like that. It makes warehousing and logistics extremely effective when you have a lead time of a couple of seconds. Think about it. No need for large refrigerators or extra space for inventory at the facilities. When you order a meal, the systems AI messages one of the hotels to teleport the food over to our fully automated kitchens in the facility where it cooks it up and sends it to you. Instant Tesla craft jumps have perks too. How do you think we reached you in space so fast?"

The four astronauts paused for a second. A barrage of questions spilled out from each of them following the momentary silence. Amy and Rachael asked about using the tech to see their family members. Adam questioned the physics behind teleportation. George asked about the vehicle applications behind the technology. Isaiah and Teancom looked at each other, hoping the other would take the lead. Isaiah grinned at Teancom. "It's your crew. Take the lead."

Teancom knew that Isaiah was right. He turned to his crew, who were still throwing out questions, and said in a loud voice. "Hold on, hold on! Settle down for a second!" The crew reluctantly stopped asking their questions as they looked at Teancom with unsettled eyes. "Look, I get that there are a lot more questions that you want to get to. I really do. You will have most of those questions answered, I promise. Right now, I think that it is very important that we start focusing on the reason why you are all here. Something happened to your ship in space and we need to find out what that was. Because that is still a mystery, time might be of the essence."

Teancom noticed that all their eyes were on him. "Thank you. First, I think it's fair to explain to you the details of your rescue. On the day of the incident, Josh and I were in our ship above the South China Sea, monitoring possible hostile activity. In the middle of that mission, we received a call stating that there was suspicious activity going on with your mission to the moon that needed immediate attention. While monitoring your transmissions to Houston, the organization noticed that Rachael started to say something, then was immediately cut off. It was radio silence on your end after that. Something had to be going on. So, we broke mission and jumped within observing distance of your craft.

It wasn't long after that we noticed one of your control thrusters started firing, causing you to go into a spin. Once we saw that your rotations were way too fast, we figured there was no recovering from it. At that point, we gained permission to intervene. Using gravity bursts, we quickly slowed the spinning to a stop and disabled the malfunctioning thruster. As we looked in the window of your space craft, we noticed that the four of you were unconscious.

We immediately swung around to the front of the ship to dock. As Josh was lining up the approach, the unthinkable happened. The main engine on your craft fired. Before your ship rammed into ours, your hatch blew open on its own. Luckily, the force from the ships colliding kept your artificial atmosphere from escaping rapidly. We were able to quickly dock, thanks to Josh's maneuvering skills and quick thinking. When it came down to it, if we hadn't been there, the spinning of your ship combined with the opened hatch would have caused fire from the engine to engulf the oxygen filled capsule, and everyone in it."

Josh spoke up. "I just wanted to make something clear. What Teancom graciously called skillful maneuvering by me was in all honesty, pure luck. The hatch was blown at just the right time where a perfect collision with our ship created very minimal loss of atmosphere inside your ship. We were at the right place at the right time on an extreme level. The fact that you're with us now is a statistical anomaly!"

The four exchanged glances, pale as ghosts. The reality that they were all on the brink of destruction sank in. Teancom noticed the change in his audience's demeanor as he continued. "Thanks for the frightening details, Josh. If anyone needs a fresh pair of pants, let me know and I'll have someone get them. What matters is the fact that we were there. Things happened the way they did, and because of that, we are able to move forward together. Continuing the story, once we were docked, we entered the Orion capsule, and immediately moved your unconscious bodies into our ship. We grabbed as much as we could, including laptops and tablets. Josh was able to download all the information from the ship's hard drives. Once we got everything we could, we sealed the hatch and rigged it to blow. We spun the ship again, got to a safe distance, and blew the hatch. Sure enough, the exhaust from the engine engulfed the inside and caused the ship to break apart."

George looked up at Teancom with focused eyes. "There're too many things that happened at the right time for this to be an accident. Someone wanted us dead." The reality of George's statement sent chills down the spines of the other three already stunned crewmates.

"That's what we thought too." Teancom continued. "That's why we brought you in the loop as quickly as we did. We need to find out what really happened and why."

With a balled-up fist and wrinkles in her brow, Amy questioned, "If you had the ship docked and under control, couldn't you have just fixed the issues? Why did you drag us out of the ship? We were knocked out. No one saw what happened. We still could have had our lives intact." Her voice was slightly elevated as she spoke.

Speaking in a soft voice, Teancom answered her. "Unfortunately, the ship was not under control. The main engine was still firing on its own. We probably would have had to do some serious repairs in order to correct the problems that we knew of, not to mention the possible unknown issues. Our footprint would have been too big. Too many questions would have been left unanswered. That's a dangerous itch to be left unscratched with an organization such as NASA. I wish we could have fixed the issue and left you to finish the mission, I really do. Unfortunately, the situation was either to take you with us or let you die. Fortunately, you now have a chance to find out what happened. If it was sabotage, we can find out who and why."

Amy's demeanor softened. She knew that there was a glitch in the programming. She saw it herself. Her eyes and head drooped down. "I know what it was. It was corruption in the programming that did this. I saw some of it right before the ship started spinning. I swear my team checked everything before we left. They must have missed it. I missed it. This is my fault." Rachael got up and hugged her as she started tearing up.

Hannah stepped forward and shook her head at Amy's comment. "It wasn't you or your team's fault. The main programming was solid. There was definitely foul play going on. We found evidence of it."

"Evidence? What evidence?" Rachael asked as she looked up from comforting Amy.

Hannah continued, "We found traces of a self-destructing virus in the hard drives data, pieced back together with our quantum AI computers. A virus crafted an unfixable scenario. First, it shut down all communications with Earth. Then, it severed manual controls followed by the spin, the hatch, and the main engine fire."

Amy looked up. "Then my team did miss it."

"Not exactly." Hannah replied. "After hacking into NASA's database, I went through the stored program that mirrored what was on the ship. I couldn't find any trace of it, until I looked at the final launch adjustments."

Amy sat up with her head down in thought. Her eyes rose as she put the pieces together. "That makes sense."

Adam looked at Amy with a furrowed brow and a tilted head. "Can you please explain to us non computer hacker-code writer experts how that makes sense?"

Amy quickly turned to Adam. "Right before we launched, the system analyzed the most current weather variables and uploaded small adjustments to the program to allow the most effective possible launch to occur. If someone wanted to slip a virus in undetected, that would be the time to do it."

"That's right." Hannah smiled at Amy as she nodded her head. "And that's where we found the same traces of the broken-up code. Unfortunately for NASA, it will take them at least a couple of weeks to piece together the code, that is if they ever find it. What I find odd is that for as advanced as the code was, it was pretty easy to trace where it originated from, at least for me."

Amy looked at Hannah with raised eyebrows. "Location? That means it was uploaded from an online source, not created on site."

"It had to have been." Hannah confirmed. "Although someone from NASA had to have inserted it into the closed network system. I tried to find out who it was but the ID's must be stored in a completely closed off system."

Amy nodded. "Yes. Ever since a couple of NASA employees were wrongfully defamed and doxed on social media by disgruntled former employees, NASA had taken what I thought were extreme steps to secure identifications of anyone that worked on the system. It was a PR prospective move. We would have to go into the network at one of the facilities in order to get more information."

George leaned forward. "So where did the code originate from?"

Josh replied, "On the southern region of Taiwan."

Teancom rolled his eyes as he sighed and lowered his head. "Of course. That's just wonderful."

Rachael looked at Teancom with a shrug of her shoulders. "Why? I thought relations were better in that area."

Teancom picked his head up as he looked over at Rachael. "I get that you guys were isolated and focused on training for the last few months but Taiwan is still a very sensitive area. Tensions are higher than ever between countries because of that area. Governments agree to hide it, stabilizing markets and economies. That's why the U.S. and China have worked out a deal where the U.S. would reduce the amount of defense weaponry it sells to Taiwan and China would back off. That doesn't mean there is actual demilitarizing near that region nor in the South China Sea. Trust me. Taiwan is a tinder box; one spark could ignite the world."

"Looks like we have another mission to prevent another world war on our hands." Mark spoke up from his seat. "Teancom, what's the play?"

Teancom paused. "We need answers fast. We'll split up to cover more ground. Josh will go with Rachael and Amy to NASA facilities to find out more about our mystery person while Hannah, George, Adam, and I go investigate the place where the code originated." He looked at Josh. "We'll drop you three off in a vehicle on our way there." He looked back at Mark. "We will need teams on standby in case something goes south."

Mark nodded with approval. "Sounds like a plan. You will have full resources if you need it. You know how to reach me." He got up and walked out the door while looking at his phone.

Adam, brow furrowed, leaned toward George. "Wait, did he just say prevent another world war?"

Hearing Adam, Teancom replied, "Yes, he did. I think it's time that we finished the tour that we started. There's a Tesla craft waiting for us. Does anyone need more time to get ready? Get something to eat or drink before we go?"

Raising his hand, Adam glared at Teancom. "I have so many more questions."

"I'm sure you do. I'm sure you all have a lot more questions. You will have the opportunity to get answers to those questions. Right now, we have a potential killer or killers out there that we need to focus on. The longer we wait, the more opportunity they have to disappear, do more destruction, or both. I hope you understand that." Teancom reasoned with the group.

Rachael stood up and spoke with a commanding voice. "We understand." She looked at her three companions. "Don't we." The three of them looked at each other as they shrugged their shoulders and nodded their heads. Rachael gave a half smile at the group. "Does anyone need anything before we go?" George and Amy shook their head no. Adam opened his mouth to say something, then noticed Rachael staring at him with an icy stare. He closed his mouth without saying anything and shook his head as well. "Great. I believe we are ready to go." Rachael smiled as she looked over at Teancom.

Teancom gave a quick nod of approval. "Great. George, take your three companions and follow me in your golf cart to the hangar. There, you'll get a basic crash course on some more tech that you will need."

George smiled. "It's about time." They all stood up and walked towards the main hallway where their vehicles were. Teancom pulled out his phone and started typing messages into it as he walked.

Isaiah stayed behind but shouted as the group left, "Good luck."

Chapter 11

The group climbed into their vehicles with George driving one and Hannah driving the other. George followed Hannah as they traveled down the hallway toward the hangar entrance. Trailing her, he noticed that he was allowed to go quite a bit faster than before.

"Did anyone else get nauseous when Mark said we are going on a mission to prevent another world war?... No… just me. Great." Adam shook his head and squinted his eyes as they drove down the hall. Everyone in that golf cart stared out the window, lost in deep thought.

Amy blinked hard, then looked down. "My world was already destroyed. I'm just looking to get some of it back."

Looking up, Rachael took a deep breath. "Look, I know we are going through a lot right now. It took me a trip to the clinic to get a grip on what's happening. And yes, Adam, I did get a lump in my throat when he mentioned a world war. Not so much nauseous. That's a you thing." Rachael smiled at Adam. "I think that's why we need to do everything possible to stay focused on the task at hand. We're not soldiers, except for George, but we are highly trained

NASA astronauts. We need to remember what we learned and be flexible enough to absorb some more. I know that's asking a lot, but the sooner we get whatever we need to do done, the sooner we can move forward, wherever that may take us."

Amy looked at George with a quick upward flick of her chin. "George, you've been on military missions before. Do you think we can trust them?"

George, eyes on the road, replied, "I don't know. What I do know is that they haven't given us any real reason not to trust them. I'm sure there are a lot of things going on that we don't know about. That's why I'm staying alert. At the same time, I think it's best to believe them for now. Right now, when it comes down to it, we don't have a choice."

The two vehicles turned the corner to the stretch of hallway that led to the hangar entrance. As they approached, the hangar door opened for both of them. They went through, turned ninety degrees, then proceeded down the long hangar. Amy and Adam's eyes widened from what they were looking at. They scanned the vast hanger. As they traveled, Adam spotted huge saucer craft hovering off the floor.

Adam, almost speechless, tapped George on the shoulder. "George, you seeing this? This is mystery science theatre type stuff!"

George had a big smile on his face as he looked as well. "If you like those, you should check out that group over there." George pointed in front of them on the other side of the hangar at the group of larger triangle shaped craft. Adam looked over and saw the ships. He almost climbed on Amy to get a better look. He was completely speechless as he gazed at the group of ships that were getting bigger as they got closer.

The vehicles pulled up to one of the triangle shaped craft. It was hovering about ten feet off the ground, slightly lower than the other ships. In the middle, there were steps which resembled a thick ladder that extended from an opening in the craft to the floor. On one of the points of the triangle shaped ship, a large rectangular panel on the bottom of the craft was missing, exposing and empty area within. The missing panel lay on the floor below. On all four corners of the panel were long metal poles roughly the size of a traffic delineator. Nothing was connecting the panel to the ship.

As the group got out of the golf cart, an electric car approached them. It was a black Tesla model X. The vehicle swung around the triangle ship and drove underneath it. It continued to drive on top of the panel on the floor, with the front of the model X facing away from the center of the ship. The driver of the car got out, shut the door, then stepped away from the panel. The surface of the panel illuminated green. The whole panel slowly floated up, back onto the ship. The edges of the rectangular panel completely disappeared as though the bottom of the ship were a solid piece again.

Dizziness struck Adam, his vision blurring briefly. He put his hand on the golf cart to catch his balance. As he got out of the car, Teancom noticed Adam struggling. He opened up the back door of his golf cart and pulled out two metal drinking bottles. He jogged over to Adam. "Are you ok?"

Regaining his balance, Adam rubbed his eyes. "Yeah, I'm ok. Just got slightly light headed for a second."

Teancom handed one of the drinking bottles to Adam. "Here, drink this. It will help. It's kind of like an energy drink that helps calm the nerves and allows you to focus. Tastes pretty good too."

Adam took the bottle from Teancom. "Thanks." He opened the top and took a big swig of the liquid. "It does taste pretty good. Kind of like rum." He took another drink and immediately felt a little better.

Teancom looked around at the others, held up the bottle, and asked, "Anyone else need something to help them feel better?"

Amy looked down at the ground as her eyes started to tear up. Her hands balled up into fists as she clenched her jaw. She marched aggressively to the steps of the ship. As she passed Teancom, she spat out, "Let's just get this over with. I have a family to get back to." Rachael and Adam followed her as Teancom lowered the bottle down.

George walked up to Teancom and took the bottle from him. Slapping his hand on Teancom's shoulder, he grinned. "Don't take that personal. She has little ones that she misses. Talks about them all the time." He popped the bottle open and took a drink.

Teancom glanced over at George. "No, I get it." They both followed the group to the entrance of the ship.

Before reaching the steps, Rachael placed a hand on Adam's back. "You, O.K.?"

Adam nodded. "Getting better with this." He held up his water bottle. "With all that's going on, how can you remain so calm and focused? I get that Amy's mind is focused on getting back to her family again and we all know that George is dead inside. But you, you're a scientist. I would think that you would be like me, with your thoughts going a thousand miles an hour. How do you do it?"

Rachael looked down, taking a deep breath. She knew Adam's words weren't true. She was still baring the fact that she lost it and had to receive treatment from the clinic. "Believe me, when I first heard about all this, my thoughts were all over the place with skepticism at the foremost. I actually passed out from an anxiety attack because of it. I had to remind myself of who I am. I'm the commander of the Artemis V mission. It's my responsibility to stay focused and aim for the best outcome. If that means temporarily stowing away some of my curiosities to move us forward, then that's what I'll do. Like George said earlier, right now, I don't think we have a choice."

Rolling his eyes, Adam replied, "Yeah, I guess. Unfortunately, I don't have that justification in which my mind can stand on. I want to start dismantling everything to see how it works. Just do me a favor and stop me if my desires come to fruition."

George walked up to Adam as he was taking another drink. "You know that drink is made out of gold. Metal."

Adam looked at his bottle while nodding his head. "Huh. Just like Moses and his people. Interesting."

George stopped walking as his jaw dropped. "How do you know that?"

The group one by one climbed up the ladder into the ship. They entered into the middle of a large dome room. There were three rows of chairs spaced out in the middle of the room that took the shape of high-end bucket seats in a car. The front and back rows had two seats and the middle row had three. The two front seats had three-sided digital control panels in front of them with a yoke steering wheel. On the right side of the seats were movable handles that acted as throttle controls. At the feet, attached to the stands of the control panels, were two peddles.

On the sides where the three triangular tips were located were three closed doors. In between each door were large work stations with two to three secured chairs on each. Each work station had a large desk with varying control panels, laptops, drawers, cabinets, and secured equipment. The room was well lit by varying light sources located on the floor and sides.

Raising his hands in the air, Teancom asked, "Well, what do you think?"

Adam walked around, studying the various work stations. "I have so many questions. I don't even know where to begin." Adam was on the edge of overload. He took another drink out of his bottle. Josh walked over to him, placed his hand on Josh's back, and pointed out the various equipment.

George walked over to the two front seats and examined the controls. "Are these controls similar to the golf carts controls?"

Hannah walked over to George. "It's pretty similar, yes."

George looked to the front of the ship, and then all around. "I don't see any windows or viewing screens. How do you know where you are going?"

Hannah smiled. "Like this." She put her hand on the front control panel. The screens on the control panel turned on. Pushing a few icons on the screen, the whole top half of the room disappeared. In its place, a projection of the outside of the ship appeared. It was almost as if there were no top of the ship at all.

All four astronauts looked up at the outside projection. Adam, Amy, and Rachael spun around as they gazed at the sight. George, who had already experienced the deck projections in their rooms, was not as impressed as the others. He nodded his head as he looked up. "Huh. Reminds me of the plane simulators that we trained on in the military, except not as detailed of course."

"Pretty neat, huh." Teancom commented to the group. "Why don't I show you a couple of items that we'll be using on this mission." While he walked over to one of the doors located toward the back of the ship, Hannah turned off the outside projection. He placed his hand on the wall next to the door and it slid open. As he walked in, the lights turned on. The others followed him into a room that took the shape of one of the tips of the ship. The area was much larger where the door was, but shrank down as they walked further in. Instead of a tip at the end of the room, there was a circular hatch, which looked to accommodate the current NASA space craft that existed. On the sides of the room were various shelves that had clamped down equipment on them as well as metallic drawers and chests.

Adam noticed a large object in the room that was covered up by a blanket. He walked over to it and lifted the cover to see what was underneath. He froze when he saw a big hairy creature staring back at him. He instantly dropped the blanket and jumped back exclaiming, "Ahh! What the crap is that?!"

Teancom laughed. "That is one of our BFA units used to scare off individuals that happen to wander into areas where we are training."

Adam grabbed his chest with one of his hands and looked at Teancom with a wrinkled brow. "BFA units? What, like Big Foot?"

"Well, the official name that some engineer gave it a long time ago was Bionic Fomenting Robot. That name didn't catch very well, so it was unofficially renamed Big Foot Robot. The upgraded version, like you see there, changed from Robot to Avatar. It's pretty fun to control it. I covered it up with the blanket because every time I walked into this room it freaked me out." Teancom explained.

Adam finished off his drink. "Yeah, I know the feeling."

Teancom laughed again. He walked over to one of the larger drawers and put his thumb against the handle. After the drawer made a click sound, he slid it open. Inside were several mannequin heads with varying wigs and hats on them. He pulled out an ordinary baseball hat with the Cardinals logo on it and held it up to his phone. His phone made a notification sound after a couple of seconds. He made several swiping gestures on the screen. "Watch this." As he tapped, the hat changed logos to different teams. The color of the hat changed with it as well. After settling on blue with the Cowboys star logo on the front, he put the hat on. "Don't freak out." As he tapped again, his face changed to an entirely different face.

The four onlookers all stared in amazement. Teancom kept scrolling and tapping on his phone. Every time he tapped on his phone a different face appeared. Amy broke her stare and said, "You got to be kidding me."

Teancom smiled. "Pretty cool, huh." As he talked the green alien face that he settled on spoke and expressed all his facial changes, from the way his cheeks moved to the lines on his forehead and eyebrow movement. It was extremely detailed. "Try it. Your phones have a hat icon. Just tap on it and the rest is self-explanatory."

Three of them grabbed a hat, while Rachael grabbed a shoulder length wig. They all took out their phones and found the icon. After they opened the application, it prompted them to hold their device next to their chosen hat. Once they were synced to their devices, they went at it. Rachael found that she could change the wig's color to any that she wanted to, but could not change the length or the style of the hair. They all put on their hats and laughed at each other as they chose various faces.

George chose the face of a flat nosed lizard. Adam immediately admired it. He searched on his device to find it but couldn't. He turned to Teancom and held up his phone. "Why can't I find the lizard face that George has?"

Teancom, still showing his green alien face explained, "Each device has its own unique choices of faces. No two individuals can have the same face at the same time. If you want, you have the option of transferring different faces to others."

Adam shrugged his shoulders. "Why is that?"

"It keeps relationships that you build with people in the normal world while wearing a specific face within one user." Teancom explained. "For example, if you wear a particular face and always go to a specific hotel, you probably build a relationship with the person at the counter and the valet. You get to know them and they get to know the persona that you make up. If someone else wears that same face and runs into the same people, they might stop and want to talk to the new user of the face. Not knowing those individuals or the details of the already established persona to the face will raise suspicion. To avoid that, we put this control in place."

"Yeah, I guess that makes sense." Adam looked down at his screen, reluctantly scrolling to find a similar lizard face.

Teancom took off his hat to reveal his true face. He put it back on the head in the drawer where he found it.

After allowing the group a few minutes to play with the hats, Teancom said, "Let me introduce you the other items that we will be using. If you would please place the hats and wig back in the drawer, I'll show you." The four of them took off their hats and wig and put it back where they found them. Teancom pushed the drawer closed and walked over to another drawer. He opened it the same way he did the first. He pulled out a pair of very thin tan gloves. "These are our chameleon gloves. When you put them on, they shrink around your hand, then project the image of your actual hand so as to look like you're not wearing anything. The main feature is that they change your fingerprints to ones that can't be identified in any records. They're waterproof, heat-resistant, and help shield against sharp objects." Teancom pulled out a pair for everyone in the room and handed them out. "Try them out. If you want, you can also change the color or pattern of them on your phone to match whatever face you choose."

Each of them tried on the gloves. After they put one on, it immediately shrank around their hand and disappeared as they projected the image of their hand.

George swung his hand around and felt the walls. "Wow. They are extremely breathable. Besides the fact that I can't feel textures, it's like I'm not even wearing them." The other three nodded in agreement as they examined their gloved hands.

"Pretty neat, huh. If you are impressed with the gloves, you're going to love this." Teancom pulled out a black leather belt with a low-profile square buckle and held it up. "This is our body armor." He placed his phone next to it, much like he did with the hat.

As Teancom put the belt on, George rose a brow and asked, "What? How is that body armor?"

Teancom finished putting the belt on, then clicked his phone a few times. "Let me show you." He walked over to a chest on the floor, unlocked it with his thumb print, and opened it up. He pulled out a Glock 19 handgun and checked the chamber to make sure it wasn't loaded. He also pulled out a suppressor made for the gun. Screwing the suppressor on, he grabbed a magazine loaded with 9 mm ammo and closed the chest. He walked over to George and handed him the gun and the magazine. "Shoot me."

George looked at Teancom with narrow eyes. "What? You sure?"

Teancom checked his phone again, then looked up at George with a grin. "Yes, I'm sure."

George tilted his head. "Ok. Your funeral." He inspected the gun, slid the magazine in, and pulled back on the slide. Against his better judgement, he raised the gun, aiming at Teancom's chest. Winching, he slowly pulled the trigger. The gun fired. To everyone's surprise, the perfectly intact bullet stopped six inches from Teancom's chest, then dropped to the floor.

Adam's eyes widened. "How is that even possible? I mean, the theme here seems to be gravity manipulation. But even then, the type of sensory that needs to be involved with something like this is insane!"

Teancom picked up the bullet from the floor and tossed it at Adam. "Unheard of is also the main theme here. I don't know exactly how it works, but you're right. It has to do with gravity manipulation. It's saved me from serious injury a few times. On a single charge it can withstand several thousand rounds as well as a few high-altitude falls."

Rachael's eyebrows rose. "High-altitude falls?"

"Yes. You can jump out of a ship and land safely on the ground with it on. As you approach the ground, it slows you down. It's a lot more discrete than having a large parachute deploy for the world to see." Teancom explained.

"On a single charge?" Adam inquired, looking at the bullet that Teancom tossed at him. "Let me guess, gravity driven generators."

Teancom nodded his head once. "We have some portable generators that work like that, yes. To power equipment that require much more immediate power, such as these ships and the golf carts, we have mini fusion reactors installed."

Adam stared at Teancom. "Mini fusion reactors? The world has barely scratched the surface on producing efficient full size fusion reactors, and you have working mini fusion reactors?"

"Yeah, they are way nicer than the older mini nuclear reactors we had before them. They were very sensitive which caused countless issues of external radiation leaks. The containment crew was extremely happy when the fusion reactors arrived. Less to cover up." Teancom replied.

"You are going to have to get me some information on all of this stuff when this mission is over." Adam pleaded.

"When this is over, you can go and have long conversations with our engineers and they will tell you everything that you want to know." Teancom reassured Adam.

Amy pointed to the cabinet that contained the hats. "How long do the hats last?"

Teancom replied, "If it is constantly being used, it should last a good week on a single charge."

Teancom looked at George with pressed lips, then looked down at the gun that was still in George's hand. George understood. With quick precision, he took the magazine out of the gun, pulled the slide back, and locked it in place. He picked up the bullet that was in the chamber which ejected out as he pulled the slide back and loaded it back in the magazine. After seeing that the chamber was clear, he handed the gun and the magazine back over to Teancom.

Teancom quickly inspected it, then walked over to the chest to put it away.

As Teancom was putting the gun away, Rachael eyed the other cabinets. "Are there any other items we get to see?"

"At this time, no. I don't think we will need anything else for now." Teancom explained as he put the gun back in the chest. He went to the drawer with the belts, grabbed four of them, and handed them out. "Before you put these on, sync them to your phone. There is a shield icon that you can open up. It will tell you the amount of charge that it has left. You can change the settings with projectile proximity, rate of fall, distance to deceleration, and things like that. Don't mess with those settings right now. I would hate for you to do something which makes the belt useless."

Each of the crew synced their belts to their device before they put them on. A picture of their body profile appeared on their phone screen with a blue glow that outlined that profile. As Adam slipped his belt around his waist, he suggested, "With all this technology, couldn't you just give us a suit that makes us have superman like powers. I mean, with the power to manipulate gravity, I would think it wouldn't be too difficult to do."

Teancom smiled. "That would be awesome. Unfortunately, the idea is to stay as discrete as possible. Flying around and openly stopping crime doesn't exactly do that."

Adam reluctantly nodded his head. "Yeah, I guess you're right."

"Come on, let's go plan this out." Teancom walked back toward the main room of the ship while motioning the others to follow.

Back in the main room, Josh was at one of the workstations tapping away at a computer while Hannah was sitting at one of the pilot seats, plotting out their path on the control panel. As the group walked back in the room, both Hannah and Josh temporarily stopped what they were doing, stood up, and walked over to the rest of the group.

Teancom looked around at the crew. "As mentioned earlier, we will break into two groups. Josh, Rachael, and Amy will go to the NASA facility in Florida to find out more about the person that injected the code. We will drop you off in the car a few miles away to avoid any attention."

"Drop them off?" George rose his brow. "Wouldn't landing a triangle shaped ship cause a lot of attention?"

"We won't be landing. The car is on a portable jump pad. We'll hover many miles above, then transport them down once the area is clear." Teancom explained.

"If we can just transport things where ever we want, why even use this ship? Why don't you just transport them from here?" Adam's hands flailed around as he spoke.

Teancom nodded. "That would be nice if we could do that. Unfortunately, there are a couple of obstacles that we would run into. First, we scan for joggers, passing vehicles, or stray animals. Second, the jump pad that we are using doesn't have enough power to transport long distances, so we need to be at least a few miles from the destination. Also, some prep time will be needed to hack into security and get access. How's that going Josh?"

"Pretty much done. We just need to insert profile pictures for Rachael and Amy from the faces that they choose. We can do that once we're on our way." Josh replied.

Teancom nodded with approval. "That's good to hear. Amy and Rachael, once you're in the facility, will you be able to get the information that we need?"

Amy spoke up. "We should be able to. I know the location where they keep the secured data servers. Once I'm in, I'm confident I can piece it together."

Teancom smiled. "Great. Once you get the information about the hacker, locate that person and find out what they know. If you need it, there will be a ship on standby to pick you up and take you where you need to go. As for the rest of us, we'll go scout out the location where the code originated from. What we know so far about that spot through satellite imagery is that it's an isolated building located on the southern region of Taiwan. We'll scan the area and figure out our next steps based on what we find. Any questions?"

Adam rolled his eyes. "Yes, but at this point I think it's pointless to ask."

Teancom grabbed Adam's shoulder. "Good call." He turned and faced Hannah. "Is our path plotted and ready to go?"

Hannah lifted her head. "As long as we leave within the next fifteen minutes."

"Sounds good." Teancom turned back to the four. "Just to let everyone know what to expect while we are traveling in this ship, we have our own controlled gravity within this space. That means you will not feel any forces pushing against you while we move around. We could be in a cork screw nose dive and it would feel like we weren't moving." Teancom pointed toward the seats at the center of the ship. "I would advise you at this time to take a seat while we gain altitude, however. The view of us moving around can get somewhat disorienting."

The group looked over at the seats. With questions still in their mind, they reluctantly walked over and sat down. Amy and Adam sat in the rear. Rachael and Teancom choose seats in the middle row. Josh sat in the pilot seat to the right. Before Hannah sat in the other pilot seat, George walked over to her and asked, "Why do we have a fifteen-minute launch window?"

Hannah replied, "We have to avoid any type of contact with the outside world. I scanned all military, private, and commercial flights as well as ships and vehicles on the surface. Based on their trajectories, we should be cleared from any contact with the path I laid out for the next fifteen minutes, although military planes are a lot of times unpredictable."

George nodded his head in understanding. "Can't we just jump to the locations in the sky? I can't imagine much to get in the way up there?"

"Yes, we can. In fact, that's what we usually do. However, if you're not use to it, jumping can really mess with your head. The farther the jump, the greater the effect. A few miles and the effects won't be as bad. A few hundred miles will be a problem for rookies like you." Hannah answered with a smirk on her face. "Don't feel bad. You get used to it. I can jump hundreds of thousands of miles and it barely fazes me."

George grinned. "Give me a couple of days and I'm sure I'll catch up to you."

Hannah smiled. "We'll see." Hannah sat in her seat. George sat in the seat behind her so he could watch her pilot the ship.

"Whenever you're ready." Teancom said to Hannah.

With a few swipes on the controls, Hannah turned on the projection for the top half of the ship, revealing the large hangar that still had very minimal activity going on. The three tips of the triangular shaped craft were visibly sticking out where the doors were located. Hannah rotated the ship so that they were facing the center of the hanger. As she did this, the positioning of the tips changed in relation to the doors.

The ship itself stayed in the same direction. The ovoid shaped center where they were sitting rotated within the ship. She pulled the craft forward to the center of the hangar to clear them from the other ships parked. She once again rotated the center, keeping the triangular tips of the ship in the same direction. While rotating, she tapped the control panel again, causing the center hangar doors on the roof to open. Slowly, she pulled forward in the direction of the hangar doors. As soon as they were right under the open doors, Hannah stated, "All systems nominal. Scanners are showing no intrusions. Our path is clear."

Teancom cracked a slight smile. "Sounds good. Let's go."

The ship began to rise straight up. As they got closer to the opened bay door, Josh looked back and noticed Adam and Amy looking up with wide eyes, while gripping their legs. He looked up and saw why. The open hangars revealed a dark void they were slowly approaching. Josh tapped and swiped at the control panel in front of him, causing the external lights of the facility to turn on. Instead of going into a dark abyss, they were now entering the giant glassless fish tank that Rachael and George witnessed earlier. Amy and Adam's jaws dropped as a small school of large fish swam by the opening.

"That is absolutely unbelievable. Is that some sort of force field tech or manipulating gravity again?" Adam asked as the ship slowly went through the doorway, into the water. An invisible barrier formed around the ship as it became engulfed by the ocean, keeping the water five feet away from the ship.

"Manipulating gravity… which in turn acts like force field tech." Josh replied. The ship was now completely out of the facility and fully surrounded by water. The lighting dimmed as there was now very little light coming in from the outside.

"Want to see something really trippy?" Hanna said as she smiled. With a few taps of her finger, the floor of the ship seemed to go transparent as the projection of what was underneath the ship appeared. They could see the bay doors close. Rock formations slid into place, perfectly hiding the facility. All they could see was ocean floor before the exterior facility lights turned off. Hannah turned her head toward George. "Always make sure that the doors are completely closed and concealed when you pull out of a facility."

George shook his head as he looked up and down, trying to hold back a grin. "I'll make sure to do that."

"Here we go." Hannah pushed the throttle forward. The ship started moving much faster through the water. The dark abyss surrounding them started to get lighter as they got closer to the surface. Finally, they broke the surface and quickly rose into the sky. Adam and Amy were speechless as they looked down and saw the details of the ocean quickly disappear. They both gripped the side of the seats hard. George had a large grin on his face as he observed his surroundings.

Rachael was shocked as she looked down at her feet to see nothing but sky. "Holy crap!" She blurted out.

Hannah noticed Rachael's cry and realized that the floor projection was a little much for her crew. She tapped the controls. The transparent floor turned back into just a floor, while the surrounding ceiling projection narrowed to a large front windshield view. Adam let out a deep breath. As he sat on his seat, wiping his brow and checking his pants, he realized that it felt like they were not moving. Thinking back on his experience with their launch out of the facility, through the ocean, and into the sky, there was no physical forces pushing against them. No movement from turns. No G-forces as they gained speed. It was as if they were not moving at all.

Adam stood up, shaking his head in disbelief. "This is unbelievable! Even with the ability to manipulate gravity, I can't even imagine the complex calculations that it would take to simulate this type of non-motion in cabin environment. I would think that even an extremely small amount of lag to counter the forces would cause some balance issues. There's none of that!"

"You're not wrong about that." Teancom looked back at Adam. "I heard stories of when they were designing and testing the system. It involved buckets of puke. Thankfully they nailed it."

Adam tilted his head, then sat back down. "And what happens if the system that controls this environment suddenly has issues while the crew is moving about the cabin?"

Teancom smiled as he stood up. "Don't worry. The engineers that designed the system were more paranoid than you. There are four separate backup systems to compensate for issues like that. And if they all go down, an emergency system will kick in that will throw the ship into auto pilot to minimize the outside forces, giving the crew a chance to buckle up."

"Huh." Adam looked down in thought. "I guess that makes me feel a little better. I'd really like to meet those engineers."

"I'm sure you would." Teancom replied. Looking toward Hannah, he asked, "What's our ETA until our inland jump?"

Hannah turned her head and looked back at Teancom. "About twenty minutes."

Teancom turned to Josh. "Josh, you have twenty minutes to finish setting up. You good with that?"

Josh stood up. "That should be plenty of time."

"Awesome. Rachael and Amy, please go with Josh to get ready. Hannah, please realign the ship so they can have access to the side doors."

"You got it." Hannah tapped on the controls. The three tips of the ship rotated clockwise until they lined up with the doors. "We are realigned. Doors are unlocked."

As Josh walked toward the back storage bay that the crew was previously in, he gave a friendly motion to Rachael and Amy to follow him. They looked at each other and slowly moved towards the door. Josh opened the door and let the two girls walk in. "You need to pick either a hat or a wig. Then, well, you need to pick a face."

Twenty minutes ago, Josh's comment would have sounded extremely strange to Rachael and Amy. Now, it made them both crack a smile as they went toward the cabinet that held the caps. Rachael attempted to open it. It was locked. She put her thumb on the door. Nothing. Josh saw her attempts. "Here, let me help." He put his thumb against the door. It clicked.

While Rachael reached out to opened the drawer, she looked over at Josh with a smile. "Thank you." The two girls tried on the different hats and wigs. After a minute, they decided that it was too much of a pain to have to tuck their hair into the wigs and both settled on a regular baseball hat.

Josh picked up a similar hat. "I tend to go with the classics as well. Go ahead and sync up with your phones." Once they were linked, Josh said, "Try to go with a plain color or a NASA logo. The idea is to blend and be forgettable." They all changed their hats to a navy-blue color. Josh and Rachael added a NASA logo while Amy went without.

"Alright. Let's go back to the workstation. Pick your face and I'll print out ID's and upload it into NASA's security data base."

Rachael and Amy scrolled through the different face options on their phones as they walked back to the main room of the ship. Josh fixed some of the displaced hats and wigs, shut the drawer, and followed them. Walking back into the main room, he noticed the two girls had their hats on and were trying out different faces. Josh motioned to the girls to follow him as he walked over to one of the workstations that he was at earlier. He sat down at the computer and logged back into the security database at NASA.

"Huh. That's interesting." Josh said out loud while looking at the screen with a puzzled look.

"What is it?" Amy diverted her attention to the screen.

Josh tapped at the keyboard. "It looks like they just beefed up the security protocols. It's no big deal. I easily got through them."

Amy leaned in. "Let me see." Josh pushed the keyboard over to Amy. Her fingers went to work as she analyzed the situation. A frown crossed Amy's face. "This isn't good. NASA doesn't have this much security." She continued to look through the code on the computer. "It looks like the FBI has taken control. They must suspect foul play in what happened. I'm sure they have locked down NASA by now. This might make things more difficult."

"Not necessarily." Josh reassured Amy. "It actually might make things easier. We'll probably need to change our approach, that's all."

Rachael's eyebrow rose. "How will more security make things easier?"

"Whenever government organizations get involved, things become sloppy. We can take advantage of that. Usually, the play is to claim that we're from a different government bureau with higher clearance, like the DOD and they let us do what we need to do." Josh explained.

"And that works?" Rachael's other eyebrow rose.

"Well, it gets us in the door and buys us time. Don't get me wrong, there's usually contention if the person in charge gets word that another bureau is invading their space, but we'll have all the proper credentials and electronic clearances in place, which is pretty easy to do from here." Josh grabbed the keyboard again and went back to work hacking the different networks. "Just give me a couple of minutes. In the meantime, finish picking your face and come up with some good names. If not, I'll pick it for you."

Rachael and Amy looked at each other to find comfort, but came up short. Instead, they were met with the same uneasy stare. The small spark of excitement from Amy shrank back to anxiety. They took a noticeable deep breath at the same time. Their synchronization of breaths made them smile, breaking some of the tension. "Let's pick our faces. I kind of liked the lizard look on you." Rachael joked with Amy. Amy shook her head with disapproval as her smile became slightly bigger. They continued to scroll through their phones.

While Rachael, Amy, and Josh were working out the details of their mission, Teancom was talking to Mark on his phone. After he hung up, he walked over to Adam and George who were standing next to Hannah. She was showing them some of the controls of the ship. Teancom frowned as he looked at the group. "I just got some information from Mark about the world political situation. It's not good. According to Suzie, the U.S. has decided to advance forces toward the South China sea."

Adam looked at Teancom with a wrinkled brow. "Who's Suzie?"

Teancom replied, "Suzie is one of our main informants planted in the U.S. intelligence agency. She has proven to be an extremely accurate source. She claimed that China showed empathy with the explosion of the U.S. space capsule. The U.S. didn't take them very seriously when China started building up their forces near the South China Sea. The U.S. decided on advancing forces of their own. Such advancements on both sides in a very unstable part of the world will result in tensions rising significantly between countries. This means it's only a small matter of time before shots are fired. Whatever happened to your ship, we need to figure it out quickly."

George shrugged his shoulders. "Can't the organization make up some cover story to explain the explosion as an accident? Isn't that what the "CTC" does?"

Teancom answered, "Yes and no. We will do that, but the cover stories need to be based off of facts. It doesn't do any good for us to insert the idea that it was an accident when the real threat starts attacking in other ways. We need to find out what really happened and eliminate the threat if any. Then we can put down a legit cover. Which brings us to Taiwan. Unfortunately, we don't have a lot of information on what is going on at the facility in Taiwan. When we get there, we are going to have to scan the area to get a better layout of what's going on and what we have to deal with."

Hannah continued to show George and Adam the different functions of the ship which she thought might be relevant to their upcoming mission. On the other side of the ship, Rachael and Amy finally picked the faces that they wanted to use and gave that information to Josh.

As Josh put in the data on the computer, he explained, "With higher security clearance, we will have to dress more appropriately. Fortunately, we've planned for different scenarios." He pointed to one of the doors. "If you go through that door, you will find the Model X parked in there. In the trunk is different outfits for all three of us. One of those outfits are low profile suits. Quickly change into them and come back here. You can leave your clothes and hats in the trunk with the other outfits. We'll probably have to switch to wigs to match our new attire."

Rachael and Amy walked over to the door, placed their hand on the wall next to it, then entered the room. Inside sat the Model X vehicle with the four poles near each of the corners of the car. They opened up the trunk to find many different outfits neatly folded and in clear plastic. They placed their hats inside the trunk and searched through the outfits. After moving aside wet suits, winter clothes, and camo attire, they found the suits with their names labeled on the clear plastic covers. Grabbing their specific suits, they quickly changed into them, throwing their other clothes in the trunk. They found shoes that looked like dress shoes, but wore and felt like running shoes and put them on as well. After grabbing their hats, they closed the trunk and walked back out to where Josh was sitting. He was just finishing up when the girls walked up.

Josh grabbed a couple of ID tags that he just created and stood up. Handing the tags to Rachael and Amy, he said, "We are now officially members of the DOD. Here are your ID's. Now let's go get some wigs."

The three walked back into the room with the equipment. Josh opened the hat drawer, collected their hats, and put them back. After they chose a wig, Josh closed the drawer again. As they walked back into the main room, Josh pointed to the room with the Model X. "I'm going to go change. Try on those wigs. Remember, you can adjust the color with the app on your phone." Josh continued to the other room and shut the door behind him so he could change. After Amy and Rachael helped each other put their wigs on, they opened the App on their phones, turned on their new faces, and experimented with the different hair colors.

Adam broke his attention from Hannah and looked over at the girls trying out their different looks. He yelled over to them, "I think you should go with the pink and green."

Rachael smirked. "Nah, we'd look too much like George's ex-girlfriends. Don't think that will help us to blend in."

"At least I've had dates." George yelled back.

"I've been on dates." Rachael argued.

"You can't count monkeys in the lab as dates." George argued back

"Then I guess that means all of the girls that went out with you didn't go on dates." Rachael replied with a grin on her new face. George liked the comeback. He smiled and nodded with approval.

"Five minutes till continental jump." Hannah announced, still sitting at the pilot's seat.

Josh came out of the room dressed in a grey two button suit, white dress shirt, and black tie and walked over to the girls. Teancom, who was looking up information at another workstation turned to the three of them and asked, "You ready to go?"

Josh looked at Amy and Rachael for confirmation. Rachael and Amy looked at each other with clenched jaws and determined eyes and nodded. Rachael looked back at Josh and nodded. "We're set up and ready." Josh replied to Teancom.

"Find out what you can and keep in communication so we can piece this puzzle together as soon as possible. Things are getting hot really quick on the world front. A lot is riding on this." As he was saying this, Teancom noticed that Rachael and Amy were fidgeting with their hands and slightly rocking. With an empathetic, yet confident voice he said to the girls, "You will do great. Have confidence in yourself and remember why you are doing this. I promise after we get this done, we will do everything we can to make things right."

Josh put his hands on Amy and Rachael's shoulders. "A walk in the park."

The three made their way into the room with the Model X. After they entered, the door shut behind them. Josh got in the car in the driver's seat. Rachael and Amy both got in the back seat. Out of habit, they buckled up.

Josh looked back at them. "In a couple of minutes, the ship will do a short transport jump over to our drop point near Kennedy Space Center to avoid any inland air traffic. At that point, they will do a quick scan of the area to make sure that it's clear of any prying eyes. Once it's clear, this car, with us in it, will transport down to the ground where we will proceed with our mission. After these jumps, you might feel a little dizzy. It will feel like you just got off a twisty roller coaster. There are some barf bags under the seat if you need them. Don't worry though, the feeling should pass after a few seconds."

Rachael looked down at the seat, then back at Josh. "I think we might be alright. We are NASA Astronauts after all."

Josh smiled. "I'm sure you will."

Amy grinned. "Well, if Adam was here, it might be a different story." Rachael laughed.

Josh faced forward and put on his wig that he picked out. He looked at himself in the rear-view mirror to make sure that it was on correctly. With a tap of his phone, his replacement face appeared. He Turned around with a grin on an unrecognizable face. "What do you think?"

Amy's eye widened as she attempted to look away. Rachael kept herself from laughing. "It's Ok."

Josh smiled. "I know. It's not as good as the original. With the wigs, the app has a function that you can activate that adds a suction to your head. That way if you trip or are hanging upside down for some reason, your wig will still stay on." Josh held up his phone to them to show them. "See. Just push this icon and you're good."

Amy and Rachael pulled out their phones and activated the function. As they were looking over the other functions of the app, Hannah's voice sounded over the car speakers, "Twenty seconds to continental jump."

Josh faced forward again and grabbed the steering wheel. "Ok. Here we go. Get those bags out just in case. Don't want it smelling in here."

The girls reluctantly followed his advice. They grabbed the bags and placed them in the middle seat. Hannah's voice came on again, "Five, four, three, two, one…"

Rachael and Amy looked around and didn't notice any change. A second later, a slight bit of dizziness hit them. They both closed their eyes and shook it off. Josh looked back and asked, "You alright?"

Both of them, now almost fully recovered gave him a thumbs up. Hannah's voice over the speakers sounded again, "Area clear. Are you ready?"

Josh replied, "Yes. We are ready to jump."

Hannah announced, "Jumping in Five, four, three, two, one…"

Rachael and Amy peered out, the world twisting like a wrung-out cloth. When the background untwisted, they were outside on a dirt road, surrounded by trees. The jarring shift and sharper dizziness bent them over, eyes shut, breathing deep.

Josh, who was unfazed, turned the vehicle on and pulled forward and off the platform the vehicle was on. Once off, he announced, "We are clear of the platform."

Hannah's voice replied over the speakers, "Sounds good. Good luck you guys." The platform with the poles on the four corners disappeared behind them.

Josh glanced back, Rachael and Amy hunched over, breathing deeply. "Are you two, ok?"

Rachael replied in-between breaths, "Yeah, give us a minute."

"No problem. Remember those bags are right next to you if you need them." Josh turned back around and turned the air conditioning on and up. It was already starting to get warm even though it was early morning. The sky was clear and the humidity outside was high. Josh activated the navigation on the vehicle's center screen. The map indicated that they were at Fey Lake Wilderness Park. He typed in Kennedy Space center for their destination. The navigation calculated a path to where they needed to go and indicated forty-five minutes till arrival. Josh turned back around to see how the girls were doing. At this point they were no longer bent over, but sitting up with their eyes closed. "Feeling a little better?"

Amy spoke up, "Yes, I am. It's passing pretty quick, like you said."

Rachael relied, "Same here. I'm good."

Josh smiled as he faced forward again. "Good to hear. If you need me to pull over, just let me know." He started driving on the dirt path that led to an empty parking lot. He continued to drive until he got onto an actual road and continued to their destination.

Rachael, now almost fully recovered, said to Josh, "It looks like that the jump didn't faze you at all."

Josh shrugged his shoulders. "You get used to it. Your body adjusts, just like anything."

Rachael rolled her eyes. "Yes, well I wouldn't call that just like anything."

Josh smiled. "In my line of business, that's normal. I can see how that can weird you out though."

Rachael let out a little laugh. "That's the understatement of the century! So, what's next through our trip through the twilight zone?" She asked sarcastically. Hearing herself, she immediately noticed that she started to sound like Adam and decided to readjust her attitude a bit. "Sorry, didn't mean to snap like that."

Josh replied jokingly, "Well, on this week's episode, a group of hero's infiltrate their ex-employer's facility on a quest to uncover a sinister plot to set the world ablaze. Once in, they hack into their system to find the identity of a potential programmer that sabotaged a mission that they were once on. Little do they know that as they journey to complete this mission, they have entered into the realms of, the twilight zone. Doon, Doon, Doooon, Don Don Don Don Don Don."

Amy shook her head as she grinned. "That was pretty cringy. You're a dork."

Josh chuckled. "I get that a lot."

Leaning forward, Amy placed her hand on the empty front passenger seat. "Don't you get nervous on missions like this?"

"I do, but like I said before, this is normal to me. In these situations, I found it best to unwind in my mind a bit. Don't overthink it. At the same time don't underthink it. Relax, and just do what needs to be done. If you can have some fun with it, do it. Of course, don't get carried away. The idea is to be noticed as little as possible. I learned that the hard way."

Amy inquired, "What do you mean?"

Josh grinned. "A few years back I was on a surveillance mission at night near a zoo that required me to be on the ground. So, I masked up and did my thing. It got really boring. My coworker, who was safely on a ship, started joking with me over the comms. For some reason that I can't remember, she told me that it was fitting that I was on this mission because I belonged in the zoo. So, I flipped through my phone and found a wolf face. I knew there was no one around, so I decided to switch faces."

"You didn't." Rachael said with a smile.

"Yes, I did." Josh replied. "I video called my coworker and said maybe this is more fitting for me. We both got a good laugh. Unfortunately, because we got distracted, my coworker didn't notice that I walked in the path of one of the zoo's surveillance cameras. It wasn't long before it was on social media. Fortunately, I was far enough away so the video footage was not very good. Of course, I had to get a talking to from Mark and some disciplinary action."

Both girls were laughing. Rachael commented, "You are a dork."

Josh grinned. "Yeah, not one of my brightest moments."

Back on the ship, they just completed their second jump back away from the mainland. George stood tall with his eyes closed, recovering from the jump. Adam, who was bent over, quickly lifted his head toward Teancom and asked with a green face, "Where's the bathroom?"

Teancom, trying to hide his smile pointed to the third door on the ship. "The facility room is behind that door."

Adam quickly darted to the door and tried grabbing at a non-existing door handle. Hannah, who couldn't hide her smile, let out a silent giggle and opened the door with the controls at her console. Adam stumbled in. Hannah closed the door behind him as she let out a much louder laugh.

After Hannah was able to compose herself, she looked at the controls and announced, "Thirty minutes till we reach Taiwan."

Chapter 12

In the distance, Josh could see a barricade with armed guards blocking the road to the NASA facilities. "Ok, we are pulling up to a check point. Remember, you are with the Department of Defense. You report directly to the office of the Secretary of Defense. The FBI does not have jurisdiction over you. I will do all the talking. If someone by chance asks you a question, your response is "it's classified."

The vehicle pulled up to the check point where a guard dressed in urban military camo was standing by. Josh lowered his window. A bead of sweat rolled down the guard's face as he looked in at Josh with a serious demeanor. He noticed the ID badge hanging from Josh's suit and asked, "Do you have an appointment to be here Sir?"

Josh looked at the guard with a straight face. "Yes, we do."

The guard glanced at the back seat. "I need all three IDs to confirm your appointment, sir."

Amy and Rachael took off their IDs and handed them to Josh. Josh added his own ID to the pile and handed them to the guard. He grabbed the IDs, ducked into a shed, and checked a laptop by a humming fan. The guard typed in their info and carefully inspected each ID. After a few seconds, he walked back to their vehicle and knocked on the back window where Rachael was sitting. "Ma'am, can you please lower your window so that I can verify your faces?"

Rachael lowered her window. The guard carefully studied the IDs and compared them to Rachael and Amy's holographic faces. He went over to Josh and did the same. After checking, he returned the IDs to Josh. "Carry on." The guard took a step back from the vehicle as the barricade lifted out of the way. Josh pulled the vehicle forward past the barricade and continued on as they raised their windows back up.

Rachael and Amy took a deep breath. Amy commented, "If the IDs failed, can this car flip to airplane mode for a quick getaway?"

Josh smiled at the thought. "No, this is just an ordinary Tesla."

Amy slanted her head. "Wait, with all the technology that your organization has, we are driving around in an ordinary vehicle on a mission to prevent the next world war?"

Raising his index finger in the air, Josh answered, "First, I wouldn't call a Model X Plaid that can go zero to sixty in two point five seconds an ordinary vehicle. Next, remember that we want to keep our technology out of the hands of the general public. If this car were to be stolen while we were in the building, the thieves wouldn't get any of that tech."

Amy closed her eyes in thought for a second. She looked up with a slight frown. "Yes, I guess that makes sense."

Josh caught her facial expression in the rear-view mirror. "Don't worry. That belt that you have on is your personal security blanket to keep you safe." Josh continued to drive down the road. They pulled up to an intersection. "Ok, now where do I go from here?"

Amy pointed to a parking lot in the distance next to a large office building. "Park over there. The data we need is in that building."

Josh pulled into the parking lot and backed in an empty spot close to the building. He turned around and looked at Rachael and Amy. "Ready?"

Both girls nodded yes.

"Ok. Let's go. Remember, stay calm. Show confidence. Try not to stick out and let me do the talking." Josh turned back around and got out of the vehicle. Rachael and Amy took deep breaths and did the same. After he shut and locked the doors, Josh waved his hand forward. "Lead the way. I'll follow behind."

The girls walked side by side to the entrance of the building while Josh followed close behind. They walked through the front entrance and up to metal detectors with moving belts that led into x-ray machines for small loose objects. Two guards stood next to the machines, ready to direct and wand them if needed. They each put their phones in a container on the moving belts and walked through different metal detectors. When Rachael walked through, she was surprised that she did not beep. She was sure that the belt she was wearing would have set it off. Amy and Josh cleared the detectors as well. They collected their phones and proceeded forward.

Rachael and Amy took a few steps before they looked up. They froze, staring at the memorial ahead. In the middle of the main foyer were four large framed pictures on stands of Rachael, Amy, Adam, and George. Above the pictures was a banner that said "Forever to the stars." Their deaths stung anew.

Josh put his hands on Rachael and Amy's shoulders and nudged them forward. He whispered, "Keep moving forward."

As they started moving again, Rachael pulled out her phone. "Oh, I got to get a picture of this." She pushed on the camera icon. A message popped up that said "function disabled."

Josh noticed. "Don't worry. I'll get it for you." He pulled out his phone and took a quick picture of the scene as they continued on their way.

Moving forward again, Rachael and Amy were back walking side by side with Josh following as they walked to the elevators. Rachael pushed the button to call an elevator. A few seconds later, an elevator door opened. After they walked in, Amy pushed the button for the fourth floor.

After the doors closed, Josh, who was still standing behind them, whispered, "Remember, there are cameras everywhere." As Amy started to look up, Josh quickly whispered, "Don't look at them. You'll raise suspicion. Keep looking forward."

Amy whispered back, "Then why mention it if you didn't want me looking? Of course, I'm going to look at them. The power of suggestion."

Josh whispered back, "Just saying, that's all."

The elevator door opened at the fourth floor. A very familiar aroma of brewed coffee invaded the girl's nostrils. The smell clicked open a very large file of memories in their brains. They continued on their way in the same formation. As they walked down the hall, Rachael and Amy saw many of their former colleagues that they have worked with for years. They fought the urge to interact. One individual walking down the hall towards them caught Amy's eye. The past couple of days instantly faded in her mind like waking up from a bad dream.

"James?" Amy said out loud as she broke off to walk towards him.

Rachael whispered to her, "Don't do it." But Amy didn't pay attention to her.

James looked at Amy and replied with a puzzled look on his face, "I'm sorry, do I know you?"

Amy was thrown back into the nightmare and remembered that she was in disguise. There was no way that James would know who she was. She quickly thought up something to say to make up for her mistake. "You're James Whittaker, right? I read on Amy's profile that your family was very close to hers."

James looked at Amy's DOD ID hanging around her neck. "Yes. My wife was best friends with Amy and I was best friends with her husband. We went on vacations together all the time."

Amy couldn't help herself and asked, "How is Amy's family doing?"

James teared up. "It's been very hard for everyone. I'd be with them now, you know, for support, if I wasn't needed here. The kids… it's been tough." James tried to hold his composure as best he could. Amy spun from James; eyes wet. "Excuse me." She quickly headed down the hall where the bathrooms were. Rachael chased after her.

Josh was left there standing in front of a slightly confused and now very emotional James. Josh explained, "Investigators often get very emotionally attached to the people that they are researching, especially in this case where Amy had young kids."

"I can understand that." James wiped away a few tears. "I'm sorry, but I better get back to work." James continued down the hallway, trying to regain focus on his tasks.

Josh took a deep breath and walked down to the bathroom where both Amy and Rachael went into.

Amy slumped over the sink as her real tears rolled down her fake face. Rachael tried comforting her with a hug. She broke off the hug for a moment to open all the stall doors to make sure that they were the only ones in the bathroom. They were.

Rachael gripped Amy's shoulders. "Amy, I know it's hard for you right now but I need you to focus for a second. Look up at the mirror. Come on, look up for a second." Amy looked in the mirror to find a crying stranger looking back at her. "The only person that is going to get you back with your family is that person staring at you right now. We need to push forward and it doesn't sound like we have a lot of time. I need you to pull it together. We can't do this without you."

Amy rubbed her face and took several deep breaths as she stopped crying. "You're right Rachael. I'm sorry. I shouldn't have lost focus like that. I shouldn't have talked to James. I'm sorry."

Rachael smiled and looked at Amy in the mirror. "It's ok. I get it. It took every fiber of myself not to go and talk to everyone that I saw. Now is not the time for that though. Now is the time to stay focused so we can finish this. Can you do that for us, for your family?"

"Yeah…yes. I can. I'm sorry. I'll get back into focus… just… just give me a minute. I'll be alright." Amy turned on the cold water of the sink and splashed her face several times.

Rachael grabbed several paper towels and handed them to Amy. "I know you will be. It will be alright. Things will work out." Deep inside Rachael knew that she had no idea if things would work out. She had no idea what was going to happen to them after this was all done. All she knew was that she needed to stay strong and positive so that they could accomplish what they needed to at that time.

Outside of the bathroom, Josh was standing next to the door with his arms folded, making sure that no one entered. When Rachael and Amy walked out, Josh noticed that Amy's eyes were red and swollen.

Josh whispered to Amy, "Amy, casually turn and face the wall and let me see your phone really quick." Amy complied. Josh opened up the face app and tapped on a few settings. Amy's red puffy eyes changed back to normal, as if she hadn't been crying at all. "Ok, you're good. Your eyes don't look red and swollen anymore, FYI." Josh handed Amy's phone back to her. "Hope you're feeling better."

Amy looked at Josh with a genuine smile. "I do. Thanks."

"No problem." Josh smiled back. "Now let's keep going."

Amy looked at Rachael and nodded. The two of them took the lead again as Josh followed behind.

As they approached the end of the hallway, Amy looked to the left at a room behind large windows that lined the wall so that you could see everything inside. Inside were several servers, tables, and computers. "There it is." Amy exclaimed as she pointed at the room. They walked over to the door of the room located at the end of the hallway. The door was locked and could only be unlocked by punching in a number on a key pad. Amy typed in a seven-digit code on the key pad and the door unlocked. She opened the door and went in. The other two followed her in as the door shut behind them.

"A seven-digit code for a secure room? Anyone could crack that." Josh commented as he casually looked around for cameras.

"It's more for identification purposes." Amy explained. "Everyone that is granted access is given their own personal code. When they enter, security is notified and validates their video image with an on-file picture."

"So, wait, you didn't just use your code, did you?" Josh asked, a little concerned.

"No." Amy replied. "I used a code that is given to outside guests. Fitting for our cover story."

"Great." Josh said sarcastically. "That just means that the FBI agent heading this operation will not only be notified that there are members of the DOD in his operation, but those members are now here in this room. We need to act quick because we are about to get company."

They moved quickly to the nearest computer. Amy sat down and went to work. Rachael and Josh stood behind her, keeping watch. Moments later, Amy snapped, "I'm in. Josh, do you have the code information from the virus?"

"Yeah." Josh took out his phone and opened up his photo album. He scrolled through the pictures and found a picture that he took of it. He opened it up and gave his phone to Amy.

Amy studied the code. "This might take a couple of minutes." She went to work on the computer.

A minute later, a man in a dark suit walked into view and was heading toward the entrance of the room. Josh rolled his eyes. "Oh, great. This guy."

Rachael rose an eyebrow as she looked at Josh. "You know that guy?"

"Yeah. I've delt with him before in other missions. He can be a big tool. Very territorial. I personally think that he's trying to overcompensate for something. Luckily, he's never seen this face." The man in the dark suit walked up to the door and started knocking. "I'll deal with this guy and buy you some time. Use my camera on my phone to take pictures of any information that you find. The faster you can get this done, the better. Remember, if he asks you anything, it's classified." Josh laughed. "That will piss him off."

Josh walked over to the door and let him in the room, but stopped him near the entrance. The two of them engaged in a conversation. Amy continued to work the computer. Two minutes later she finally reached the file that she was looking for. The code belonged to a recently retired NASA programmer. All his information appeared on the screen. She picked up Josh's phone, opened up the camera, and took a couple pictures of the screen. After putting down the phone, Amy noticed that there was a laptop on a table next to the desktop she was on. She paused in thought for a second, then reached for the laptop. She opened it up. It was already on. She looked in the lower corner and saw what she was hoping for, the icon showing that it had internet connection. The computers in that room were not supposed to have internet connection to avoid any outside hacks.

Rachael looked at her and whispered, "What are you doing?"

Amy ignored Rachael's question and opened up the internet. She typed in a URL which led her to her NASA email account. After logging in, she opened up a new email. She typed in her husband's email name as the receiver and typed in the words in the subject space, "I'm still alive!"

Rachael saw what Amy was doing and squeezed her shoulder to get her attention. Amy looked up to see Rachael mouth the word "No." Amy looked back at the laptop screen and continued to type an explanation as to what has happened to her. Rachael squeezed Amy's shoulder again. Amy looked up at her as she mouthed the words "Trust them."

Time seemed to slow down for Amy. She eyed the laptop, then passed it. Josh's argument grew loud. She looked back down at the laptop at the unfinished explanation. Amy knew that this might be her only shot to communicate with her family. If she didn't send it, she would be relying on an organization that she knew very little about. Her mind became a complex program that she was trying to fix. There were so many conflicting codes that caused her to malfunction. She knew at that moment that the only way to prevent herself from completely breaking, she was going to have to dump some of those codes.

She closed her eyes and took a deep breath. Dragging the mouse icon on the upper right x on the email, she clicked it. A message appeared asking her if she wanted to discard the draft. Her face wrenched in pain as she clicked yes. In her mind, she felt as if she just deleted her husband. She dragged the mouse icon on the upper right x on her email web page and clicked. Her kids were now gone. Tears filled her eyes, making the screen blurry in front of her. On the screen she thought she saw her own reflection staring back at her through her teardrops. As she wiped the tears away, her reflection turned into a face of what used to look like a stranger. She realized that this face was now her new identity. Her own face was now just an illusion. As she came to that realization, the urge for tears disappeared and was replaced with focused anger. Clenching her teeth, she quickly went to work clearing all the history of what she did on the laptop. Once done, she closed the laptop and turned her attention to the desktop, doing the same thing.

As soon as she was done, she aggressively stood up, grabbed Josh's phone, and turned to Rachael, still with clenched teeth. "I'm done. Let's go." She walked quickly over to where Josh and the man were arguing, walked up to the man, got in his face and said with a loud voice, "It's classified!" then stormed out of the room. Rachael turned to the two men, shrugged her shoulders, and followed Amy out the door.

The incident put a huge smile on Josh's face. With that huge smile, he looked at the man. "You heard the lady." Josh walked out of the room leaving the man in the dark suit dumbfounded.

Josh and Rachael power walked to catch up to Amy, who was walking briskly to the elevator. She was already half way there before the two of them caught up to her and got back into formation. Rachael looked over at Amy and just saw a serious stare, focused on her destination. When they reached the elevator doors, Amy pushed the button to call an elevator. The door immediately opened. After they walked in, Rachael pushed the button to go back down to the lobby.

As soon as the elevator doors shut, Josh turned to Amy. "Amy, that was amaz…"

Amy cut him off and shoved his phone against his chest. "Here's your phone back. I took a picture of all the information that the system had on that scum bag."

Josh took the phone, taken aback at Amy's reaction. "Thanks." He put the phone in his pocket and turned back around to face the elevator doors. In a less enthusiastic and more serious voice he said, "Great job Amy. We'll check it out when we get back to the car. Don't worry, we'll get him because of you."

They reached the lobby and casually made their way out of the building and back to their vehicle. Once they got in the vehicle, Josh turned it on to get the air conditioner going, then took out his phone and examined the photo's that Amy took.

"Jack Herbert, retired eighteen months ago, last known address in Houston. Ring any bells?" Josh asked while still studying the photos.

Amy replied with a hardened demeanor, "No, haven't heard of him."

Rachael thought for a second. "A year and a half ago. That was when NASA received major budget cuts because congress questioned the validity of the Artemis program with all the other private companies making greater gains in space exploration. A lot of people from all departments were either laid off or forced into early retirement. He was probably one of those people."

Josh looked back at Rachael. "So, you're thinking revenge as a motive?"

Rachael nodded her head. "Could be."

Amy sat up and spoke with a harsh voice. "Wait a second. How do we know that it was even him that did it? The people that were laid off or forced to retire were not top tier employees. This guy was a programmer, and probably at terrible one at that. There's no way he would be talented enough to create a program as complex as what was injected into the system. Someone could have been using his ID."

Rachael lowered her head in thought as she thought about it again. "Can't you hack into security videos of the building at the time it happened?"

"That's a good idea." Josh picked up his phone and called Teancom. By this time, Josh had already pulled out of the parking lot and was heading down the road.

The phone rang over the car speakers. Teancom answered, "Josh, did you find out anything?"

Josh replied, "The code was allegedly injected into the system by a man named Jake Herbert. He might be holding a grudge from being forced into retirement a year and a half ago."

"So that's our guy?" Teancom's voice sounded over the speakers.

"Maybe." Josh answered. "Although, Amy thinks that this guy wouldn't have been smart enough to create something this complex."

"So, he could have had help. He could be the delivery boy, so to speak." Teancom suggested.

"Could be." Josh replied. "Rachael suggested that we confirm with video footage of NASA's security system. I'll send you a picture of the guy. Just use facial recognition to go over all the video within the past month, and it should find out if he was on the premises or not."

"Sounds good. Send the picture and I'll call you back in a few minutes." Teancom said as the call ended.

"A few minutes?" Rachael looked at Josh with a crinkled face. "That type of search should take a lot longer than that."

Josh smiled. "Not with our computers. With only a months' worth of video footage, it should only take a few seconds, and that's with video enhancement of each frame."

Josh sent Teancom the information. Five minutes later, Josh's phone rang. "Did you find anything?"

"Barely." Teancom answered. "He was in two videos. One was the footage of him walking from his car to the building in the parking lot. The other was of him walking back to his car from the building a short time later. I found that kind of odd that there was no other footage of him inside the building, so I dug in further. I tried to find the video of that time frame and couldn't. There were clips of the videos deleted in each section of the building where he would have been."

"Which means he's our guy and he had help." Amy said with an icy stare.

Teancom replied, "Yes it does. Drive back to where we dropped you off and I'll send another ship to pick you up and take you where he lives. Find out what he knows. Keep me updated. Great job all of you on finding him."

The phone call ended as they drove back to their insertion point. All three of them were anxious to meet Jake.

Chapter 13

Back on the ship, George, Adam, Teancom, and Hannah were hovering two miles above the Taiwan facility. Teancom hung up with Josh as the others completed the facility's scan.

Teancom walked over to the rest of the crew who were sitting at one of the work stations. Hannah finished compiling data and pushed a button that displayed a small holographic projection of the facility above the table. "This is what we know about this place. The facility is located on an open grassland relatively isolated from other communities. Forest surrounds the grassland, which will provide cover for your insertion. On the outward appearance, it looks to be a factory where they make fireworks. We know this because there are several rooms that show signs of explosive material and equipment used to manufacture fireworks. This is more than likely a front, however."

She zoomed into a room located in the middle of the facility. "This room seems to be what they are trying to cover up. We've detected several computers, none of which seems to be connected to any outside network. This wouldn't be an issue if not for five armed guards inside, considering that it's both the middle of the night and the middle of nowhere. The next big indicator of suspicious activity is that in the connecting room, there are lots of paper files, munitions, and a C4 bomb that has an electric detonator. The explosion from the C4 itself would only be big enough to destroy the contents of the room. What makes this bomb devastating is the explosive-laced walls and floors throughout the facility. Detonating that bomb would take out the whole building. The silver lining to the situation is that the only thing that could light the explosive material injected within the facility walls is that bomb. The walls and floor are made of stone. So even if the other fireworks in the building were to go off, it wouldn't trigger the explosive material within the walls and floor."

She expanded the projection to show the whole facility as well as the immediate surrounding area. "The only other people in or around the facility are three-armed guards patrolling the outside and a large room that looks to be sleeping quarters which currently have eight other men inside. They appear to be sleeping."

"Must be the day shift. This place seems to be protected round the clock. Sounds like we need to find out what's on those computers. Looks like we're going in." Teancom concluded.

"Wait, didn't you hear Hannah when she said armed guards and explosions that will take out the whole building?" Adam asked in a very concerned tone.

George gave Adam a hardy pat on the back. "You only live once, or in our case, twice. Besides, you have your magic belt to protect you."

"That's half true." Teancom corrected George. "The belt will keep the bullets away but the explosion will definitely take us out. Don't worry, Hannah can deactivate the C4 detonator from here. Right Hannah?"

"That's right." Hannah replied. "With a flip of a switch it will be de-armed. I'll even rescan the building after I deactivated it just to make sure. You know, to make you feel better Adam."

"That's reassuring." Adam said sarcastically. "So, what. After the guards run out of bullets from firing at us, we reason with them to let us check out the computers? Or are we going to… you know… take them out? Do you do that sort of thing?"

Teancom saw the moral concern on Adams face. "What, kill people? Only if it's absolutely, one hundred percent necessary, with no other choice type situations. In this case, we have rounds that will put them to sleep."

Adam looked at him with a blank face. "Huh. Neat."

George clapped his hands together. "So, what's the game plan? What's our plan of attack?"

Teancom replied, "Well, first step is that we either teleport or jump down half a klick from the facility."

George noticed Teancom's use of the word klick. "Klick? You speak like you served in the military."

Teancom nodded. "We've adapted the best tactics and training from military forces from around the world and incorporated it into our own operations."

Adam spoke up, bringing the conversation back to the options that Teancom laid out. "I think we should teleport. You know, to get down to the facility. I've never been a fan of dangling from a parachute."

Teancom grinned. "Are you sure? You made quite the mess in the bathroom the last time we teleported. There won't be any toilets on the ground and we can't leave any traces of DNA behind. As far as dangling from a parachute, you won't have to worry about that. We don't use parachutes. They can be spotted too easily."

Adam looked at Teancom with a tilted head. "So, what do you use?"

Teancom grinned, gripping his belt. George matched Teancom's smile while nodding his head in excitement. "Yes. That. Let's try out the belts."

Adam's eyes became very wide as his eyebrows shot up. He quickly shook his head. "No, no, no, no. I'm still getting used to the idea that little green men from other planets is just you guys playing dress up. I don't know if I'm to the point where I can trust an object that, in my past experience, is meant to hold up my pants let alone stop me from falling to my death."

Teancom's smirk became a little bigger. "It's perfectly safe. I've done it hundreds of times. You have nothing to worry about."

Adam looked at George, who was nodding enthusiastically in favor of the free fall. Rubbing his head, he stood with his mouth open as he watched George's enthusiasm. He shook it off and gave his attention back to Teancom. "I'm sure you have and I'm sure I don't. Nonetheless, I would much rather teleport down. I know some breathing techniques that I've learned from NASA's training. Besides, I think that my screaming on the way down would give us away."

Teancom let out a hardy laugh. "Alright, we'll teleport down. Just know, if you puke, you're carrying it." Teancom turned to George, who was smiling at Adam's comments, and gave him a pat on his arm. "Maybe next time."

Teancom pulled out his phone and tapped at the screen a few times. He put it back in his pocket and turned his attention to his watch on his arm. He clicked the side button, swiped at the face a couple of times, then tapped the glass. A small hologram of the facility appeared above the watch face. There were three very small guards moving around the extremely detailed projection of the building. Teancom tapped the glass again and the building turned into a blue outline, losing all its details but causing the shape of the building to be more prevalent. The guards turned into red outline figures that stuck out more. "Once we make it to the facility, we will have to take out the three outside guards. Hannah hacked into the security system so the security cameras will not be a problem."

"Wait a second. If Hannah was able to hack the security system, couldn't she just tap into the computers and find out what's on them without us having to do all this?" Adam inquired.

"If only it were that simple." Teancom answered. "Unfortunately, like Hannah mentioned earlier, the majority of those servers are on a closed and extremely secured network. Whoever designed this place knew what they were doing and did not want anyone from the outside to know what's on them." Teancom inserted his closed hand into the hologram and slowly spread out his fingers. As he did that, the hologram zoomed in to expose the layout of the inside of the facility. "Once we're in, we'll head to this room here where the day shift is sleeping." He pointed to a room that had eight red figures laying down. "We'll hit them with sleeper rounds while they are asleep. We'll then make our way over to the secured computer room and take out the remaining guards. From there, we find out what's on the servers, then go over to the next room and find out what's on the paper files. Any questions?"

Adam rose his hand. "And if we find out that, I don't know, let's say China is responsible for blowing our ship up. What then?"

Teancom tapped on his watch and the hologram disappeared. "Well, if China is stupid enough to leave a trail to this lightly secure building located in a place that is hostile to them and store damning evidence on servers instead of erasing all evidence, we will cover it up to prevent the next world war and go after those responsible covertly. More than likely, there is a more complex back story to this mystery. We just need to figure it out before more damage can be done."

"So, what you're saying is that this might be the first step on a long trail." Adam looked down at the floor and closed his eyes. For the first time all the distractions of the organization and the advanced technology that it carried faded from his mind. His thoughts suddenly became focused on his family that currently held the idea that he was killed in space. He looked up at Teancom with a long face. "It might be a while before we actually get to figure things out with our families, whatever that means."

Teancom sensed Adams tone. He knew at that moment Adam could easily break down in despair over the situation. With empathy in his voice, Teancom replied, "I know this must be a tough situation for you and I'm sorry you had to be thrown into it. Understand that you're both here now because of your intimate knowledge of the space program that someone maliciously diverted. Hopefully whatever information we find down there, the next steps after won't have to involve you. We will get you back with your family as soon as possible. I promise."

Adam looked down again for a second, then looked up at Teancom with a slight smile. "Thanks. I believe you.

You know what helped is that drink that you gave me earlier. You have any more?"

Teancom smiled. "Yeah, I think we have some in the room with our gear. Let's get ready and I'll get you some. George, you want a bottle too?

George nodded. "Sure. I'll take some more, thanks."

Teancom walked to the equipment room followed by Adam and George. Although George had come to like Teancom, he still had his suspicion about what was going on. He admired how Teancom controlled Adam's emotions from getting out of hand. However, he saw it as just a tactic to maintain control. He couldn't tell if there was any genuine concern about his family. Because he couldn't tell, he maintained his suspicion of manipulation so that he wouldn't get caught off guard. For his benefit, he hid his suspicions and went along.

Teancom walked over to a cabinet that was next to the covered up BFA and pulled out three metal drinking containers. He handed each of them their own container and kept one for himself. The three of them took the lids off and rose their container simultaneously in the air before they took a drink.

Satisfied with his drink, Teancom wiped his mouth with his sleeve while walking to another cabinet. He put the lid back on the container and placed it on the floor next to the cabinet before opening the doors. Reaching in, he pulled out two sets of pants and shirts. He handed them to George and Adam. "Here, put this on." He turned back to the cabinet and grabbed boots and socks on the bottom shelf to go along with it.

As Teancom was about to hand them their boots, Adam spoke up. "And I suppose that there is an app for these too."

Teancom took Adams comment as another attempt at sarcasm and smiled. "Not this time. No color changing options with these, although they do hold unique and possibly life-saving properties to them."

George unfolded the olive camo-patterned pants and examined them. They looked like ordinary combat pants with pockets down the side and sturdy yet it was also soft to the touch. He examined the long sleeve turtle neck shirt. It felt as if it were made of the same material. The sleeves and neck were the same color pattern as the pants while the main body was a solid olive color. He tried to see what life-saving properties Teancom was talking about but came up short. "What life-saving properties are you talking about? I don't see anything special about them."

Putting their boots on the floor in front of them, Teancom answered, "You should know by now, things are deeper than what they appear to be. Besides being extremely breathable, it is also completely water proof. Not only that, the fabric blends graphene with off-world elements. It is impenetrable to sharp objects such as knives and shrapnel, although you still will get bruised up from the pressure caused by the objects hitting your body."

Adam shook his head as he rose an open hand toward Teancom. "Wait a second, I thought these belts were supposed to protect us."

Teancom replied, "The belts were designed to stop high velocity objects such as bullets and yes, some shrapnel from grenades, but not all. Too many objects at once will overload its capabilities. That's why you now have the clothes. It will protect you from the rest, although I wouldn't go jumping on grenades. The pressure from the blast wave could do a lot of damage to you. The boots and socks are the same, with the souls being extremely slip resistant. Try them on. They are really comfortable."

Adam, while putting on the shirt, sarcastically replied, "Well, as long as they're comfortable." He felt the soft breathable material of his shirt was actually extremely comfortable. "Yeah, actually it is pretty comfortable. Soft."

Teancom tried really hard not to roll his eyes at Adam again. Instead, he quickly turned back to the cabinet and reached up to grab a combat helmet. He flipped the helmet upside down and used it to put in a neck gaiter, tactical gloves, watch, and sun glasses that he grabbed from the cabinet shelves. Turning back around to face George, who was just finishing changing, he handed him the helmet full of equipment.

George examined the objects and noticed that the Helmet, neck gaiter, and gloves were the same color and pattern as the rest of the clothes. The helmet didn't seem out of the ordinary except for side extensions that completely covered the ears. It also came equipped with a chin strap. The neck gaiter seemed slightly thicker than usual, but very soft as well. The gloves were thin on the palms and finger tips but the knuckles were hard, meant to do damage when punching. The watch seemed extremely durable, similar to the one that Teancom had on. The sun glasses looked to be designed to fit snug to someone's face and had a thin strap to help prevent them from falling off.

Handing Adam his helmet full of gear, Teancom explained, "The helmet comes with ear protection which also acts as a comms device. If needed, it can also project a new face for you. The gloves are thin enough for touch screen functionality, with the added protection around the knuckles. Remember, even though you probably forgot, you still have your chameleon gloves on. You might want to take them off before you put these on. Just don't touch anything if you decide to take your new pair of gloves off while we're down there. The neck gaiter is my favorite. Usually, I don't like objects around my mouth and nose because it restricts breathing. This, however is different." Teancom turned to the cabinet and grabbed his own neck gaiter, put it around his neck, and lifted it over his face, covering his ears and nose. "Once you put it on, just push this little sensor on the side with your fingertip and it will not only harden, but will expand around your mouth and nose allowing you to breathe easier while keeping a tight seal around the edges." He put his finger tip on a barely noticeable spot on the neck of the gaiter. The gaiter slightly expanded around the contour of his face, while keeping it tight around the edges. "This will filter mostly all toxic gasses that we might possibly come across. Not only that, the part around the ears will not only amplify sound, but will muffle any loud sound, protecting our hearing." Teancom turned to the cabinet again and grabbed his sunglasses. After he put them on, the strap tightened around the back of his head, securing the glasses to his face. "The glasses have multiple functionalities. They act as fast transition sunglasses, keeping any brightness and glare away while amplifying your sight. They also act as night vision and infrared when needed. It has the capabilities to zoom in and out and take video while also acting as a heads-up display, providing details of objects that you see and directions when needed. All of these things are controlled by your watch, which is connected to your phones."

After giving his brief descriptions of the equipment, Teancom took off the glasses and gaiter and placed them on the shelf of the open cabinet. He turned to the cabinet next to the first and opened it with his hand print. Inside were multiple rifles and pistols as well as many magazines of varying sizes. He pulled out a black rifle with a strap attached to it as well as a magazine and held it up to George and Adam. "This has the exact appearance of an M-4 Carbine military issued rifle. It aims and shoots in all the same ways as any rifle. In reality, it is an electric rail gun. There is no gun powder used, hence, no ballistic traces left. In this magazine is one hundred sleeper rounds. The rounds are basically gel tablets that is encasing the material that will put the target in a deep sleep. When fired, the electric charge from the rail gun will infuse with the gel tablet traveling with the round itself. By the time the round hits the target, the gel itself will have all but dissolved, leaving the sleeper material and electricity infused together. The electricity is actually the delivery system that will travel through the human target and deliver the sleeper material into their system. This not only eliminates any worries of bullet proof material that the target might be wearing, but leaves no evidence of any type of puncture anywhere, making things easier to cover up."

Handing the rifle and magazine to George, Teancom went back to the cabinet and grabbed another rifle and magazine. He walked over to Adam and held the rifle and magazine in front of him. Adam reached out and grabbed the rifle with one hand and the magazine with the other. When he went to pull it in, his action was stopped from Teancom still holding onto the equipment. Teancom stared Adam in the eyes with a serious look on his face. In a very stern and sober voice, Teancom asked Adam, "Have you shot one of these before?"

Adam, feeling somewhat belittled by the gesture replied, "Yeah, I've shot a rifle similar to this. I know the rules. Keep your finger off the trigger unless you are shooting it, never point it at anyone you are not going to shoot, always treat it like its loaded and so on."

Teancom kept staring at Adam. With the same serious tone he continued, "Understand, there is nothing that we have on that will protect us from these weapons. If I were to get hit by one of these rounds from friendly fire, I would be instantly put to sleep. Do you understand?"

Adam looked at the gun, then looked at Teancom with a straight face and a nod. "Yeah, I…I understand."

"I'm glad we have an understanding." Teancom released his grip from the rifle and magazine. As soon as he turned his back to Adam, he smiled. He started to really enjoy messing with Adam, although, in that case, there was a lot of actual concern.

Walking back to the gun cabinet, Teancom grabbed another rifle for himself as well as a tablet that was mounted on the inside wall of the cabinet. He slung the gun strap over his shoulder and used both hands to activate the tablet. With a few gestures, he synced all three rifles to the app on the tablet. He placed his right hand, on the screen and lifted it off after it beeped. He did the same with his left hand. He looked at the other two. "Put each hand on the screen. These weapons are biometrically configured. Once we sync our hand prints to our gloves and gloves to these guns, we will be the only three that will be able to fire them. If someone else tries to use them, a round will go off, putting the would-be user to sleep."

"That could come in handy." George replied as he put each hand on the screen. Adam did the same.

Teancom linked their gloves to the system, then confirmed activation and returned the tablet back where he found it. Grabbing a couple of magazines for himself, he shut the cabinet and made sure it locked. "Alright, gear up." Going back to the first cabinet, he grabbed all of the same items that he gave to George and Adam, as well as a low profile, sturdy backpack, then closed the cabinet. He quickly changed and put on his gloves and glasses. He put his neck gaiter around his neck without pulling it over his face. By this time the other two had all of their gear fully on. Both of them were playing with their watches, trying to figure out the features.

Teancom put his helmet and backpack on the floor. Pulling his phone out of his pocket, he said, "Let me show you how to work those things." He spent a few minutes going over the different functions of the watch and how to control their equipment from it. He also showed them how to interact with the different active functions with hand gestures, such as zooming in and out when in scope mode. After he was somewhat confident on their abilities, he picked up his helmet and backpack. "Alright, let's do it."

George and Adam followed Teancom out of the room and back into the main room of the ship where Hannah was still sitting at the workstation. Teancom walked over to Hannah and opened up his backpack. "Hannah, can you hand me one of those computers."

"Yeah, no problem." Hannah closed the far laptop on the desk, disconnecting it from the charging cord, and gave it to Teancom. "Need anything else?"

"No. Just keep comms open and be ready to do your thing. You know the drill." Teancom slid the laptop into his backpack.

"You got it boss." Hannah commented with a big smile, knowing that using the word boss would get to Teancom. She knew that he always had an issue with authority. Now that he was an authority figure, she took the opportunity to give him a verbal jab.

Teancom froze. With a smirk on his face, he turned to Hannah. "Thanks." He zipped up his pack and looked at George and Adam. "Ready to go?"

George gave Teancom a confirming nod. Adam shrugged his shoulders. "Sure, why not."

Teancom gave Adam a hearty pat on the back. "You'll do fine." He made his way to the other room where the Model X was previously stored. George and Adam followed.

On their way to the door, Hannah shouted, "Good luck, Boss!"

Teancom shook his head in disapproval and replied again as he walked through the door, "Thanks."

The three of them entered the now vacant room where only the platform with the four poles sat. Teancom stepped onto the platform and stood at the center. Adam and George followed. Putting his helmet on the floor, Teancom reached into a smaller pocket in his backpack and pulled out two small bags made from a material that seem to be mixed between cloth and plastic. He gave both Adam and George a bag. "Just in case you decide to lose your breakfast. I wasn't kidding when I said you're carrying it with you."

George shoved it into his pant leg pocket without much thought. Cringing at the thought of having to carry around his vomit, Adam also slid his bag into his pocket. After zipping up his bag again, Teancom slid his arms in the straps. Once on, he grabbed a couple of clips on the inside of each strap and pulled on them. A separate smaller strap came out as he clipped the two together forming a chest strap. He did the same with two clips located on the side, but toward the bottom of the bag and fastened them together around his hips. His pack was now firmly attached to his torso. Pulling his neck gaiter over his nose and ears, he pushed the sensor, solidifying the material. After grabbing his helmet off the floor and strapping it on, he explained, "Once we're down there and clear of the platform, switch on your night vision and HUD with navigation. From there we'll book it to the facility. You good to go?"

George nodded in confidence. Adam, still thinking about having to carry around his puke, said, "As much as I'll ever be."

George looked at Adam and said, "Hey, remember to pull your mouth cover off of your face before you hurl."

Both George and Teancom chuckled. Teancom followed up with, "He's right, you know. Don't forget that you can't take it off until you push the neck sensor. But hey, if you don't take it off in time, I have an extra neck gaiter in my bag for you. The smell does linger however."

Adam shook his head. "Thanks. I'll keep that in mind."

"Hannah, we're good to go." Teancom said out loud, knowing that she was listening.

Hannah's voice rang in their ears from their comms. "Transporting in ten, nine, eight…"

As Hannah continued the count down, Teancom looked at Adam and said, "Hey, close your eyes and don't open them until we are down there. It will help a lot. I'll tug on your arm as soon as it's over."

Adam took Teancom's advice and clenched his eyes shut as he heard Hannah echo the words "three, two, one." A wave of dizziness struck him. He kept his eyes clenched as he took deep breaths behind his mask. Feeling the continual tugs at his arm, he opened his eyes to find that they were in a dark and damp forest. He stumbled off of the platform onto the forest brush. Feeling a warm sensation creep in the pit of his stomach, he pushed several spots on his neck before he found the sensor. The fabric loosened as he pulled the cloth down. His lungs filled with the warm, moist, tropical air as he fought with all his might to keep from puking. After many deep breaths, the sensation started to fade. Gratefulness engulfed him as he overcame the scenario where he had to carry his vomit.

Adam looked around to find that as he was hunched over, Teancom had his hand on his back while George had his puke bag in front of him, ready to catch whatever came out. Adam looked at them and said, "Thanks guys. I'm feeling better. I'll be alright." Gaining his senses back relatively quick, Adam did notice that this jump was not as bad as the previous jumps were. He concluded that he must be getting used to it.

Teancom squeezed Adams shoulder as he straightened his stance. With a quiet voice, Teancom said, "Hannah, the platform is clear." Seconds later, the platform disappeared. Looking at George and Adam, Teancom said, "Gentlemen, turn on your eyes if you haven't already. Adam, you good to go?"

Adam, feeling much better, replied, "Yeah, it didn't last very long, thank goodness. I'm good to go." He tapped and swiped at his watch face a few times to activate his night vision. The damp dark forest suddenly became lit up as if it was the afternoon. He was expecting to see a monochrome green tinge scenery but was shocked to see everything in full crisp colors. He tapped on his watch twice more. The navigation and object recognition systems turned on. There was a faint light blue path with arrows that appeared to point him the way to go. All of the sudden the near-by plant life had digital labels on them, identifying what they were. He looked at George and his name appeared over him. The amount of information that was in front of him was very overwhelming. With a few swipes and a tap on his watch, he turned off the object recognition system. The labels disappeared but the artificial path remained, showing him the right direction.

Teancom and George already started to make their way down the artificial blue path as Adam finished adjusting his settings. He pulled his neck gator back over his face, pushed the small sensor to harden it, then began to follow behind. As he walked, he noticed that there were numbers right above the path that reduced as he walked forward. It was the distance that he had left to go before he reached his destination. His mind started to wonder how these ordinary looking glasses could fit so much tech into it. There was so much technology that he wanted to tear apart. As his mind was dissecting the engineering behind it, he tripped on a root sticking up, causing him to stumble. Fortunately for him, he caught himself before he fell on his face. Luckily, the other two didn't notice. They were, however, started to make some distance from him. He became more focused at the task at hand, slightly jogging to catch up with the others.

The three of them moved quickly but cautiously through the damp tropical evergreen forest. Drips of water bounced off of their waterproof clothes as they fell from the canopy above. Occasional deer ran off as they came close to their vicinity. As they neared their destination, the faint blue path veered to the left. They followed it. It took them down a steep rocky hill. George was amazed on how much grip his boots gave him on the wet mossy rocks they were stepping on. When they got to the bottom of the hill, they turned to their right to see a large rectangular building made of stone at the end of a spacious grassy field. Outlining the back side of the building was the bottom of a massive cliff that stood at least five hundred feet tall. There was a single road paved with loose gravel that went from the facility, through the large open field, and then into a large partially man-made opening in the forest.

Squatting down and in a whisper, Teancom turns to George and Adam. "Turn your thermal Imaging on." Raising their wrists, they tapped on their watches. Two distinct figures highlighted in red appeared. One to the left and the other to the right of the building.

Hannah's voice came over their comms devices. "Sending you the ships thermal readings of the third guard now." The third guard appeared in red standing behind the building. He was sitting on a tree stump, and appeared to be smoking a cigarette. Hannah spoke again. "Scanning building for explosives. Stand by." Thirty seconds passed. "Same results as before. One main centralized explosive. Cloning signal data output of trigger… replicating signal… signal replicated. Shutting down trigger. Scanning to confirm all explosives neutralized." Another thirty seconds' pass. "All explosives neutralized. Tapping into security and looping video feed now. You are clear to advance."

Adam's heart started to beat faster at the go ahead to advance. He saw Teancom give hand signals to George, but could only guess what they meant. All he could do was stay low and wait for them to make a move so he could follow.

George was given instructions from Teancom to take out the guard on the right. He remembered that Teancom showed them a zoom function on his glasses before they were sent down. He swiped at his watch face and tapped on scope mode. Raising his rifle, he put it up to his shoulder and looked down the sights toward the target. He held it in place with his right hand. With his left hand he made a fist and brought it close to his left eye. As he slowly pulled his fist away from his face, his view zoomed in to where he was looking. Once he fully extended his arm, he opened up his hand and brought it back close to his face. Repeating the action of clenching his fist and extending it, the view of his target got bigger and bigger. He did it one more time to get a perfect up-close view of his target. Even though he was zoomed in, there was still incredible detail that he could make out. He brought his left hand back on the rifle to steady it. The cross hairs were sitting right on the guard's chest.

Careful not to move, George whispered, "Ready two."

Teancom had his rifle aimed at his target. "Ready one. Execute in three, two, one."

Both Teancom and George fired at the same time. There was virtually no sound or recoil that came from the guns. The only way they could tell that it fired was from both their targets falling to the ground. They taped their watch faces again to turn off the zoom function.

Teancom whispered, "Both targets down. Clear them out."

Hannah replied, "Copy that. Clearing them now."

The limp bodies rose, vanishing into the sky. Adam's jaw dropped as he watched the two bodies fly away. His shock lasted all but two seconds before he shook it off and realized that this was one of the hundreds of unusual things he saw today.

"Let's move before our third friend notices that his companions are missing." Teancom whispered as he got up from his prone position. He started jogging, rifle in hand, toward the right side of the building. George was right behind him.

Adam took a deep breath and said under his breath, "Here we go." He got up and started jogging through the wet grassy field as well.

They got to the side of the building and stopped at the corner of the back side. The guard was still sitting on the stump lighting another cigarette. Teancom made some more hand signals. George nodded to confirm while Adam looked at him with a puzzled look. Before Adam could ask, Teancom was on the move, rifle ready to fire while George followed right behind him with his rifle at the ready as well. Before Adam could follow behind, Teancom took a shot and the third guard fell over.

"Target three down. Get him out of here." Teancom whispered.

"Copy boss." Hannah replied.

Teancom winced at the name boss that Hannah purposely kept using. "I really wish you would stop calling me boss."

Hannah laughed. "Would you rather me call you Chief?"

Teancom smiled. "You know that's Marks title. Let's just get back to the task at hand."

"Copy that. Extracting third target my leader." Hannah replied.

Teancom shook his head in disapproval as the third guards body lifted up into the air and disappeared into the sky. "Ok, what's the layout?"

Hannah's voice echoed in their ears. "No changes. Five guards in the computer room and eight lying in bed. Sending you directions to each now." Two different paths appeared in different colors. One blue with the word "Quarters" on it while the other was purple labeled "Computers".

Teancom looked at George and Adam. "Alright, let's go." As they made their way to the front entrance, Teancom explained, "We'll first hit the guards that are sleeping. Then we'll clear the computer room."

They approached the front door. Before they could reach the door knob, Hannah announced, "Front door unlocked. You are clear to enter."

The three of them entered the facility. It was pretty plain inside. It had a medieval castle feel to it with the stone walls and floor. There was a medium sized desk for a receptionist and two hallways that extended to the left and right. The paths separated at this point. The "Quarters" path went to the left while the "Computers" path went to the right. Teancom led the group to the left. After making their way down a series of different hallways, they neared the room. Before they turned the corner to the entrance of the sleeping quarters, the door opened. Teancom stopped and pushed the other two back. He peaked around the corner and saw a guard stumble through the door. The guard continued down the hallway toward another room. Teancom assessed that it was probably the bathroom. After the guard went into the bathroom, Teancom turned George and whispered, "I'll take Adam and hit the guards in the barracks. You think you can take out the guy in the bathroom?"

George, with confidence, replied, "No problem."

After nodding with approval, Teancom took Adam and disappeared into the sleeping quarters while George went down the hallway toward the bathroom entrance. At the door, he paused and listened. There was no sound. He gripped his rifle a little tighter with his right hand, while carefully placing his left hand on the door handle. With a quick and fluid motion, he opened the door and turned the corner, ready to fire at the guard that he thought was relieving himself. Instead, to his surprise, the guard was waiting for him as he entered. The guard grabbed George's rifle, wrestling his arm. He spun around and hurled George over his shoulder attempting to disarm him at the same time. Unfortunately for the guard, George held tight, causing the guard to tumble on top of George as he landed on his back.

George quickly pushed the butt of the gun against the guard to knock him off. The guard, however, still had a firm grip on the barrel of the rifle with one hand, keeping it aimed away from him. With his other hand he pulled a knife out from a side leg sheath. With a quick motion, the guard swiped the blade hard against George's abdomen. The blade sliced the strap of the rifle, cutting it lose from around George. Fortunately for George, the blade did not penetrate his clothing, but he definitely felt the pressure from the swipe.

George gripped the rifle harder, positioned his legs, then twisted the rifle to attempt to get the guard off of him. The attempt did not work. Instead, the two of them rolled to the side. The guard took the knife and jabbed it as hard as he could into one of George's forearms, which was now against the floor. Again, the blade did not penetrate his sleeve, but the immense pressure from the knife caused George to lose his grip from the rifle with that hand. The guard was now in position where he rammed his knee into George's crotch, causing George to lose the grip of the rifle with his other hand. The guard now had full possession of the rifle.

As George attempted to get up, he was met with the butt of his own rifle against his face. Luckily the blow was greatly reduced by his protective gear, but it still did cause George to become dazed and fall back onto his back. In his ear, George could hear Hannah's voice. He couldn't make out what she was saying, but he could tell she was frantic. He looked up from his daze to see the guard standing over him with is rifle pointing straight at his face. The guard said something that George couldn't understand. He pulled the trigger. Instead of the round shooting through the barrel of the gun towards George, it went off in the chamber, causing the electrical charge to travel to the guard's trigger hand and into his body. The guard collapsed and fell on top of George.

Just then, Teancom and Adam came charging into the room. Noticing the guard lying unconscious on top of George, Adam paused and quickly rose his eyebrows. "Well, this is awkward. Should we give you two a minute?"

George looked up at Adam, shook his head, then pushed the guard off of him. He was somewhat embarrassed, but definitely appreciated the nature of Adam's comment.

Teancom reached over to help Adam up. "Are you ok?

While George got up, he replied, "A few bruises, mainly my pride. I know I'm rusty from my tour with NASA, but these guys aren't just off the street rent-a-cops. This guy noticed us in the hallway, yet had the discipline to wait for me to come to him. Not only that, he knew how to fight effectively and carried a knife with him to the bathroom. They are ready at all times and well trained. At least this guy is."

Teancom lowered his head in thought. "Control, I need you to scan those three guards you have up there with you. Find out who they are."

Hannah answered, "Copy that. I'll go scan them now, then run it through the database. It might take a few minutes."

"How'd your end go?" George asked Teancom while rubbing his abdomen.

Teancom replied, "The day shift is knocked out even more than before. Let's get this guy back in his bed with the rest of his crew."

George nodded in agreement, then picked up his rifle off the floor. He tied a knot where his strap was cut, then extended the strap to compensate. After he threw his rifle back around his torso, he helped Teancom and Adam carry the knocked-out guard back to his bed.

Once the guard was dumped, the three regripped their rifles and proceeded to follow the purple path toward the computer room. Several hallways later they arrived to the outside of the room. The door was closed. The room was silent from the outside. Teancom moved in front, George right behind, and Adam in the rear. Teancom again gave some hand signals. George squeezed his shoulder. Adam, once again, had no idea what was going on.

Adam walked up on the side of them, threw his hands up in the air, and whispered, "I have no idea what you are saying."

Both Teancom and George rolled their eyes. Teancom rose a finger up to his lips, then pulled out his phone and held it up. Adam to pulled his out. After Typing a message on his phone, Teancom hit send and the message appeared on Adams phone. It read "We are going to breach the room. I will go in and position myself on the wall with the door. George will position himself on the opposite wall. You will follow me and position yourself on the same wall as me. You will fire on the guards as soon as you walk in. Do not shoot George or myself!" After reading the explanation, Adam gave Teancom a thumbs up and took his position back behind George.

Once again Teancom and George were ready to enter the room, rifles in hand. Adam awkwardly stood third in the line, trying to mimic the other two as best as he could. A flood of emotions swept through him. He knew that Teancom told him that the belt he was wearing would protect him, yet the image of George on his back on the bathroom floor left him with some doubt. What if Teancom was lying? What if he wasn't lying but there was a glitch in the equipment? What if he tripped and the guards start beating him? He physically shook his head to try to get the thoughts clear from his mind. Gripping his rifle, he prepared himself.

Teancom opened the door and disappeared around the corner. George followed right behind. Adam clenched his jaw and charged in. As soon as he took a step in, he was met with a bullet straight to his head. He saw it spinning right in front of his eyes. At first, he thought that his mind was playing out the final moments of his life in slow motion, but then the bullet dropped to the floor. Two more bullets made his way toward his abdomen before they stopped, then dropped. A surge of confidence mixed with adrenaline built up within. Teancom and George flanked the walls, firing. Adam took aim at one of the guards, glowing red in his sights. Before he could pull the trigger, the guard fell to the floor. He looked for another target, but they were all knocked out. The room was cleared. Before he could lower his rifle, Teancom had a hand on his gun, lowering it for him. Adam gave a big sigh of relief.

"All targets down." Teancom exclaimed.

Hannah replied, "Confirmed. You have the building. Great job!"

The three of them surveyed the room. It was a large rectangular room. There were several desks, each having a desktop computer. On the far wall were several smaller PC units, acting as their local server. What was odd was that they were individually encased in very thick cement boxes, with a thick clear plastic door in the front for access. On the side wall was multiple screens showing video of different rooms within the facility as well as a few shots of the outside. Because of Hannah's hack, the outside video showed the guards still standing at their post.

Teancom sat down to one of the desks and went to work on the computer. "Let's see what this place is all about."

He looked at the screen. They were in another language. With a swipe and a tap of his watch, the words were interpreted through his glasses. He went through several folders. As he was searching, he found a folder labeled "Space". He opened it. There were several sub folders. One was labeled "Facilities." He opened it. There were several pdf files. One was labeled "Houston." Another was labeled "Kennedy Space Center" as well as several more NASA facilities. He opened the Kennedy Space Center file. It was detailed blueprints of the facility.

"I think we found what we were looking for." Teancom announced. He went back to the subfolders to find files of NASA employees, protocols, rocket details, China owned bank accounts. He even found a file that had the virus that was downloaded into the system.

Both George and Adam were standing behind Teancom as he revealed all the data. They couldn't believe what they were looking at. George, in disbelief said, "Everything's here. All the info. Contacts, bank accounts, their whole plan laid out."

Just then, Hannah's voice sounded in their comms. "I got the results from the guard's identities. It seems that all three men are in the Chinese Army. It shows on file that they are all assigned to a classified assignment. Digging further into the heavily classified databanks indicate these men are deserters. My guess is that China doesn't want the image of disloyal army members so they probably put them on a classified assignment on record to keep up appearance. Weird."

Adam's face turned red as he slammed his fist on the desk. "Those sick psychos! They planned it all! They planned our murder right here! Then they kept it like some sort of trophy. I bet those paper files have all the details too." Adam made his way to the attached room where there were supposedly paper files.

Teancom looked puzzled. He couldn't figure out why there was so much information all in one location. It was almost too easy. As he thought, he glanced at George. He froze. His mind went back to the conversation that he had with George when they were in the golf cart together. About how George told him that he was too trusting of the people in the organization. His mind processed the information on the computer, the servers in cement boxes, the Chinese deserters. A chill ran up his spine as suspicion struck. He looked over at Adam who was almost to the door. He quickly stood up and yelled out, "Adam. Hold on. Come check this out. I need you to check out these blueprints."

Adam stopped his progress toward the side room and turned around to see Teancom frantically waving him back over to the computer. He turned back around. When he got to the computer, Teancom put his finger on his lips. Pulling out his phone, Teancom turned off his glasses and comms link. He motioned to the others to do the same. They did. He stripped off his glasses, neck gaiter and helmet, then dialed a number on his phone.

A couple of rings later, Hannah answered on the other end, "The fact that you're calling me on this secured line can't be good."

Teancom replied, "Please tell me you froze our comms line."

"As soon as I heard this line ring, yes. I did. What's going on?" Hannah asked.

"Things aren't adding up like they should. I need your help in playing out a hunch. I need you to rescan this building for any explosive devices or material." Teancom said in a serious tone.

Hannah replied, "I just did that after…"

Teancom interrupted, "Just do it. Humor me. Please. After all, I am your boss."

Hannah let out a quick laugh. "All right boss. Scanning now."

George pointed toward the knocked-out guards. "I'm going to search these guards while you do, whatever you're doing."

Teancom nodded. "Good idea. I'll help." He put the phone on speaker and placed it on the table. They both searched the guards while Adam sat down at the computer desk confused.

A few seconds later Hannah's voice came over the phone. "You won't believe this, or then again, maybe you will. Sensors picked up a chemical bomb on the other side of that door big enough to set off the C4."

Adam's jaw dropped. "What!? Another bomb!? I thought you said the building was clear! You even bragged about scanning the building again for my comfort!"

"It was clear." Teancom commented. "Hannah, can you tell what the trigger is yet?"

Hannah replied, "There is no sign of electrical trigger. Doing a deep scan of the room now. Hold on." A few seconds of silence passed. "Just finished. It looks like there is a switch that gets thrown as soon as you open the door. That switch sets off what appears to be an electric sparker."

"Can you deactivate it?" George inquired as he stared at the phone.

Teancom asked, "Can you use the laser to detach the switch?"

After a few seconds Hannah replied, "Yeah… yes. That should do the trick. Firing the laser in three, two, one." There was a small sizzle sound from the other side of the door. "Alright. It should be detached now. You are good to enter."

Teancom grabbed his phone and took it off speaker. "Thanks Hannah. I'll call you back after I check it out." He hung up the phone and stuck it back in his pocket. He jogged over to the door and carefully opened it. On the floor he saw the burnt-up switch that would have flipped as soon as the door was cracked. An attached wire led up the wall over the ceiling and down to the sparker. The sparker was positioned inside a very large container of liquid. On the side of the container was a tube that led up to a now empty smaller container. An opened trap door sat at the bottom of the container that would have held the liquids from mixing together when closed. Attached to the trap door was a device that was linked to a timer.

Teancom turned around and called out, "Adam. Can you tell me what this is?" Teancom pointed to the device.

Adam walked into the room to see Teancom pointing to the device. He studied it for a moment. Lowering his head, he scratched his chin. The corner of his eye spotted the C4. Turning his head, he walked closer to it to examine it. "Earlier when Hannah said that she was cloning the signal, was she talking about the signal from the physical trigger to the remote trigger?"

Teancom answered, "Yes."

"And my guess is that she duplicated that signal from the ship to make it appear that the physical trigger was still intact, correct?" Adam hypothesized.

"Yeah, what are you getting at?" Teancom asked.

Adam pointed to the device in question. "This device is a direct line of sight receiver. In other words, if the signal is not coming from that physical trigger from that direction, it will sense it. When the physical trigger was deactivated, it set off the timer. Once the countdown of the timer ended, it opened the trap door, letting the two liquids combine. It's like a fail-safe for the bomb. What I don't get is why even bother with a timer?"

George looked at Teancom. "Because whoever set this up knew your organizations protocols."

Teancom nodded in agreement. "That's my thoughts. It's protocol to scan the building again after neutralizing a threat. Earlier when Hannah deactivated the trigger to the C4, she rescanned the building to make sure that the bomb was truly neutralized, following standard protocol. That receiver activated the timer which delayed the two liquids from mixing long enough for that second scan to show as clear. Eventually the timer ran out, releasing the liquid from the top into the liquid at the bottom, creating a separate liquid explosive. Whoever set this up knew the protocol. This was an inside job."

Adam took a step back in shock. "Wait a second. You telling me that the very people that you have been trying to convince us to trust is the ones behind this whole thing!?"

Teancom continued to explain, "Think about it. Why would they encase servers in thick concrete boxes unless they wanted to protect them from a large blast? Why would they store this much information in one place? Wouldn't they delete this stuff once the job was done? Why would they store paper files in a room right next to the electronic files?" Teancom walked over to the files and looked through them to find that they were all blank sheets of paper. He held the blank sheets up.

George answered, "Bait. Something to give us reason to go in here."

Teancom threw the blank sheets to the floor and continued, "Why would they recruit deserters from the

Chinese army, knowing that the Chinese records would show them on a classified mission? They wanted to frame China. They knew that the Taiwan government would investigate an explosion and find Chinese guards lying outside, knocked out from the blast. They would find all the incriminating evidence on the protected hard drives and immediately give it to the U.S. government."

Adam shook his head in disbelief. "Why would someone do that?"

George explained, "Because they wanted to start the next world war."

Teancom pointed his index finger at George. "That's right! Things are so heated right now that the U.S. wouldn't question why they didn't delete the information. When they go to question China about their men, there's no way they would admit that they were covering up all their deserters. Even if they did tell them, the U.S. wouldn't believe them. Too many politicians in Washington have been biting at the bit for war in the name of defending democracy. Instead of deescalating with truthful explanation, they would stay silent and build up their defenses. From there it would be just a matter of time before the U.S. justified retaliation, and that would be it. Countries would join their allies in an all-out war."

Adam's brow furrowed as he shrugged his shoulders, now even more confused than before. "But why would anyone want to start a world war?"

Teancom shook his head. "I don't know. Let's find the dirtbags who did this and ask them." He pulled out his phone and dialed Hannah. "Hannah, this was an inside job. Be on standby while I call Mark." Before Hannah could answer, Teancom hung up and dialed Mark.

Mark answered, "It's never good when you call me from this line. What's up?"

Teancom replied, "Fox in the hen house. We were being set up." Teancom explained to Mark the events that occurred and what they found. He also explained what the other team found out.

Mark was sitting at his desk in his office, digesting all the information. He was disgusted. Controlling his anger as best as he could, he soberly replied, "This is terrible news." He rubbed his head for a second in thought, then continued, "We need to be smart about this. We need to not only expose whoever did this, but catch them before they fly the coop. I'm going to send Alice, who's stationed in another base right now, to pick you up secretly in a different ship. Load all the computers, guards, and whatever else is relevant as quick as you can. Once your clear, trigger the explosions. Keep up the appearance that their plan worked, which means Hannah needs to follow protocol and call in a search and cover team once the explosion happens. She needs to act frantic and in shock, you know, like she cared about you or something. Fill Josh in on all of this. Hopefully they can extract useful information from this NASA guy before you set off the explosion and we can find our snakes. If he identifies our targets, we'll know who to watch. If they don't, we'll have to do this the hard way and lock all facilities down and bring everyone in for deep interrogation. Hopefully that will trigger a response. If not, it will set operations back for a long time. The only people that will know about this will be Alice, Jay, and myself. Jay will be our control. Reach out to him for help if needed. Teancom, be careful. Keep your team safe."

Teancom quickly processed the plan. He said in confidence, "You know I will." They both hung up at the same time. Teancom immediately called Hannah and put her on speaker. After explaining the situation and the plan to the group, Teancom asked, "We will be the only ones that know about what's going on. I want to get back to the base quickly just in case Mark needs support if the culprits get exposed. You think you can handle a few more longer distance jumps?"

George replied, "I'm sure I'll be fine. I can't speak for Mr. Green over here."

Adam bowed his head down with his eyes closed and took a deep breath. After opening his eyes, he said, "Look, if it helps catching whoever it is that put us in this situation, let's to it. Just point me to the bathroom."

Teancom cracked a smile while gripping Adams shoulder in appreciation. "Why don't you two start moving these computers and guards down toward the entrance." He took his backpack off and swung it around. Opening one of the pockets, he pulled out a small pouch and handed them to Adam. "Here, these will help.

Adam opened the bag to find several small flat disks. "What are these?"

While zipping up his bag, Teancom replied, "Those are hover disks. Put them on the bottom of something and they will hover off the floor. It will make it easier and faster to move this stuff."

Adam and George went to work, each grabbing a table, putting the disks on the top, then flipping them upside down to make a push cart. While they went to work, Teancom dialed Josh.

Chapter 14

As the Taiwan crew tackled their mission, a ship picked up and whisked Josh, Rachael, and Amy to Texas where their suspect lived. Shortly after the ship dropped the team and their car off, Josh's phone rang through the car speakers.

Josh glanced at the caller ID: Teancom's secure line. Josh rubbed his face with his hand before he pushed the button to answer the phone. "I love it when you call me on this line. What's going on?"

Teancom's voice rang over the car speaker. "Fox in the hen house." Teancom proceeded to explain the situation to the group. After a few minutes of explaining, Teancom added, "Things will go a lot better if you can get names from this guy that you're about to visit before we blow up the building. I am going to delay the explosion as long as I can. Just know, the longer I wait, the more suspicious it will be. Did you get a confirmation on this guy's location?"

Josh answered, "Yeah, we got satellite confirmation that he's at his home. We're only a few minutes away."

"Good." Teancom replied. "Make him squeal. Let me know what you get."

"I'll keep in touch." Josh said right before the line disconnected.

Rachael and Amy were listening to the conversation intensely. Rachael stared at the back of the seat, mind racing. Amy, however, started grinding her teeth as she listened.

Amy slammed her fists on the seat. "It was people from your organization that did this!?"

Josh looked at the rear-view mirror to see Amy lit up in anger. He knew he had to say something to deescalate the situation. "Yes. It was. Keep in mind, just because one crooked cop does something horrible, it doesn't mean that the whole police organization is bad. Quite the opposite. These people did everything that this organization is against and tries to stop on a daily basis. What they did to you is inexcusable. Now we have the opportunity to expose them and make them pay for what they did."

Rachael looked over at Josh with inquiring eyes. His explanation could just be another cover to hide the actual truth. She didn't know whether to fully trust the organization yet, but Josh had definitely helped throughout the mission. She felt as if she could trust him. She also knew that Josh's comments were meant for Amy. Rachael knew that Amy needed to calm down, so she went along with it. "What's our plan to get this Jack guy to talk? It doesn't seem like we have a lot of time."

"Let me do the interrogating. Make sure he doesn't try to run. Also, try to look intimidating." Josh replied. Seeing that Amy's looks of anger were no more directed at him, but rather on the target, Josh added, "Yes, Amy. Just like that. That look will do."

Amy caught his humor and almost cracked a smile. It was quickly subdued however by her anger.

They pulled up to a small single-story home with a small front yard. Patchy yellow grass choked the yard. The front door was open. In the driveway was an older Prius that had the trunk and driver side door open. In the trunk was a large duffle bag. Josh studied the scene and knew what it meant. Jack was about to flee. Reaching in his suit pocket, Josh pulled out some thin, black gloves and put them on. He opened the center console and pulled out a utility tool. Josh walked over to the Prius and looked inside at the driver's seat to see if this guy was stupid enough to leave the keys inside. He didn't. He popped the hood, lifted it. After disconnecting the car's battery with his utility tool, he carefully closed the hood to avoid too much noise. Pocketing the tool, he carefully closed the trunk and the front door of the car and walked over to the open door of the house. Cautiously stepping inside, the two girls followed right behind.

To the right from the entrance was a living room with a large TV mounted on the wall, a leather couch, a leather recliner, and a small table in the center. Straight ahead was the dining room that housed a decent sized wooden dining table with six chairs surrounding it. Right behind it was a sliding glass door that led to the back yard. The glass door was half covered by wooden blinds. Looking through the glass, the back yard was small and just as poorly maintained as the front. To the left of the entrance was a wall with a door on it. Josh peeked in. Just a closet with a vacuum and some coats. Taking a few steps in, he turned to Rachael and motioned with his hand to close the door and lock it. Rachael obeyed. They walked into the dining room around the wall to find a hallway that led to a bedroom. The door was opened to reveal an open half-packed suitcase sitting on a neatly made bed.

As the three of them carefully advanced, a heavier set man appeared in view, frantically dumping more neatly folded clothes into the suitcase. With his body facing the suitcase, he froze. His ears seemed to perk up like a dog that just heard a disturbing sound in the distance. Slowly turning around, the heavier set man's eyes met Josh's eyes. He bolted at them, stumbling, outstretched, and breathless. Josh made a claw with his left hand and gripped the man's shoulder right before they collided. The man froze as if he were hit by a bolt of electricity. With his right hand, Josh reached over and swung one of the dining rooms chairs around. He pushed the man onto the chair. The man looked terrified. Attempting to get up, he was met with the claw and immediately fell back down.

"Hurts, doesn't it." Josh commented. "Trying to escape will just bring more of it."

The man's eyes were frantically looking at each of them. He was in a state of complete panic. With a very shaky voice he said, "Who are you? What do you want from me? Why are you here?"

Josh locked eyes with Jack, probing for truth. "You know why, Jack Herbert."

Jack panicked. He attempted to get up but was met with a jolt of pain once again. Frantically, he blurted out, "I didn't know. It wasn't my fault. I had no idea. Please, I didn't know."

Still staring into his soul, Josh replied, "Jack, you can save yourself a lot of pain if you cooperate and start laying out the details of your contact."

Still frantic, Jack exclaimed, "Look, I was desperate. NASA screwed me. Forced me to retire. All my plans were wiped out. I needed the money. He said that…" He paused for a second. Looking down, his eyes went wide as he shook his head. "I can't. He said he'd find me if I talked. I can't, I can't, I can't." Jack started crying.

Amy snapped, rage boiling over. His words confirmed that he was the one responsible for taking her away from her family. She exploded. Pushing Josh aside, she grabbed a book sitting on the table and bashed it into his skull. Both the book and Jack came crashing down on the floor. Amy didn't stop there. Yelling out, "Don't tell me you can't!", she jumped on Jack's stomach with her knee and rained frantic fists wherever they'd hit.

Jack desperately tried to block Amy's angry attacks. He reached out and was able to get a firm grasp of her wig, which he thought was her hair. He yanked it off as he pulled in his hands to block his face from getting hit. Josh and Rachael grabbed her and pulled her up as she continued to swing and kick at the now thoroughly beaten man. Amy was now at her feet, looking down at her target.

Jack looked up at Amy and saw who she really was. His bloodied face became distorted as his eyebrows rose. "What the hell?"

She looked down at Jack and noticed that he made a terrible mistake. He was lying on the floor with his legs wide open. When Josh and Rachael loosened their grips from her, she broke free and kicked the man right in the crotch. As Jack winced in terrible pain, Amy spat on him and turned away. Looking forward, her vision became blurred from rage. As she calmed down, her vision came into focus. She noticed that she was staring at the sliding glass door. The reflection from the glass revealed to her that she was no longer wearing her disguise. She had her true face on. Staring at her reflection, she reflected on herself and what she had become. Her mind went back to the things she told to her kids. When protestors from her husband's business would vandalize their property, she'd tell her kids violence wasn't the answer. She had turned into her own bad example. Tears started building up in her eyes. She made her way to the living room where she covered her wet face with her hands. Rachael immediately started to follow.

Before Rachael could get to Amy, Josh called out, "Wait!" He reached down next to the balled-up man, still crying in pain, and grabbed Amy's wig off of the floor. He turned to Rachael and threw it to her. Rachael made her way over to Amy and wrapped her arms around her to comfort her.

Josh took a deep breath and turned his attention back on the man lying on the floor. Jack, still in terrible pain squeaked out, "How is that possible? She died in space. How is that possible?"

Josh thought quick. He knew that this guy's memory of this was going to be wiped and he didn't deserve an explanation. He also knew that he still needed to get information out of him. Reluctantly, he explained, "It's her twin sister. As you can tell, she's pissed at what you did to their family."

Jack asked, "How did she change faces like that?"

Annoyed with the man, Josh rose the tone of his voice. "You've seen just a glimpse at what we are capable of doing. It would benefit you to start answering my questions, unless you want another round with the pissed off sister."

Jack raised his hands, bracing for another blow. "Ok, ok. I'll talk."

Josh picked the tipped over chair up and helped Jack back on it. He bent his knees and looked directly into his eyes again. "How did you get involved in this?"

Still catching his breath, Jack answered, "It was a few months ago. I just finished a double shift as a janitor when a man with a suit and a brimmed hat approached me on my driveway. He asked me if I wanted to truly retire in luxury. I was nearly broke so I said yes. He gave me a memory stick and said that all I had to do was insert this code into the system right before the launch and I would be given ten million dollars in an off shore account."

Josh lowered his eyebrows. "Did you look what was on it?"

Jack frantically shook his head. "No, he told me that it was better if I didn't look at the contents or tell anyone about it, or I would pay the consequence."

Annoyed, Josh stood up and yelled, "So you injected unknown code into the system, not knowing what it would do."

Frantic again, Jack answered, "I was desperate. My life was a joke. I was actually thinking of killing myself."

Josh took a deep breath and lowered his tone. "Was that the only time you had contact with him?"

"No." Jack explained. "He called me on an unknown number just a little bit ago telling me to leave town."

Josh leaned back into him. "How long is a little bit ago?"

Jack closed his eyes in fear. "I don't know, like an hour ago."

Josh grabbed the back of the chair. "What else did he say?"

Turning his head away from Josh, Jack answered with a shaky voice. "Nothing! It was really quick and to the point. He hung up before I could say anything."

Josh stood up straight again. "When exactly did you meet this person?"

Jack looked down and closed his eyes tightly, trying to remember. "It was the last day in February, around eight at night."

Josh pulled out his phone and dialed a number. Jay answered on the other line, "Control. What do you need?"

Josh turned away from Jack. "I need you to do a search. Tell me who was off base on the last day of February near this location."

"Give me a second." Jay replied.

As he was waiting, Josh looked back at Jack to make sure he wasn't trying to escape. Jack was breathing heavily, frozen on the chair in fear.

Jay's voice answered, "No one was even in that state on that day. There were only five people in the country during that time, all five on vacation."

Looking up at the ceiling, Josh thought for a second. "Track the movement of those five and see if you see any out of the ordinary movement."

After a few seconds, Jay replied, "Everyone was in their general location moving as if they were visiting the sights except for one guy, Eric Calvin. It shows him in his hotel room for two days straight during that date. Records show that he claimed to be sick."

Josh played out the scenario. "Let's say it was him. He would have had to somehow figure out a way to either remove his tracker or would had to make it seem like he was somewhere else. That has never been attempted before. It's a pretty big accusation. How do I prove that it was him?" Looking around in thought, Josh glanced over at Amy, now holding her wig in her hand. He all of the sudden remembered how she typed in the seven-digit code to get into the server room. He remembered her explaining how everyone had a unique code so they knew who entered the room. The holographic masks worked the same way. Everyone had their own unique faces. "Send me pictures of the faces he had linked to him at that time. I think we can link him."

Jay replied, "Smart. Sending them now. Let me know."

"Thanks." Josh ended the call. Immediately after he hung up, the pictures of the faces appeared on his phone. He turned back to face Jack, still in pain and fear. He snapped his fingers in front of Jack's face to get his attention. "Jack! Look at me! I need you to focus for a second." Jack shook his head and looked at Josh. Josh showed Jack his phone with a picture of one of the faces. "I need you to tell me if one of these faces was the man that talked to you. This is the only way you will get out of this in one piece. Do you understand me?"

Jack nodded his head slowly and looked at the picture. He shook his head no. Josh moved on to the next picture with the same results. At the sixth picture Jack's eyes widened as he looked at it. "That's him. That's the guy."

Josh looked at the picture. "Thanks for your cooperation, Jack." He sent the specific picture back to Jay, then called him again.

Jay answered, "Got the picture. Is that confirmation?"

Josh replied, "It's him. Spread the word."

After hanging up, Josh turned to the two girls. "We got him, let's go."

At this point, Amy had calmed down and had her wig and face back on. Rachael looked over at Jack, who was again attempting to get back up. She pointed to him. "Ah, ah, ah."

Josh turned around and caught the man by the shoulder with his claw grip just as he was attempting to get up. "I thought you learned your lesson. You do have the right idea however. Get up. You're coming with us."

Jack's gaze bulged. "Where are you taking me!"

Josh yanked on Jack's arm. "No more questions. Continue to cooperate and you won't need to worry."

Jack grudgingly got up as Josh continued to pull his arm. Josh led him out the front door. The two girls followed right behind. As they were walking to the Model X, the man's next-door neighbor, who was standing on her front lawn, stared at them.

She was an older lady, in her seventies. She looked at Jack as she slowly approached them. "Jack! What's going on? Who are these people? Where are they taking you?"

Amy, without hesitation answered in a bitter voice, "This man's a pedophile ma'am. We're taking him away."

Sensing that Jack was about to argue against the statement, Josh squeezed his arm. Josh knew that Amy just created another situation where a cleanup crew would have to clear this old lady's memory of this event. So, he went along with it. He added, "The man acted very inappropriately with little boys. Scumbag like."

Rachael held back her smile. With a serious face, she looked at the lady and gave a confirming nod.

The old lady stopped approaching them and looked down for a second in thought. She looked up with a shocked face. "Oh dear."

Josh opened the back door and sat Jack down. After putting his seat belt on him, Josh made the hang loose sign with his hand and touched his pinky and thumb on Jack's chest. Jack was instantly knocked out. Josh closed the door.

Josh took his gloves off his hands and put them back in his jacket pocket as he walked over to the driver's door. Before he could suggest it, Amy got in the front passenger's seat instead of the back. After Rachael and Josh got in the car, they drove off.

Chapter 15

George, Adam, and Teancom loaded the last guards and equipment onto a platform outside of the facility. The second ship that Mark sent was hovering fifteen feet above them as the platform rose into the ship with all three of them on it. As the ship's doors shut below, Teancom's phone buzzed.

Teancom answered, "What's up?"

Josh on the other end of the line replied, "Did you hear the news?"

Teancom smiled. "Got the message. Well done. We've just now loaded up and are about to blow this place, pun intended."

"Ha, ha, ha." Josh replied in a sarcastic voice. "We're driving back to the rendezvous point with our culprit knocked out in the back."

Teancom nodded with approval. "Sounds good. Just remember, don't say anything about this to your ride. If they tell you that we were just killed, act accordingly."

"You got it. See you back at the base." Josh said as they hung up.

Teancom looked at George and Adam. "Let's clear off this platform. We're going to need it to transport back into the base." They pulled down their face coverings and glasses and went to work.

As George and Adam were clearing off the guards and equipment, Teancom called Mark. Mark picked up. "We're about to head back now. We should be back in five minutes. Once we're back, I'll signal Hannah to blow the building. Do you have eyes on Eric?" Teancom questioned.

Mark was sitting in his office with Jay on the other side of his desk on his laptop. Jay had an earpiece in, listening in on the call. When Teancom asked about Eric, Mark looked over at Jay for the answer. Jay turned his laptop around so that Mark could see surveillance video of Eric sitting at the end of his dining room table in his quarters. His back was to the glass sliding door that led to his deck. He was also on a laptop, although from their view they couldn't see what he was doing on it.

Mark gave a nod to Jay. "Yes. He's in his quarters. There's an empty room located three doors down from him where you can transport in. I'll have Jay send the location to Alice so she will know where to drop you off. Your golf cart will be right outside for you to use when needed."

Teancom looked over at Adam. He had his hands on his knees, bent over, preparing himself for the trip by taking deep breaths. Teancom asked on the phone, "Does that room have a bathroom in it? We will be doing several jumps and there's still some adjusting going on."

Mark let out a slight laugh. "Yes, it does. It's an emptied out living space, so it has plenty of room for the platform to transport in. The shower is functional if he, you know, makes a mess."

Teancom smiled. "I'm sure he'll appreciate the accommodation."

Mark continued, "Once Hannah reports the explosion, I'll be out of reach. It will be full alert as I coordinate a recovery and cleanup team. Between your team and Jay, keep Eric in check. Hopefully he'll expose to us the rest of whoever is involved in this."

"Will do." Teancom hung up the phone. He looked at George and Adam. "You ready?"

George gave a confirming nod. Adam, taking a deep breath, replied, "Hold on a sec." He reached into his pocket and pulled out his barf bag. Gripping it, he took a knee and braced himself. Wincing his face and closing his eyes, he said, "Ok. Do it."

Teancom announced out loud, "Alice, we're ready to go. Did you get the coordinates?"

Over the ship's speakers, Alice replied, "Yes, just got them from Jay. Taking off now."

The triangular ship started to rise straight up in the air. As it picked up speed, Alice announced, "Initiating orbital jump in three, two, one." The ship disappeared, then reappeared one hundred miles above. Immediately after, it bolted to the planet's far side. This was the longest jump that George and Adam experienced yet, and they were feeling the effects. Dizziness caused George to take a knee. After a few deep breaths he was surprised on how quickly he was recovering. Adam struggled, knees and forehead pressed to the floor. He gripped his head, fighting the puke. He started to heave, then got control of himself and rolled on his back. After a few deep breaths, he started to feel a little better and the urge to throw up slowly left him.

After a few minutes, Alice's voice came over the speakers again. "Thirty seconds till we reach our destination.

Once there, we'll jump back down to earth. Immediately following, I will transport you via platform down to the designated room. Once down, clear the platform asap so I can transport it back and get out of the area before someone notices me."

At this time George was almost fully recovered while Adam was still on his back, barely starting to recover. Teancom stood unphased. He was standing to the side, far enough away from Adam to avoid the vomit if it came up, but close enough to grab him if he accidentally rolled off of the platform. Adam reluctantly rolled back onto his knees and braced for the next jumps. The dreaded words echoed in his ears. Alice announced, "Jumping in three, two, one."

The ship jumped straight down from space, ninety-five miles into the earth's atmosphere. One second later, the platform transported into the living room of the empty living quarters. Adam, holding his mouth, recognized the layout of the quarters to be similar to his. Stumbling, he ran as fast as he could across the dining room and into the bathroom. George stumbled off of the platform and sat on the floor with his hands on his head and his head between his legs, taking deep breaths.

Teancom walked casually off the platform and took out his phone. With vomiting sounds coming from the bathroom, Teancom spoke on the phone. "Alice, the platform is clear. Thanks for the help."

"You bet. Good luck!" Alice replied as the platform disappeared from the room.

Teancom hung up on Alice and called Hannah. When she answered, he said, "Ok. We're back. Trigger the bomb."

Hannah, listening to Teancom's voice on speaker, replied, "You got to boss." She pushed an icon on the screen which caused a laser to fire through the Taiwanese facilities roof and into the explosive liquid, causing it to go off with a fiery blaze. The concussion from the blast triggered the C4 that was sitting near it, causing a much bigger explosion that resonated through the stone floor and walls. That explosion ignited the explosive powder that was packed within the veins of the whole building. The chain reaction that started in the C4 room now reached every part of the building, causing a huge explosion. Chunks of stone mixed with fire was thrown throughout the immediate area. The sound wave extended for miles.

"It's done." Hannah's voice sounded over the phone.

Teancom replied, "Alright. Now turn the tears on and remember how much you care for your now dead boss as you call it in. I'll see you when this is over." Teancom hung up on Hannah, then called Jay. "Alright Jay, it's done. You should see the red alert notification soon. Let's see what our accomplice does."

Jay, staring at the video of Eric, replied, "I'm watching him now." After a minute, he got an alert on his phone, as well as a large notification on his laptop of the red alert, signifying agents had been killed in the field. He found it odd that Eric had no reaction to the situation. Looking closer, he noticed a reflection of the computer screen on the glass door behind Eric. Jay split his screen in two, both having the video stream. He clicked on the video to the left causing it to rewind. Once he got to the time right before the notification went out, he paused it and zoomed in on the refection. Pushing play, he watched the screen to find that no notification appeared on the reflection. He rewound it and watched it again, then a third time. Nothing. Zooming in on the reflection of the computer on the live video, he closed the rewound video and opened up a chat screen. He messaged

Eric's computer several times. This should have triggered the chat screen to pop up on Eric's computer. It didn't.

"I think we have a problem." Jay said to Teancom with a concerned tone. "The video that I'm watching of Eric is a recording. It's not a live feed."

Teancom felt his stomach sink. "Are you sure?"

Jay replied, "Pretty sure. Tracking his location now." Jay minimized the video of Eric and opened up a program that tracked the location of all personnel. He pulled up Eric's location. It showed that he was in his room. Eric sat puzzled for a second. He immediately smacked himself in the head with the palm of his hand and said out loud, "Idiot." He remembered that Eric was able to disconnect himself from his tracker months ago when he originally contacted Jack. He was doing the same thing now. Frantically, he opened another program that showed the whole facility. Clicking a few buttons, he filtered out heat signatures and isolated the signatures that was not attached to a personnel ID. He found him. There was a heat signature moving rapidly toward the end of the hallway.

"I think I found him." Jay said excitedly. "It looks like he's heading north on your side of the hallway."

Teancom thought for a second as to where he might be heading. It was the opposite direction of the entrance of the hangar. He remembered. There was a food and supply teleporter room in that direction. It was fully automated, so there would be no one to notice him if he entered. "Jay, shut down the teleporters for the food and supplies."

"Got it. Doing it now." Jay clicked into multiple programs and shut the teleporters down. "Just to let you know, it looks like he's moving in a golf cart with the ID tracker shut off. I think you might have some experience with that."

Teancom replied sarcastically, "I don't know what you're talking about. So, if we can't track him in his golf cart, why can't we just track his personal location signal."

Jay replied, "Yeah, he knows how to turn that off. Josh figured it out. That's how he was able to meet with the NASA guy without anyone knowing about it. Right now, I'm tracking him by his heat signature. Once he figures out that we shut down the teleporters, he's going to book it to the hangar. If he escapes, we'll lose that heat signature. There will be no way we could track him."

"Got it." Teancom replied. "Keep tracking him and send that information to my golf cart."

Focused with the task at hand, Jay said, "Alright. Sending it now."

"Thanks." Teancom said quickly as he hung up the phone. He looked over to George who now had his head up. "George, how you feeling?"

The dizziness faded. He was only feeling slightly off. Having caught some of the conversation, George replied, "I'll live. What's going on?"

Teancom motioned his head toward the door. "Time to catch the bad guy. Let's go." He moved toward the exit into the hallway. George clenched his muscles, got up, and followed Teancom. As they were heading out the door, Teancom asked, "You good to drive?"

"Always." George replied with confidence, even though he didn't feel one hundred percent.

Exiting the room, they found Teancom's golf cart waiting for them. They got in, with George in the driver's seat and Teancom in the passenger's seat. Teancom put his hand on the center screen and the vehicle powered on. Tapping the screen, a map of the facility appeared, showing their location as well as Eric's. It showed that Eric stopped at the location where the food and supply transporter was. Teancom knew that it wouldn't be long before he started heading in their direction. To prepare, he opened the glove box in front of him. With his right hand, Teancom placed his palm on the top of the inside of the glove box. A click sounded and the top wall of the glove box lowered down, revealing a holstered hand gun with two magazines beside it. He pulled it out along with both magazines. The gun looked just like a Glock 19. The magazines, however were different. Looking at one of the magazines, there were four columns that stretched up the front side. The four columns were labeled in small letters "Lethal", "Sleeper", "Stun", and "Tracker." A switch at the bottom triggered which rounds were active. Teancom switched the magazine to Tracker, then inserted it into the gun. He took the other magazine and switched it to Sleeper, then stuck it in his pocket.

Closing the glove box, he noticed on the screen that Eric's dot was heading their way. Teancom looked at George. "Here he comes. Follow him as he passes. Get as close as you can to him so I can tag him with a tracker."

George saw on the screen how fast he was going. He quickly swung the vehicle around and started moving in the direction that Eric was going. As he picked up speed, Eric's golf cart sped by them from above, riding on the ceiling. George quickly accelerated as he swiftly moved to the wall, then ceiling. He was pleasantly surprised that unlike his previous venture on the ceiling, internal gravity settings in Teancom's golf cart were turned on so it felt as if they were right side up.

As George caught up to Eric, Teancom put on his glasses that were still dangling from his neck. The straps tightened around his head. Getting a tight grip of his gun, he leaned out the window of the vehicle. They were going close to two hundred miles an hour. The wind pushed Teancom's back against the door as he aimed as best as he could at Eric's smaller two-seater golf cart. Teancom pulled the trigger. Much like the rifles, the gun projected the small tracker dot with an electric rail system instead of gun powder. Unfortunately, the shot missed due to his aim being off from the forces of the wind. He gripped harder and fired eight more rounds. All rounds missed except for two. One stuck on the back of the passenger's seat and another stuck on the bottom of the rear bumper. Pulling himself in, he took off his glasses and tapped on the center screen multiple times. The dot on the screen that indicated Eric changed from one big dot to two smaller dots coming from the trackers. He slid and tapped the screen a few more times to call Jay.

Jays voice came out of the speakers from the vehicle. "You are quickly approaching the entrance of the hangar."

As Teancom was changing magazines, he answered, "Please tell me you locked the bay doors shut."

Jay replied. "I tried, but he must have jammed the system. They are stuck open. I'm working on it."

Teancom hit the door of the vehicle with the side of his fist. "Of course he did. Keep us informed if any other surprises pop up."

Teancom hung up just as the two vehicles slowed down to bank around the corner. They both moved from the ceiling to the wall as they turned the corner, then back to the floor. The hangar door opened. Eric turned to head down the hangar towards the exit with George following close behind.

As they approached the opened hangar doors, Teancom said, "I'm going to switch us to submarine mode when we get to the exit. The steering will be just like flying a jet."

George nodded his head in understanding. With a few swipes and taps on the screen, Teancom got to the icon where all he had to do was tap it to activate submarine mode. As they got closer to the doors, Teancom said, "Alright. Submarine mode in three, two, one." He pushed the icon. The steering wheel loosened up. George immediately pulled back on the wheel as he followed Eric up and out of the facility. George almost clipped the side of the bay door as they exited. Swerving behind Eric's vehicle, it took George just a moment before he started to get the feel for the controls.

Bubbles encased both vehicles, blocking the water from pouring in. As they picked up speed, the front and the back of the bubbles stretched to points to replicate the shape of an almond. George stayed right behind Eric's vehicle. He didn't need the tracker dots. He was close enough to retain visual contact, even with the lack of light. That didn't last long however. Eric sped by a group of whales. He went close to their large bodies and maneuvered up and around them. George went below the whales, but quicky caught up right behind Eric. Swerving in all directions to try to lose them, Eric pulled the vehicle toward a large school of fish.

His vehicle disappeared in the large cloud of fish. George followed, wincing as he went in. The fish were pushed aside as their vehicle plunged blindly through the school. They were relying solely on the two beacons. The dot started to pull away as timidness overcame George as he navigated through the fish. George's timidness faded as he noticed the gap. He sped faster to catch up. As he did, the bodies of the fish slightly broke the barrier of the bubble. The tracker dots made an abrupt turn downward. When George matched the maneuver, a couple of fish broke the barrier and came flapping in the back seats. One flopped out the other end while the other remained in the back seat. A third fish broke the barrier where they were sitting, landing on George's lap. He quickly released the steering wheel and grabbed the flopping fish, throwing it out and back into the water.

Their vehicle moved out of the school as disgust overcame George from the fish smell that now covered his hands. He quickly reached outside of the vehicle and engulfed his hands and forearms into the water to wash it off. Grabbing the steering wheel with his wet hands, he focused back on the tracking dots that was still heading down. The distance grew.

George accelerated down into the dark abyss ahead of them. While they were heading down, Teancom swiped and tapped at the screen to activate the vehicles sonar. In the windshield appeared an outline of an underwater mountain range that the system mapped out. As they got closer, the outline added more and more detail, making the terrain visible in the dark void. The two dots now appeared in the windshield as well. He was still some distance ahead, now navigating through the valleys of the mountains.

Having visibility of what was ahead, George accelerated faster. The distance reduced as he continued to pursue Eric into the mountainous valleys. It was extremely eerie to navigate through the un-weathered underwater mountain range. The peaks were sharp and rigid, yet covered in underwater plant life. Because George was able to navigate the terrain faster than Eric, it wasn't long before George was right behind him again. Eric closely maneuvered around the peaks of the mountains, trying to shake George and Teancom's vehicle. Because of his experience as a pilot, George was easily able to follow. With a quick maneuver, Eric's vehicle did an immediate one-eighty-degree turn, causing George to quickly maneuver to avoid hitting him. Before George could get back on track, Eric's vehicle disappeared into a cave. The tracking dots went down into the earth. The system didn't register the layout of what was inside.

Teancom looked at George. "Pull up to the entrance of the cave and I'll scan the cave system."

George pulled the vehicle to the entrance as Teancom tapped at the center screen. A long system of tunnels now appeared in front of them. The tunnels were very tight in some places. George cautiously pulled forward as he followed Eric, who was now deep into the caves. As they were traveling through the tight tunnels, George and Teancom noticed that Eric's vehicle stopped. Seconds later, a dot vanished. His vehicle started moving again.

"He must have found the tracking dot on the back of the seat." Teancom commented.

"Yes, but I don't think he knows that there is a second one or else he wouldn't still be moving." George replied. He stopped the vehicle and thought for a second. "Can his vehicle track where we are?" George asked.

Teancom, trying to figure out what George was thinking, answered, "Yes, I'm sure he enhanced his sensors to pick up our signal from farther away."

George asked, "Can we manipulate that signal to make it seem like we are going in another direction?"

Teancom thought about that question. He knew how to turn the signal off, but wasn't sure about making a decoy signal. "Let's find out." Teancom called Jay.

Jay answered excitedly, "Did you get him yet?"

Teancom replied, "Not yet. I have a question. Would you be able to manipulate our golf cart ID signal and make it seem like we are heading in a different direction than we are actually going?"

Jay went silent for a moment. He then replied, "Yes, it looks like it would work. I can do it."

"Great." Teancom replied. "I'm going to send you our navigation info. We are in a cave system. Keep our signal wandering through this system, leading us down paths away from where Eric is." Teancom tapped on the screen, sending Jay the navigation information.

After a minute, Jay replied, "Ok. I did it. You should see a green dot on your screen. That is the pretend you. I'll navigate it down the caves, away from Eric."

Seeing the green dot appear on the screen, Teancom replied, "Great! I'll keep you updated." Teancom hung up and turned to George. "There's only one way in and out of these caves. Let's wait outside for him to come out."

"Agreed." George replied as he carefully turned the vehicle around.

As they were heading out of the cave, George asked, "How are we going to stop this guy? I mean, is there a harpoon or something attached to this thing so that he can't keep getting away?"

Teancom, holding up his gun, replied, "No, but if you get us close enough, I can hit him with a sleeper round."

George cringed at that idea. He knew that would be a very difficult shot. "I don't know how well that's going to work." George looked at the center screen. It reminded him of his first ride in his vehicle and how he explored all of the different settings and vehicle controls. A thought popped into his mind. "Why don't we just ram him?"

Teancom looked at George like he was crazy, yet slightly intrigued with his suggestion. "You do realize that we are at the bottom of the ocean. We could drown if we lose our life support."

The vehicle pulled out of the cave. George flipped them upside down to reveal a jagged ridge. "Look, I'm not saying that we do a head on collision, but just bump him into those rocks." He pointed to the fish that was still in the back seat, now barely moving. "This bubble can obviously be penetrated by outside objects. I'm sure those sharp rocks would penetrate his. We just need him down long enough where you can get a clear shot at him. I know that there is a control function on this thing where it delays your direction when you turn the vehicle. We can use it so that we don't crash into the rocks with him."

Teancom grinned. Nuts but brilliant. "Alright. Let's do it. The strongest part of the golf cart is the rear bumper. If we hit his roof, we should be alright. Which means that we will have to approach him from above. Once we're in position, I'll activate the Center Turn control and delay acceleration to three seconds, which means after you swing the vehicle around, it won't go in that direction until three seconds has passed. That will allow us to hit him with the rear bumper, then allow us to escape. We will have to time it just right."

"Sounds good to me." George flipped the vehicle right-side up and headed into position, high above the cave entrance. Once there, George positioned the vehicle so that the front was facing down. Teancom adjusted the settings. They were ready. They watched for several minutes as the two dots navigated the cave tunnels in different directions. Finally, they saw Eric's dot start to head out toward the caves entrance.

Teancom pointed at the dot. "Alright. He's making his way out. Get ready."

The two of them watched as Eric's vehicle exited the cave. Teancom nodded his head and George pushed the throttle forward. They quickly sped in Eric's direction. The distance between them was displayed on the screen. Teancom watched the number carefully as they got closer to their target. As soon as it got to the desired distance, Teancom yelled out, "Turn now!"

George flipped the vehicle's direction around one hundred and eighty degrees. They were now facing upwards. Numbers appeared on the screen as soon as he turned. Three, Two… As soon as the one appeared, their vehicle crashed hard into the roof of Eric's vehicle. Screens glitched. Electronics sparked. Before both vehicles collided hard into the sharp rocks below, George and Teancom's vehicle took off upwards. George quickly decelerated until the vehicle came to a stop.

They both sat for a second before looking at each other, then behind them. All they could see was a dark void, mixed with clouds of dirt. They looked back on the center screen. Eric's tracking dot was no longer showing on the screen. Teancom tapped the center screen to put the vehicle back to normal steering. After motioning for George to turn back around, George went down into the cloudy abyss to see the fruits of their plan. As they came closer to Eric's vehicle, Teancom raised his gun, aiming at Eric. The Golf cart was mangled. The roof had a giant dent in it where they collided. The bubble was still active, but had several places where water was slowly pouring in. The bottom of the golf cart was sitting on a smashed pile of rocks.

When they looked in, they saw Eric unconscious on his seat. The water level was to his waist and rising quickly. George pulled up to the crippled vehicle so that Teancom was right next to Eric's seat. Teancom leaned over and put the gun up to Eric's neck and shot him with a sleeper round, just in case. Leaning back in, Teancom tapped at the center screen, then put all five fingers on the screen and opened his hand. The motion caused the bubble that surrounded their vehicle to greatly expand. Both vehicles were now encased in one large bubble, with an additional couple of feet around them.

Getting out of the golf cart, Teancom reached in Eric's vehicle and put his fingers on Eric's neck to check for a pulse. Eric was alive. Noticing the bruise on his head, Teancom figured that he must have bumped his head on the steering wheel. Teancom looked over at George. "Help me get him in the back seat so we can take him back to the base. We have some questions for him that need to be answered."

The two of them got Eric out of his smashed vehicle and into their back seat, next to the now dead fish. They searched Eric's wreck to find nothing odd, then drove back to base.

Chapter 16

Eric sat unconscious on a hard wooden chair, his hands bound behind him with metal wrist bands, designed wider and tighter than traditional handcuffs. A single light positioned in the center of the square room illuminated the scene, right above where Eric sat. Josh and Teancom stood in front of him, ready to interrogate. Teancom had a rectangular device in his hand that was the size of a handle at the end of a jump rope. He jabbed it onto the side of Eric's neck, causing a small electric jolt to deliver a substance into his body to revive him.

Eric's head snapped up, eyes wide. He looked around to discover that he was in the interrogation room. Although there were only two people in the room, he knew that one of the four plain walls surrounding him was see through from the other side, and that he no doubt had a much bigger audience. Looking at the two men in the room more carefully, he noticed that one of them was Teancom. With a casual, and somewhat defeated tone, he said, "Hi Teancom."

Teancom had worked with Eric on past missions. He was a controller in the background, acting as tech support for Teancom when needed. Teancom shook his head. "Why?"

Eric looked at Teancom with contempt. "You of all people should know why. How many times had we complained about the people running the operations? How often have we seized control to do what was right? You know how many people die while people of the organization sit around and watch. How many people in the world suffer when we can end it quickly with our technology? Our resources? Earth's progression is nonexistent. I did what needed to be done."

Teancom glared, voice sharp with disgust. "Just because I disagreed with the method, doesn't mean I fought against the purpose. You're right. The world is jacked up. And you want to hand them more tools in which they can jack it up even more. We exist to help the world, to save people, not to be the means in which we bring war where millions will die!"

Eric snapped back with a similar tone. "What do you think I was doing? I fight for the same purpose! To bring ultimate peace and order to the world!"

Josh jumped in with an extremely puzzled look on his face. "What are you talking about? You know how close you were to starting another world war? Is that your idea of peace?"

Eric replied, "And what we have now is yours? We live in a world where all it takes is one election in one key country and the world turns upside down. From the brink of world peace to the brink of nuclear war. From billions living in prosperity to billions living without basic energy and freezing to death. The world is so stable to you that we can turn that quickly?"

Teancom's tone rose even more. "So, what were you thinking!? That might as well wipe out those governments with a world war and start over!?"

Eric looked at the two of them with a glassy stare. "After every world war, the world has come closer together. The U.S. for the most part wanted to stay isolated from the rest of the world's problems until they were dragged into World War II. During the Russia-Ukraine war, NATO became more powerful with more countries joining. The world has demonstrated that it needs conflict to truly bring it together."

With a wrinkled nose and predominant frown, Josh humored Eric by asking, "And when the world comes together, who's going to decide how to govern it?"

Eric revealed a small smile. "We have always been the ones pulling the strings. We can guide it in the right direction. All we have to do is redirect project New World Order from the coverup team to the operational team."

Teancom walked closer to him and looked him straight in the eyes. "Every tyrannical dictator that has been on this planet has thought exactly the same way. Taking control by means of strict world laws is insane. But let's put that aside for a second. You were going to kill me and my team! According to your plan, millions would die in a war!"

Eric looked down. "Yes, and I'm sorry about that. I really am." He looked up at Teancom. "Transition has to come with sacrifice."

Squeezing his eyes shut while shaking his head, Teancom took a couple of steps back. "I know someone that doesn't quite agree with you on that. Bring her in."

The door opened. Amy took a step into the room. She had on a pair of gloves with thick knuckles that Teancom, George, and Adam were wearing while in Taiwan. With the look of death on her face, she charged at Eric who sat there helplessly. Her right fist smashed his cheek bone. His head was thrown to the left from the blow. She followed with a left, then a right again. Finally, she swung and made contact square in the nose, breaking it.

Josh and Teancom quickly pulled her back. Teancom grabbed her arm, "Three punches, Amy. That was the deal." As she was being pulled back, she spat in his broken face. She reluctantly turned around and stomped out of the room, slamming the door behind her.

Satisfied with the work that Amy did on Eric's face, Teancom asked, "Who are you working with?"

Hurting from the blows, Eric looked up. "I work alone."

Teancom rose his voice. "Who's working with you!?"

Again, Eric replied, "I said I work alone."

A voice in Teancom's earpiece chirped, "According to sensors, he's telling what he believes to be the truth." The light that was shining down over Eric was not just a light. It was scanning him for multiple readings. Among them were polygraph readings.

Teancom looked at Eric in disgust. "I think you need to see what it's really like living in a country with a tyrannical government in charge." With a nod of his head, two men came in the room. Lifting him out of the seat, they dragged him away.

Behind the see-through wall, Mark and Isaiah stood watching and listening. Isaiah commented, "You know, he's not wrong about the elected officials. All it takes is one election to flip the world around."

Mark looked at Isaiah and nodded his head. "True, but you don't get rid of tyranny with more tyranny. A governance shouldn't be born out of fear of destruction, but from hope of a better life. People should be free to choose what is best for them. And when that goes sideways from corruption, well, that's why we're here to act as damage control."

Isaiah replied, "I agree." They both turned to walk out the door. As they were walking, Isaiah commented, "Unfortunately, there might be more individuals in this organization that don't see it our way. Scans caught faint signs of recent brain surgery on Eric. Someone could have erased some of his memory."

Mark stopped walking. He paused, then said, "I'll have to look into that."

"You understand that if it is an inside job, they probably have access to the AI protocols. Your activities would be heavily monitored."

"I have an idea of how to get around that. In the meantime, keep your eyes open." They continued to walk out the door.

Eric woke up drowsy. He was lying on the ground of a dirt road in the middle of a desert city. The sun was pounding down on him. His face hurt for some reason. He didn't know why. In fact, he couldn't remember anything, not even his name or who he was. He sat up to see a small circle of people around him, staring at him. As he glanced around, baffled by his surroundings, he noticed writing on a wall. His foggy mind finally clicked as to what it said. It was written in Farsi. The writing said "Death to America. Praise to the Supreme Leader. May he guide Iran to paradise."

Now sitting up, he looked down at himself to get a clue as to what was going on. He was wearing alcohol covered shorts, tennis shoes, and a dirty white shirt with a bald eagle and an American Flag on it that said "Proud to be an American" in big bold English letters. There were several empty bottles of alcohol surrounding him.

As he was trying to make sense of his situation, two armored military vehicles pulled up near him. Heavily armed Iranian soldiers stepped out of the vehicles. Two of them walked up to Eric, grabbed him by the arms, and dragged him to one of the vehicles. Confused and scared, Eric cried out in English, "Wait! What's going on!? What's happening!? Where are you taking me!?"

They threw him into the vehicle's back seat. All the soldiers got back in and slammed their doors shut. They sped off, dust billowing.

One month later.

Rachael and George pulled up to Rachael's quarters in George's golf cart. Training drained them, mind and body. Rachael got out of the passenger's seat, followed by George from the driver's side. As Rachael opened the door and was walking in, George quickly reached his hand inside and placed it on the wall next to the door.

The lights turned on, followed by a greeting with the voice that sounded like Rachael that announced, "Welcome to my home King George. I am so grateful that you are here. You make everything awesome."

Rachael, tired, shook her head in disapproval. "I can't believe you convinced an engineer to lock that setting so I can't change it."

With a big grin on his face, George replied, "Pays to make friends with the right people."

Rachael, somewhat annoyed replied, "Alright. Go home and rest that brain of yours. Maybe it will help you with your programming skills tomorrow."

George replied, "And maybe rest will help you with your combat training."

George was in the middle of turning to his golf cart when Rachael asked, "I forgot to ask, have you heard from Amy recently?"

George turned back around toward Rachael. "Last time I heard from her was a couple of weeks ago when they were still working out the details of her family."

Rachael, a little disappointed, replied, "Oh. Me too. Ok. See you tomorrow." George turned back around, waving goodbye as he headed to his vehicle.

Closing the door, Rachael went to her kitchen and pulled out a bottle of liquid gold from the refrigerator.

As she opened the bottle and was about to take a drink, her phone buzzed to indicate that she received a message. She looked at her phone and saw it was a message from Teancom. It read, "Turn your TV on to channel five ASAP."

Rachael grabbed her drink and sat down on her couch. She sipped her drink, flipped on channel five. A weather forecaster was on explaining the forecast for the next five days. A few moments later, a news anchor appeared on the screen. She stated, "In other news, retired NASA programmer, Jack Herbert, was arrested today on Pedophile charges. Jack, who amazingly enough, won the lottery a month ago and has been spending his time in Hawaii. Authorities raided his home and arrested Jack after finding strong evidence of his involvement in this heinous crime. The head officer had this to say."

An officer appeared on the screen and said, "After finding many pictures of Mr. Herbert with young children, we acted quickly to apprehend the suspect. There is no doubt that he will be going away for a very long time."

Rachael almost sprayed out her drink in laughter after seeing the news report. After composing herself, she looked up to see the news anchor interrupting the story. "We have a breaking report coming from Ortega Highway in Southern California."

A news reporter appeared on the screen standing on the side of the road with several emergency vehicles surrounding the scene. "I'm here on the side of Ortega Highway in California where a man named Sam Williams and his three children went off the road in their vehicle into the valley below. I've been told that Sam and his children were the family of recently deceased Astronaut Amy Williams, who died just over a month ago when a small meteoroid hit her ship as they were traveling to the moon. Witnesses said that the family was driving down the highway when a group of bikers wearing jackets that had the words "Reparations for Nature" on them forced the family off the road, into the ravine. Before they forced them off the road, witnesses say that they broke the back windows of the car and threw bottles full of liquid into the vehicle. Authorities are saying that the liquid was no doubt a form of accelerant. When the vehicle hit the bottom of the ravine, it went up in a huge ball of fire. The fire burned with extreme temperatures, leaving very little traces of any remains. The RFN organization is said to be the protesters that have been harassing the Williams family for years over Sam Williams architecture business that specializes in cabins in the woods. Authorities are on the hunt for members of the group as we speak."

Rachael set her drink and remote on the table, burying her face in her hands. Tears slipped through her fingers, spotting the rug. After a few moments, Rachael lifted her head up, removing her tear-soaked hands to reveal a big smile on her face.

The End

Epilogue

One year later.

A warm summer day hit the mid-eighties. Amy sat on the porch of a large home in the middle of a lush forest. A small lake glimmered nearby. A Mountain range was only a few miles away in the background. In front of her was a small table where her laptop sat. She was typing away at a report that she was working on. The title of the document was labeled "Dark Network." Typing, she caught a small glitch on the screen that caused everything to go fuzzy for a split second. Amy smiled and shook her head as she minimized the document and opened a blank word document. On the document, she typed, "Getting sloppy."

Seconds later, words typed themselves. "Dang it. Let me guess. The screen went fuzzy."

Amy typed, "Yes, it did. Don't be too hard on yourself. It must have been hard to sneak on the property unnoticed and tap into my secured home network. Let me guess, we have a fresh load of supplies in storage."

The words typed again by itself, "Yeah, you're all set for another month. You know, if you were to join us back on the base, you could help me get rid of my flaws."

Just as Amy read the reply, her three kids came running from the side of the house to the front, holding water guns. Sam chased them, water gun blazing. All of them were laughing as they hosed each other with water.

Amy smiled at the sight. She watched them, grateful for what she had. Returning to her laptop, she typed, "I'm good here. That life is not for me. You are doing an amazing job without me. But, for reference, if you want to get rid of the glitch, all you have to do is…" Amy continued to type on how to fix the glitch.

Two miles above the house, a triangular ship hovered. Inside, Adam completed a project at a workstation. He turned around and asked, "Ashley, are you all done and ready to go."

Ashley was sitting at a computer on an adjacent work station. She just finished reading Amy's explanation and typed, "Thanks. I'll have to try that on you next time." Once she was done typing, she turned to Adam and replied, "Yeah, Dad. I'm all done."

Adam faced Teancom in the ship's center seat. "Teancom, we're all done here."

Teancom replied, "Sounds good. Hannah, let's get out of here."

Hannah, in the pilot's seat, replied with a smile, "You got it boss."

The ship disappeared out of sight.

www.ingramcontent.com/pod-product-compliance
Lightning Source LLC
La Vergne TN
LVHW090556110826
845146LV00001B/152

* 9 7 9 8 9 9 3 6 0 4 4 1 1 *